KISSING MICKY

*Washington Guardians
Hockey ~ Book #1*

By Ellen Devlin

Kissing Micky

Limitless Publishing, LLC
Kailua, HI 96734
www.limitlesspublishing.com

Formatting: Limitless Publishing

ISBN-13: 978-1-64034-546-1
ISBN-10: 1-64034-546-9

Dedication

Dedicated to anyone who has ever wanted to breathe life into their daydreams and fantasies.

Chapter One

"You cannot possibly be serious, Paige. Look at him! He's like a walking fantasy! My *personal* walking fantasy." Liz looked at her best friend as if she'd lost her mind and laughed. "There is no way I'm going on a date with *that*. I wouldn't be able to remember his name. Hell, I wouldn't be able to remember *my* name."

Paige laughed with her. "I know, right? It's like someone drew a picture from your personal wish list!" She hooked her arm into Liz's elbow. "But really, Liz, I am serious. He's Chris's best friend. They've known each other for years; they're like brothers. And they're finally on the same team again. Chris was the one who suggested it." Liz looked sideways at her and raised one eyebrow skeptically.

Paige let go of her elbow and put her hands up. "I swear!" She laughed. She put her right hand over her heart and became very serious. "I swear that I have never once told my husband that a big, tough, six-foot-four defenseman with shaggy light brown

1

hair, broad shoulders, and blue eyes is your personal fantasy." She smiled at Liz. "He really does think that you guys would get along. And he wants Micky to at least meet someone who isn't on the team."

"Micky" was Tom McCullin, recently traded to the Washington Guardians from the Montreal Lynx. At thirty-two, he was well into a successful NHL career. He was no superstar, but he was a strong player, respected by his teammates. He was also an enforcer—the guy on the team ready to drop the gloves in the game when it was time for a fight.

Tom had been best friends with Chris Beckman since they were teenagers playing together on national level and college teams. Chris had signed a long-term contract with the Guardians about five years earlier and had met and married Paige while playing with the team.

Chris and Paige had eloped—Justice of the Peace and a trip to Hawaii—so in an odd twist of fate, coupled with crazy hockey schedules, their two long-time best friends had never actually met each other before now.

Paige put her hands on her hips and looked mockingly stern. "Liz Williams, are you seriously refusing a request to be friendly and hospitable to a new person—Chris's *best friend*—and join us for dinner? I will even have him wear name tags, one with his name and one to remind you of yours."

Liz recognized defeat. Now she just made a snarly face at Paige while Paige laughed. "Come on, grouchy, let's go say hi."

They started across the backyard pool deck. They were at Chris and Paige's house at the pool party they hosted in the last half of July to welcome the new team members and generally get the guys and their families together for a little fun. It had become a summer tradition; it was never a huge party because folks went their own ways during the off-season, but it was always a great time.

Halfway to where Chris and Tom stood talking with a few other guys, Liz was literally swept off her feet by Jakob Zimmerman, a young right winger and good friend of hers. He grabbed her around the waist, put her across his shoulders with a triumphant shout, and then half-ran to the end of the diving board. There were yells from the partygoers—some giving him a hard time for harassing her, many encouraging him to dump her in the water, and most encouraging him to jump in with her.

The latter came mainly from the kids in the crowd—he was doing this mostly for their benefit, and Liz knew that. She had shrieked once in surprise but had started belly laughing as soon as she realized what was going on. Zee was a ham, and his love of making people laugh was one of the reasons they got along so well. He tended to go for boldly dramatic physical humor, while she leaned more toward the "I gotta tell you what happened to me today" variety.

Tom had looked over as soon as he heard the shout and shriek and saw one of his younger teammates grab a woman in khaki shorts and a dark blue t-shirt and run off with her. He watched the show along with everyone else but was paying attention to the woman rather than the guy. After the first shriek, she hadn't seemed upset at all, and she wasn't fighting him, not even in jest. There was no fake protesting, no begging not to throw her in, no extra touching to make it more of a show. She was just...*is she laughing?*

Paige continued over to Chris and Tom, and the three of them watched the show going on at the pool. By this time, Zee seemed to have decided that the votes had gone in favor of him releasing Liz, so, amid groans of protest from the kids, he put her down on the diving board. She put her hand on his arm, thanked him sweetly, and then caught the back of his knee with her leg enough to get him off balance and hip checked him off the end of the board amid cheers.

Having received their parents' permission, the kids were now all jumping in the water to play with Zee, and Liz, forgotten by the masses, walked over to join Paige.

Paige asked, "Do you think he's ever going to grow up?"

"God, I hope not! The world needs fun. He's such an idiot, you've just gotta love him," Liz replied. She had a huge smile on her face, and her blue eyes were shining brightly as she turned and faced Chris and his best friend. *Wow, it should not be legal to be that good looking.*

His light brown hair was mostly straight but thick and longish, coming to his eyebrows. It had a sort of permanently tousled look, as if he'd just run his fingers through it or just toweled off. His eyes were a rather startling shade of dark blue. He was clean shaven, which made him look somewhat younger than he was; she knew they were the same age. She realized with a start that Tom was holding out his hand.

She took it and shook it, hearing him say, "Tom McCullin, really nice to meet you finally. It feels weird that we have known the same people for so long and never met."

"Liz Williams. Same here. I blame them for eloping," she said, gesturing with her head to Chris and Paige. "I would have been willing to travel to Hawaii for a small wedding." She hadn't let go of his hand, and she felt slightly lightheaded at the contact.

He laughed. "Me too! I have never been."

The handshake seemed to linger for a while before they both noticed and let go at the same time.

"I was excited to see you traded here. You're a fun player to watch, but it was difficult for me to fully appreciate your abilities properly while watching you flipping one of my guys end-over-end in the middle of the ice. I have a feeling I'm going enjoy that a lot more when you're doing it to, say, somebody from Pittsburgh."

Tom looked surprised and pleased. "You're a fan?"

Liz laughed and said, "Definitely. Ever since I was a kid. I remember the first hockey game I ever saw on TV. There was a fight, and the refs were just standing around watching. I was like, 'Why aren't they doing anything? Those guys are *fighting.*'

"Long story short, I ended up deciding that hockey is the best, most honest sport. Fast paced, with a limited amount of play stoppage; strength, speed, and an amazing level of skill required; gritty, rough, full contact, with none of the injury-faking bullshit you find in something like soccer…" She seemed to be really getting into what she was saying. "…and insults and fighting are part of the fucking game, which is why I think it's honest. Who wouldn't love the opportunity to beat the crap out of someone at their job every now and then?" She looked around and caught the look on Paige's face. "I did it again, didn't I?"

"Yup."

Tom's mouth was hanging open slightly in surprise. Liz looked at him briefly and blushed.

Paige gaped. "You're *blushing?* I didn't think you had it in you, Liz."

"Really, Paige? Do you think that's helpful right now?" She turned to Tom. "Sorry. I usually try very hard not to scare off new folks by dropping random f-bombs in the first five minutes. I may have just set a new record."

Chris laughed, clapped Tom on the shoulder and gave him a huge grin, took Paige's hand, and asked her to help him with the food. Liz squinted up at Tom. He had recovered and had a devastatingly cute smile on his face, including the hint of a dimple in one cheek.

Her stomach flipped. *That really isn't fair. He doesn't even have the decency to be missing a few teeth.* "I'm assuming you know already that they have the four of us going out to dinner. Are you actually okay with that?"

Tom gave a strong laugh and said, "Are you kidding? You just convinced me I'm going to have a great time."

She tamped down the flutters that she felt when he laughed, brightened, and said, "Excellent." Pretending to write a note on her hand, she added, "Note to self: does not shy away from random f-bombs."

At the sound of a particularly loud laughing shriek, they turned to look at the pool, where kids had lined up to have Zee pick them up and throw them. All the kids, including the big one doing the throwing, seemed to be having fun.

"Hey, why didn't you try to get him to put you down earlier? You didn't seem to try to sway the vote either way."

Liz chuckled. "It wouldn't have mattered. He had decided before he picked me up what he was going to do. If I had been wearing a white shirt, I would have known he wasn't serious, because this was for the kids. He wasn't trying to start a wet t-shirt contest." Tom's eyes widened slightly at the visual that presented. "But with the dark blue shirt, I had no idea if I was going in or not."

"So, what if he had thrown you in?"

She turned and looked at him, like she wasn't sure she understood the question. "I would have gotten wet…? That's the way that usually works."

"You're not wearing a swimsuit."

She shrugged. "Chris and Paige have a dryer. Maybe I could borrow a t-shirt from Chris. He's tall enough, so one of his shirts might make a passable dress. Whatever. In any case, I wouldn't melt, and the outcome would be the same. Still funny, just with different players involved." She squinted her eyes a little. "I would have made sure that he got his, though. No doubt about it."

Tom caught himself looking at her curiously, genuinely surprised at the idea of a woman who wouldn't be pissed off at being dumped into the pool at a party. She was definitely cute—tall, at around five-foot-nine, with her dark blonde hair in an easy ponytail. Her figure was average, nothing that would have called his attention from across the room, but when they met and she had turned to him with that smile...well, that had been something altogether different.

While they were talking, Zee had finally gotten out of the water and wandered up, dripping wet.

"Speak of the idiot and he shall appear," she said.

Zee clutched his chest. "I'm wounded."

"Oh, sweetie, if you were truly wounded every time I called you an idiot, you would have died the death of a thousand cuts already." She turned toward Tom. "Tom McCullin, Jakob Zimmerman. Jake, Tom. And I'm quite certain that will be the last time you two will hear your given names for a long time."

The two players grinned and shook, introducing themselves as Micky and Zee.

Liz rolled her eyes and said, "Sometimes I wonder if it is physically impossible for hockey players to call each other by their given names."

Zee took Liz's hand and said, "And you remembered my name. I knew you cared."

"Some of us use our brain cells for things other than just pranks and hockey plays, Zee."

He blinked. "Well, that seems like a waste of good brain space. Why on earth would you do that?"

She sighed and looked at him in a long-suffering way that told Tom this was a conversation they had repeated many times. "So that you can call me after a bad game, and I can tell you stories about funny crap that happened during the day and make you laugh, and then you'll remember that there's some weird thing that you want to put in someone's sock tomorrow, and you'll feel better. That's why."

"Oh, that's right."

He smiled at her with a grin that was far too large. Her eyes got wide, she said, "Shit!" and tried to dodge, but he caught her in an enormous, extremely wet bear hug. "Argh! Oh my God, you are a such pain in my ass!" But she was laughing while she said it. Zee gave her a fat kiss on the cheek and let her go.

She saw Paige starting to move some food out of the house and took the opportunity to escape. "I'm going to go help Paige. Nice to finally meet you, Tom." She walked off, still chuckling, plucking her now-wet shirt away from her body.

They stood and watched her go. Tom was surprised, and oddly pleased, that she had called him by his given name rather than Micky.

Zee turned to Tom and said, "Great to meet you, Micky. Welcome to DC." Then he ran back to the pool and cannonballed into the water, to the delight of the kids still swimming.

Tom walked over and found Chris hanging out near the beer cooler. He was introduced to a few more people, drank another beer, ate a burger, and generally enjoyed the party. But he did find himself regularly looking around, trying to catch a glimpse of a woman in a dark blue, slightly damp t-shirt. She appeared to be at least passing friends with most of the people at the party. Every time he looked at her, it seemed she was either hugging someone, laughing with someone, or talking in an animated way, obviously telling a story that had everyone around her laughing. He hadn't really meant to, but he caught her eye.

She blushed, and he felt the corner of his mouth turn up. His smile widened as she blushed a bit deeper and looked away.

***

Liz had just been talking with the wife of one of the players about their five-year-old son's latest obsessions, and they had been sharing a laugh together, when the woman suddenly asked, "So have you met the new guy? I think his name is McCullin?"

Startled, Liz replied, "Yes. He's actually Chris's best friend, so Paige introduced me earlier."

Her friend leaned in. "Am I imagining things, or is he seriously good looking?" Liz choked on the drink she had just taken. "I was just wondering if you realized that he's been looking at you all day."

Recovering her composure, Liz replied, "I'm quite sure you're imagining things, but you are very sweet to think that."

"He's looking at you right now."

Liz turned before she could stop herself and caught Tom's gaze. She felt herself blush and saw him smile. She could feel herself getting redder and felt her heart rate speed up an unreasonable amount.

Her friend laughed and said, "See? He's all kinds of adorable, Liz. I'm just sayin'."

Liz hugged her friend and got up to move toward heading home. "I will take that under advisement," she said, looking very serious. Her friend burst out laughing.

Liz went looking for Chris and Paige to say her goodbyes and thank yous. The party had been a huge success again. She found Chris first. He was standing with Tom, which she probably should have expected, but it still caught her just a bit off guard and made her feel slightly lightheaded.

"Hey, Chris, I'm heading home. Thank you so much. I had a blast, as usual. You know I love coming to your house." She wrapped him up in a big hug, which he returned. Chris and Paige were family to her.

"Of course, Liz. Wouldn't be a party without you. Hey, I'll text you about going to dinner, okay? Maybe tomorrow night, if you can swing it. Micky was just asking me how soon we could go."

Liz turned to Tom to say goodbye and caught him looking briefly wide-eyed at Chris. He recovered quickly and turned to Liz. "It was great to meet you."

"You too." She smiled, looked into his stunningly gorgeous blue eyes, and noticed that they were framed by unreasonably long, thick lashes. She started toward him as if to give him a hug, gave a small lurch, and held out her hand for a handshake, all the while feeling like there was a small group of creatures cavorting through her insides. Possibly otters. "See you soon."

Tom had leaned toward her for a goodbye hug— hadn't he seen her hug almost everyone at the party the entire day? He saw her outstretched hand and caught himself short, staring at it. He took her hand, shook it as he had when they had met earlier that day, and repeated, "See you soon."

As she made her escape, Tom shot a questioning look at Chris. Chris couldn't decide between shock and laughter. "Don't look at me, Micky. I have no clue what that was about. I have seen her hug a perfect stranger, because 'it seemed like the right thing to do.'" He used air quotes for emphasis. "Which it was, by the way. I can't ever figure out how she does that. But honest to God, Mick," he had started laughing by this point, "I have *never* seen her do that. Maybe the stink of the Montreal locker room hasn't washed off yet."

"Fuck off, Becks," Tom said, laughing. The insulting banter made him feel more comfortable, which was exactly what Chris had intended.

***

"You did *what?* You didn't. I don't believe you." Paige and Liz were standing by Liz's car.

"Why would I make this up? I. Shook. His. Hand. I feel…I can't even think of words that express how stupid I feel." Liz covered her eyes.

"Fatuous?" Paige suggested. "Silly? Idiotic?

Absurd?" Paige was a high school English teacher.

"Stop! Yes. All those things." She looked through her fingers. "I told you this was a bad idea. I looked in his eyes, and I panicked. They're really blue. Really, really blue. With long, dark lashes."

Paige's phone chimed with a message. She looked quickly and smiled. "Well, you're stuck, because we're going out tomorrow night. Chris just made reservations in Old Town." Another chime. She laughed. "And he wants to know what the hell is wrong with you."

Liz sighed. "I promise to be better tomorrow night. I will focus." She put her hand up sideways in front of her face in a visual representation of how focused she would be.

Paige hugged her friend. "We'll have a good time tomorrow night. Micky is smart and funny, Liz. You will like him, not just the way he looks. I promise."

As she turned and walked back toward the house, Liz heard her saying, "She *shook his hand.* Unbelievable."

Chapter Two

The four of them met the next evening at a nice restaurant in the historic DC suburb of Old Town Alexandria. Tom was at the meeting place when Liz arrived; Paige and Chris were running a few minutes late.

She took a deep breath as she walked up, said, "Hi, Tom," with a big smile, and gave him a solid, normal, this-is-how-I-greet-my-friends hug. She stepped back and took another deep breath. "Sorry about last night. That was exceptionally weird of me. I would hate to start this evening out awkwardly because of it."

He gave her a really big smile...*does he look relieved?*...and said, "Thanks. I was starting to develop a bit of a complex. Becks was trying to convince me I smelled really bad. Something about spending too much time in Montreal."

Liz laughed and gestured for him to lean down so she could check. She put her face close to his neck and breathed in...and then wished she had thought about that move before she had done it,

14

because oh, he smelled good. So good. She lingered for a moment breathing him in—there was a little cologne, something outdoorsy that made her think of a forest, and the clean smell of soap or shaving cream—but mostly he just smelled…male. Like she wanted to bury her face in his neck and just breathe him in.

She took a breath to speak, which was not as silent as it should have been, and said, "No. You smell very nice, Tom. That's definitely not an issue." Her voice was deeper than normal. She didn't know how that had happened, and she felt a little dizzy.

Tom closed his eyes, enjoying the feeling of her warm breath on his neck. He was thinking he should probably stand back up again when he heard her small gasp, and by the time she had spoken, he was thinking he might have started enjoying this a little too much. And there was definitely something about the way she called him Tom, rather than Micky. It somehow felt as warm as her breath, and distracting.

He stood up, and they both turned as they heard Chris and Paige call out in greeting, and the spell was broken. Paige and Chris both solemnly walked up to Liz and offered their hands for handshakes. Liz swatted them away, called them both intolerable bastards, and gave them both hugs while the four of them laughed together.

The restaurant was on the waterfront with a beautiful view, and the menu featured interesting variations on standard American fare, with a nod toward East Coast seafood. The company was excellent, and time flew by with laughing and storytelling, mostly Tom and Chris sharing hilarious team stories, some of which were even new to Paige.

After the dinner had been cleared away, Paige excused herself to the ladies' room, and for a moment the topic turned to fandom rather than playing. "So do you get into all the player stats and trades, all the nitty gritty details?" Tom asked Liz.

"Absolutely not," she replied with a laugh. "Honestly, I just enjoy watching the game. I understand what's going on, you know, but I have almost zero idea what play the coach should be calling when or even what any of the plays are or why they would be called. When it comes right down to it, I'm always impressed that you guys can do what you do, and on freaking ice skates. And stats are just a bunch of numbers to me."

Chris laughed, and Tom looked at her oddly.

"What?" she said.

"Just a bunch of numbers?" He made an attempt to look haughty and offended. "I'll have you know I was an econ major."

"Seriously?" she asked. She looked totally incredulous, as if such a thing shouldn't be possible.

Now he did look slightly taken aback. "Not just a dumb jock, Liz."

"No! No, that's not at all what I meant," she quickly corrected. "It's just that if I had the choice between majoring in econ, or statistics, or anything math-related and, say, poking myself in the eye with a sharp stick, I would have a seriously difficult time choosing."

Tom laughed. Chris was simply sitting back enjoying the banter between his two good friends.

Paige reappeared at the table, bustling a bit. "Okay, guys, I've ordered coffee, and some really great dessert, and paid the bill already, including a nice tip. Unfortunately, Chris and I have to go, because there's a thing I have to do tomorrow, and I have to prep tonight. I'm so sorry."

Liz's mouth dropped open in shock at her friend as Paige came around the table and gave her a big hug.

Chris said, "What thing? Wait, we don't get dessert?"

"It's something I forgot about completely, honey. I'm so sorry. All my fault. We have pie at home." She gave Tom a long hug from behind his chair, pressing her hands across his chest. "Have a great time, you two! Dinner was wonderful! Love you both!"

She grabbed Chris's hand and practically dragged him away.

Liz looked across the table at Tom as the waiter brought coffee and dessert. It did look amazing, but Liz didn't see it, because all she could do was stare in pure, abject horror at the two nametags that Paige had stuck to Tom's chest during her hug. The top one said:

"Hi, My Name Is Micky"

The one immediately beneath it had been altered to read:

"Your Name Is Liz"

"I feel like there might be something here that I'm missing." Tom's deep voice pulled her out of

17

her thousand-yard stare. She looked up into his handsome face, which was wearing quite possibly the most endearing smile she had ever seen in her life. There was simply no getting out of this.

"You're wearing two nametags," she said, the corners of her mouth lifting into a smile. "It's Paige's way of trying to be a good friend while simultaneously being a colossal, meddling pain in the ass. She knows there's no reasonable explanation for these," she waved at the nametags, "except for the real one and that I'm a terrible liar anyway. So she's forcing my hand." She shook her head, sighed, picked up her fork, and waved at his dessert plate. "Start enjoying, and I will share my tale," she said expansively.

Tom was astonished at the rapid turn of events. First, Paige had pulled Chris away so quickly and left them together. Second, Liz had looked completely panicked for a minute, like a deer in headlights, but now looked calm, almost resigned. He picked up his fork and started eating, waiting for any of this to start making sense.

"So," Liz began, "I don't know if guys do this, not being one myself, but I will tell you that almost every girl I have ever met in my life has built for themselves some sort of fantasy at some time or another." She took a bite. "There is usually a leading male role in these fantasies. It might be a different guy in each different storyline, but probably the same basic formula for the guy. It's a stereotype, but think, 'tall, dark, and handsome.'

"Some girls get more specific than that. Think, 'tall, blond, doctor, and loves dogs.'" She took a sip of coffee. "And then there are some girls who take their fantasies to an entirely different level when it comes to specifics. So here's where you need to follow along carefully, think 'six-foot-four, shaggy light brown hair, blue eyes, broad shoulders, defenseman on a hockey team, enforcer, amazing smile.' I could go on, because believe it or not there are a few more, and they all fit, but I'm hoping you've gotten the idea by this point."

Tom was staring at her, his fork halfway to his mouth, wondering if she was kidding.

"So you show up, Paige tells me *you* are the Micky I've been hearing about for years and says Chris has decided that we would get along great and wants us to go out for dinner. I very carefully pointed out to her the details I just mentioned— which she knew, being my best friend for, oh, I don't know, *forever*—and explained that it was a terrible idea, because I wouldn't even be able to remember your name. She suggested a nametag. I said I wouldn't be able to remember my own name…and here we are."

Tom finished the last of his dessert quietly, sat back, and looked at her. "So, if I'm understanding this, what you're saying is that I am your personal fantasy."

Liz blushed yet again. *Three times in two days is definitely a new record.* "Yes. Down to the fact that you have really long, thick eyelashes. That's what I noticed last night, right before my epically awkward handshake." She giggled. "Seriously, this has wandered so far off into the realm of the ridiculous."

"You shook my hand because I have nice eyelashes." Tom was trying not to laugh, but his eyes were starting to shine.

Her giggling was getting louder. "Oh God, can we please leave, because I'm going to laugh really hard, and we might get kicked out otherwise." Her eyes were bright, and she was shaking.

Tom stood up and grabbed her hand, leading her outside. They made it just around the corner before completely dissolving into paroxysms of laughter. Liz had to lean against the wall of the building, and she was holding her side. She looked up and realized Tom was still wearing the nametags, which started a new fit of giggling.

"You can take those off now. I promise I will be able to remember your name. And mine. Most of the time, anyway. You do know that you're way too good looking for your own good, right?"

Tom barked out another laugh. "Thank you. I do appreciate the compliment, and you have truly done wonders for my ego this evening. I'm gonna need a bigger bucket this season."

They both leaned back against the wall, catching their breath.

"God, I can't remember the last time I laughed that hard." Tom turned to look at Liz. Her eyes were still dancing.

"Excellent. Then my embarrassment is well spent." She giggled again.

"Don't start!" He gave another half laugh. "Your laughter is clearly contagious. Very dangerous." His smile was devastating. He looked at her for a moment and then asked, "Where are you parked? I can walk you to your car."

When they reached her car, Liz looked at him and suggested on impulse, "Would you be interested in taking a quick drive around to look at the memorials? It's actually quite pretty at night. They're all lit up."

Tom readily agreed. He was having a very good time and was surprised to find himself reluctant to end the evening. Liz was great company, and he felt more comfortable with her than he had with a woman in a long time. Even before Paige left him with two nametags, they seemed to be finding an effortless flow of conversation and laughter. It was fun.

They got in Liz's car, and she drove around to some of the various memorials and important buildings along the National Mall, pointing them out as she drove. The Jefferson Memorial and Lincoln Memorial were both beautiful at night. She pointed out where the Korean and Vietnam War memorials were located, even though they couldn't be seen from the car, and suggested he visit them during the day.

She continued onto Constitution Avenue and drove back toward 14th Street, past the World War II Memorial, suggesting that one was also worth a visit during the day. They passed the rotunda side of the White House and then turned right onto 14th Street, where she parked the car in front of the Washington Monument.

"You've got to get out and enjoy this one for a few minutes," she said. "I have a blanket in my trunk. If you don't mind, we can just hop across the street and sit on the mall for a little bit. I hardly ever take the time to do this anymore, but it really is a view worth savoring. That okay with you?"

Tom agreed. When they were out of the car, Liz popped the trunk, bent over, and began to rummage around for the blanket. "Sorry," she said from inside the trunk, "my trunk is always a complete mess. Don't judge me."

"I'm judging your ass right now," Tom said very quietly under his breath, enjoying the view.

Liz turned around, blanket in hand. "What does it rate?"

"What?"

"My ass. What does it rate?"

Tom put his hand over his eyes and said, "Holy shit, I did *not* just say that out loud."

"You did. What's the rating?" she asked. She was trying to look serious, but there was a twinkle in her eye that made him think she might be enjoying his discomfort.

Tom wasn't sure how to handle this situation. With a look of embarrassment mixed with confusion, he said, "…Eight?"

"Excellent!" Liz smiled brightly and winked at him. "Although I'm pretty sure you gave me an extra point for sheer embarrassment. I'll take it, though. Come on, walk across the street with me."

I have no idea what just happened, he thought, following her across the street. This whole evening had to be the strangest interaction with a woman he had ever had.

Liz walked a little way onto the grass on the other side of the street before spreading the blanket out. They spent a moment looking toward the brightly lit Capitol building, and then she turned around, sat down, and held her hand out for him to join her. Tom took her hand and sat down beside her.

She released his hand, and they sat side by side looking up at the visage of the Washington Monument, on a slight hill, surrounded by American flags, lit from below and all around. Liz lay down on the blanket, crossed her feet at the ankles, and put her hands behind her head. Tom did the same. He somehow expected her to say something about his ass comment, but it never came up again.

"It really is beautiful, isn't it?" she asked. "It's easy to forget when you live here. I drive past it every day. People come from all over the world to see something that is so commonplace to me that I practically look through it." She was quiet again for a little while. "Thanks for coming here with me. I needed the reminder.

"DC is hot and swampy in the summer, and it doesn't get enough snow in the winter." She chuckled. "And when it does snow, people lose their minds because they don't know how to drive in it. Traffic in general is a nightmare almost all of the time. And the football team has sucked for a quite a while now." She sighed.

"But…spring and fall are spectacular. I mean, really gorgeous. And even the few square feet of earth we are lying on right now could truly be ground walked on by the feet of George Washington, or John Adams, or Abraham Lincoln."

She turned her head to see him looking at her and finished with, "And the hockey team is awesome. Welcome to Washington, Tom."

She stood up, offered him her hand, and helped him to his feet. He stood silently while she gathered up the blanket and then followed her back to the car and waited as she put the blanket in the trunk. They both got in her car and rode back toward the restaurant in what felt like comfortable silence.

Tom turned to her and simply said, "Thank you. That was a neat experience. And unexpected."

Liz pulled up next to his car in the parking lot and turned off the engine. "You're welcome. Really, thank you for indulging me." They both got out of the car to say good night.

"So," she said with a smile and wink, "I really did have a great time tonight, and I want to thank you for wearing two nametags. It was very helpful."

Tom laughed and said, "You are very welcome. I will gladly wear two nametags any time. I had a lot of fun, Liz."

They exchanged a warm hug that lingered perhaps just a moment longer than strictly necessary. As they released each other, Tom looked down at her face and on impulse placed a quick kiss on her lips.

At least, he intended it to be a quick kiss. But when he moved his lips away from hers a fraction, he just couldn't bring himself to move them away further. One kiss turned into two.

The third kiss wasn't quick. His lips pressed to hers and gently opened as he moved his hand to cup along her jawline, and she opened her lips to his. He tilted his head and stepped closer to her, bringing his other hand to her waist. The kiss was soft, slow, and gentle.

Tom felt her hand on his chest and was sure she could feel his heart racing. He had not meant to do this. But that first kiss had felt so damn good. So *right.* And every second was making this more difficult to end without, well, without how things usually ended. He had started getting hard by the third kiss.

She had given him no indication that she was interested in jumping in bed. She was *still* giving him no indication that she was interested in anything other than this kiss that was melting his brain as if he were eighteen instead of thirty-two. He certainly wasn't going to try to take advantage of Paige's best friend on a set-up first date. That seemed like a recipe for all kinds of disaster.

But her lips were soft. Her tongue was soft. *Shit, when did tongues get involved? Did I start that or did she? Damn, I don't want this to stop.*

He had no idea how long they stood there in that slow, soft, amazing kiss. Tom finally forced himself to end it and moved his lips away from hers. He kept his eyes closed and took a few breaths to try to steady himself. He kept his hand on her waist to keep a little distance between them; if she pressed up against the bulge in his jeans, he was making no promises about his actions.

Liz swayed slightly, trying to force her brain to reengage. Every nerve in her body had been tingling since his lips brushed hers, and her heart was beating so fast she was afraid he could hear it. By

25

the time he moved away, she was trying really hard *not* to act on the fierce instinct insisting that she should shove him against his car and kiss him deep and hard.

They stood for a moment, breathing hard, then managed to step back away from each other. "You okay to get home?" Tom asked, his voice husky.

She nodded, heart still racing, and gave him bit of a teasing sideways glance. She asked, "You?"

He ran a hand through his hair, took a deep breath, smiled, and nodded. He started to get into his car, stopped, turned back for a second, pointed his keys at her, and said, "Two nametags for you next time."

Chapter Three

When Liz had arrived at their house in the morning, Paige had dragged her in and practically shoved her out the back sliding glass doors to the table by the pool, saying, "Tell me everything!"

"I can tell you that you're an incredible pain in the ass. Until I have a cup of coffee in my hand, that's all you're getting out of me."

With a sound of annoyance, Paige scurried off for the coffee, passing Chris as he came out of the house carrying his own cup. The week after the pool party had become a tradition for the three of them; Liz took at least a few full days off, coming over early-ish for coffee. They would spend time together—sometimes going out on day trips or an overnighter, sometimes just hanging out by the pool. Morning coffee was always for three, so this morning was no exception.

Paige returned with Liz's coffee, and Liz took her time, making sure it was correctly prepared, with too much sugar and too much cream. Paige kicked her under the table. "Come on!"

Chris said, "Please let me know how much I have to apologize to you and/or Micky for whatever the hell happened last night."

Liz's face registered the comment with shock and turned to Paige. "You didn't tell him. Seriously, Paige? I'm going to enjoy this. Deeply." She turned back to Chris. "No apology due to me. I ended up having a great time. Tom is a lot of fun." She heard Paige make a small victory whoop. "I will let you talk with Tom about whether any apology is due on that side." She turned and looked pointedly at Paige. "And *now,*" she said, "I am going to absolutely love watching your wife explain to you exactly what she engineered last night."

Paige said to Chris, "I told you, honey, it was just a little personal joke between Liz and me. I put a few nametags on Micky when I hugged him." She shrugged. Chris raised an eyebrow and looked to Liz for input.

"Really, Paige? Really? Out with it. Do not spare the details. I certainly didn't. Stop!" She put up her hand in protest as Paige looked like she was going to interrupt. "I swear if you say one word about embarrassment on my behalf, I will kill you. Every shred of embarrassment I have on this topic was burned away in a fiery crucible last night. Now I just want to see you explain this all to Chris. Go." She sat back, gesturing from Paige to Chris with her hand.

Trapped, Paige told Chris the whole story. Liz watched his eyes get bigger, saw him valiantly trying to fight laughter at her expense, and heard at least one "Oh, sweet Jesus" under his breath.

Paige left off at putting the nametags on Tom at the restaurant, and Liz picked up the story. When she got to the part about the eyelashes, Chris finally lost it entirely, laughing so hard he was gasping for air. Paige was laughing with tears on her face but managed to ask, "What happened?"

Liz, who had stayed in storytelling mode to this point, broke a bit and giggled. "Exactly what just happened. We both started laughing so hard we had to leave. We walked around the corner and leaned against the wall until we could breathe again."

After a few more minutes of coming down from a laughter high, Chris wiped his eyes and just said, "Holy shit, Liz. Only you."

She smiled at him and said, "Ah, but your life would be dull without me."

"So true."

Paige chimed in, now that they were back to normal conversation, "What happened next? Did you guys go anywhere after dinner?"

"I drove him around DC to look at the monuments."

Paige smiled and said, "What does that mean? Is that a new euphemism that I don't know about? 'Looking at monuments?'" She used air quotes and gave her friend a knowing look.

Liz looked at her and said very slowly and plainly, as if Paige needed special help with comprehension, "It means I *drove him around* and we *looked at the monuments.*" She returned to her normal speech habits. "I don't want to know what weird shit you two are getting up to in your personal life."

She left out the part about the kiss. That amazing, unbelievable, please-let-this-never-end, my-toes-are-curling kiss. Paige would be so disappointed when nothing went beyond that way-too-hot kiss; Liz suspected Paige had already decided they would make a perfect couple. Besides, she really wasn't sure she wanted to share it, as if talking about it would suddenly break the spell. She hadn't felt this way in a very long time, and she just wanted to quietly enjoy it while it lasted.

Chris looked up briefly from his coffee. He had mostly stopped listening when he heard them slip into best friend banter. "You really did end up having a good time, right? Micky behaved himself?"

Liz smiled inwardly, loving Chris for providing her with this perfect opportunity. She paused, trying to time her comments with Chris's next sip of coffee. "Of course," she said. "He was a perfect gentleman." *Wait for it...*"And he rated my ass an eight!"

Chris choked, glared at her, coughed coffee onto his shirt, tried to breathe through his nose, and finally swallowed. He wiped his face off. She heard him say, "God damn it, Liz," under his breath as he headed toward the house to change his shirt. She was pretty sure she caught, "Every fucking time," as he was closing the sliding glass door.

Paige sighed. "You two are ridiculous."

"It's fun. It gets harder to do every time. He's gotten very cagy. But that was five in a row. I'm on a roll. That's my best streak ever."

"You keep score? Seriously?"

Liz stared at her. "Of course. What's the fun otherwise? I try to make him spew out his coffee when we're all here. He tries not to. There are rules."

"Rules."

"Well, they're all in my head. We've never actually discussed this. It's my game. My rules. Leave me my pathetic amusements, Paige."

Paige turned the topic back to Tom. Again. "Did he ask for your phone number?"

"What? Oh. You are relentless about this. No, he didn't."

"Did you ask for his phone number?"

"No."

"Did you offer him your phone number?"

"No." Paige looked at her strangely. "What? I don't think either of us was particularly worried about never seeing the other person again, seeing as we have best friends in common. I assumed I would be seeing him around."

"So you guys aren't, say, planning on going to a museum or the zoo?"

Liz paused. "Oh. Shit. I'm sorry, Paige."

Every time Paige had introduced her to a new person in town, sometimes someone from the team, sometimes a new teacher from her school, or a new neighbor, Liz had always, *always,* invited the person out to go to the zoo or a museum. It was just something she did, and Paige was rather astounded that she had not done the same for Tom.

"Damn it, every single conversation with this guy seems to involve me apologizing for inconsiderate behavior." Liz sighed. "I guess now I need his phone number."

"I'm pretty sure this isn't considered thoughtless behavior by anyone's standards except your own, you idiot," said Paige. "I was just really surprised. You do *not* have to do this. I promise, Liz. Don't do this for me."

Liz smiled. "I'm not. I'm doing it for me. You know I love going to the zoo. And we really did have a good time last night. He's smart and funny. Still too damn good looking, though."

Chris poked his head out of the sliding glass door, wearing a different shirt. "Liz, Micky just texted to ask for your phone number. Okay to give it to him, yeah?"

"Yup. I was just getting his from Paige. Thank you for asking, though. I appreciate it."

Paige kicked her under the table again. Liz said, "Shut up." She tried to ignore how Chris's announcement had made her stomach flip around oddly.

She got Tom's number from Paige's phone and put it into her own, took a deep breath, and called it. No point in waiting. This stuff never got better with age. She tried to ignore Paige watching her every move.

He picked up quickly and said with a note of surprise, "Liz?" His voice was deep, and sent that odd flipping sensation into overdrive.

"Hi. I'm sitting at Chris and Paige's house. I'd just asked for your number when you texted and asked for mine. I took it as a sign I should call."

"I'm really glad you did." He had just finished entering her name into his contacts when it had popped up ringing. He could feel a smile on his face he suspected was much larger than was warranted by a simple phone call.

"In keeping with what seems to be a theme with me these days, I'm calling to make amends."

"I can't imagine what for."

She smiled and tried to ignore Paige shifting to get a better look at her face. "When Paige introduces me to friends of hers who are new to the area, I have a long-standing tradition of inviting them out to go to a museum or the zoo. She pointed out to me this morning that I did not do that for you." She turned to face Paige as she added, "Which I am going to blame on the whole nametags incident, by the way. Threw me way off my game, so this is actually your fault, Paige. Oh, man, my day just got a whole lot better realizing that." Tom laughed on the other end of the line. "Seriously, though, any interest? Museum or zoo, your choice. You are absolutely allowed to say no. I will not be upset. It's the offering that was the important part to me."

Tom said, "Well, I was actually calling to ask you if you would like to go to a movie sometime. As a kind of apology for the intense awkwardness. If that makes any sense." He paused, suddenly wondering if he was making any sense or making things worse. She had been awkward because she thought he was attractive, so he's apologizing? *Nice, Micky. Smooth.*

"Sure. Any time." *Because it won't be at all distracting to be sitting next to you in a dark movie theater.* There was a pause in the conversation, and

Liz closed her eyes, lost for a moment in the memory of their kiss.

She caught his next sentence a few words in. "…beautiful today. Are you free now? I would love to go to the zoo."

Tom held the phone up away from his mouth and cursed quietly to himself. *Sound desperate much?* He hadn't stopped thinking about kissing her since he had walked away last night, but this was ridiculous.

"Hang on a second." Liz muted the phone and turned to Paige. "Please answer this question without additional commentary: Would you mind if I bailed on our plans and went to the zoo today?"

Paige made a joyful squeak. "No! Not at all! Go forth! Have fun!"

"All right, shut up already." She unmuted the phone. "I have double checked, and I am free for the day. I'm all yours!" *Shit! So not what I meant to say!*

"Great, I'm looking forward to this!" They finished making plans to meet and hung up the phone. Tom sat down on the couch in the house he shared with two other guys on the team, put his head back, and closed his eyes.

Paige's best friend. She is Becks' wife's best friend. It doesn't matter how amazing that kiss was. He opened his eyes again.

Shit. I can't even lie to myself.

Chapter Four

They had a wonderful time at the zoo. Liz always enjoyed taking people there, and Tom had fun being with her. She was enthusiastic about…everything, it seemed to him. He seriously didn't know what to make of this woman. She was showing him around the zoo with the excitement of a kid.

"Oh, the pandas!" She told him about the pandas and the arrangement that the Smithsonian has with China, and when they moved on to a different part of the zoo, she got just as enthusiastic about the next animal. And so on.

In between, she asked him about life in Montreal, snow in Minnesota, the differences between college hockey and the NHL…certainly all things personally relevant to him, but nothing personal or intrusive. He found himself telling her about all sorts of things, one topic running into the next with an ease he found surprising.

He turned to her after telling her about poutine and said, "You can't really be finding this interesting."

"Why not?" she replied, looking completely serious. "I've never been to Montreal. I've certainly never eaten poutine." He looked at her curiously for a moment, but they were arriving at the next animal exhibit.

"Do you know details about every animal in the zoo?" Tom asked with a laugh, after Liz told him joyfully about the small-clawed river otters.

"It's a sickness." She laughed. "I like learning stuff. About things. All kinds of stuff about all kinds of things. Think of me as a font of mostly useless knowledge. Although it occasionally does come in useful, like on trivia night. Or zoo visits."

They had decided to call it a day and were heading toward the lower parking lot and their cars. "So what you're saying is I definitely want you on my team if I'm playing any kind of trivia game, or *Jeopardy,* or anything like that."

Liz turned toward him, stopped, and looked at him intensely for a moment. "Yes. In all seriousness, we will kick their asses. Word games too. I have also never been on a losing Pictionary team. My competitive side is small but highly focused." She smiled. "And if you decide to be my adversary in any of these things, consider yourself fairly warned."

They stopped as they reached Tom's car. It was mid-afternoon, and they'd eaten lunch at the zoo a few hours earlier. There was no real reason to continue to be together, and yet, neither one of them was making any move toward leaving.

On sudden impulse, Liz asked, "Would you like

to hang out at my place this evening and watch a movie? The latest Avengers flick is available for rent, and I've been looking forward to seeing it. I missed it when it was out in the theaters. I've got a big screen, nice speakers, a comfy squishy couch, footrest, beer, and popcorn," she said, ticking off the important points on her fingers. She felt her heart racing a little.

Tom felt a small leap in his chest at the idea of seeing her again so soon. "Sounds good to me," he replied. "Avengers, though? Really?"

"Yeah!" Liz sounded excited. She stopped and looked suspiciously at him. "Why, do you not enjoy superhero movies? Because I'm afraid this evening might be over before it even starts if that's the case."

Tom put his hands up in a defensive gesture. "No, that's not it, I promise," he said, laughing. "I like them as much as the next guy, I guess. I'm just not used to…" He paused and looked at Liz.

She crossed her arms and lifted one eyebrow.

"You know," he continued, "it's not often that women are really into…"

The corner of Liz's mouth curved up in rather dangerous-looking smile, although there was a twinkle in her eye.

"I am sorely tempted to make you finish that sentence and then make you stand there in awkward silence." She paused briefly to emphasize what awkward silence would sound like. "But since you're still new here, I guess I'll let you off the hook. However, this has made me realize I need to know some things about you."

"Okay," he said, not sure what he was getting into.

"Star Wars," she said.

Tom just looked at her. "What about it?"

"Star Wars," she repeated with emphasis. "Yes? No? Seen any of them? Seen all of them? Like them, hate them? I need information."

"Oh. Right. Yes, I've seen them. All of them. Like them, not in love with them. Before we get too far into this conversation, please remember that I've lived and breathed hockey my entire life, so don't judge too harshly."

"Fair enough," she conceded. "Point taken. But you do like superhero movies, right? I don't actually want to bore you this evening."

"Yes, I do," he said with a smile. *I'm pretty sure I won't be bored.*

"Okay, then," she said brightly. "This should be quick and painless. Marvel or DC Comics?"

Tom thought a moment. "DC Comics," he said, glad to be able to give an answer, although he didn't really have a strong feeling one way or the other.

Liz squinted at him and pursed her lips. "X-men or Avengers?"

"X-men."

She sighed, looking a little defeated, and said, "You are so lucky you're cute."

Tom laughed. "I've already been downgraded from 'fantasy' to 'cute?' I'm crushed," he said, grabbing his heart in mock despair.

Liz laughed with him, both relieved and pleased he was already comfortable joking with her about what could have been such an awkward subject.

"I'm afraid you were downgraded at the DC Comics answer. I thought maybe you could make up a few points if you chose the Avengers on the Marvel side, but what can I say?" She shrugged. She looked very serious for a moment and put her hand on his arm in a comforting gesture. "You are still really cute, Tom. It's okay." Liz tried to ignore the fact that touching his arm made her slightly dizzy.

"Oh, thank you. I feel much better now." Every hair on Tom's arm was standing up. *I'm not a teenager. This is insane.*

She gave him her address, and they decided on a time and prepared to part. Tom asked, "Can I bring something? A bottle of wine?"

Liz looked a little sheepish and said, "Only if it's something you'd particularly like. Wine just isn't my thing. I'm more of a beer chick. I've got some Fat Tire at my place, but you're welcome to bring something different. See you tonight!" And she turned and walked to her car.

Tom watched her walk away, admiring the view, of course, but a little lost in thought. She was keeping him off balance in surprising little ways, but he couldn't remember the last time he felt this comfortable with someone this quickly. There was an ease between them that was really nice. "Right." Like they fit. He smiled.

***

Tom knocked on her apartment door, holding a six-pack with a few craft brews he particularly liked. She opened the door and threw him a thousand-watt smile, and he felt an unexpected flip in his stomach.

Liz had obviously showered—her hair was almost but not entirely dry and hung in soft, dark blonde waves past her shoulders, rather than being up in a ponytail or a loose bun as it had been other times he'd seen her. She was barefoot and wearing well-worn jeans. Her t-shirt was obviously shaped for a woman, as it hugged her curves, but not tightly. It looked like it fit perfectly. All in all, she looked completely at home, completely comfortable.

"Hey!" she said brightly, giving him a welcoming hug. "Come on in! Welcome to my humble abode." Liz put one foot slightly forward, bowed formally, and gestured around her apartment with one hand. "I hope you have enjoyed your tour, because that's pretty much it."

Tom laughed. "I'm a thirty-two-year-old man temporarily living with roommates. Again. This looks like a little slice of heaven to me."

Liz thanked him for the beer, and they each grabbed one. While she moved the rest to the fridge, she gestured to the couch. "Please, go take a seat on my very favorite piece of furniture. The squishiest, most comfy little couch ever. I've got the movie queued up, and the popcorn is ready. I'll grab it and bring it over."

The couch was really an oversized, overstuffed loveseat, covered in a soft microfiber, with matching ottoman. Tom flopped his large frame down into a corner, kicked off his flip-flops, and propped his bare feet on the ottoman, guessing from

Liz's attire that this would be acceptable, and rested his left hand holding the beer on the armrest. He briefly tilted his head back and called out, "Okay, Liz, you're right. This might be the best couch ever."

"I know, right?" she replied as she came around the side of the couch holding a bowl of popcorn and her beer. "I've had it for years. It just keeps getting better."

She put the bowl of popcorn on the ottoman for a moment to turn out the main light, then sat back down, cross-legged, next to Tom and moved the popcorn bowl to her lap. She hit "play" on the remote, picked up the bowl, and uncurled to sit on the couch normally.

Without thinking, Tom moved his right arm over in a natural invitation to have her sit close beside him.

Without thinking, Liz snuggled next to him, turning slightly toward him, feet drawn up close on the couch and her knees pulled up partially on his lap. She was holding her beer balanced on her knee and placed the popcorn bowl in his lap by the armrest. Her head was against his chest near his shoulder. He pulled her in close, dropping his right hand down her arm to her elbow and hip, as if it were the most natural thing in the world. As if they had done this a hundred times before.

The first scene was well under way by the time they both fully recognized just how closely together they were sitting.

Liz became more and more aware of the warmth of his body beside her. She felt the size and strength of the arm that was around her shoulder and was almost painfully aware of the feel of him slowly moving his thumb against her elbow in an unconscious caress. He was wearing a soft t-shirt, and she was having trouble resisting the urge to turn her head and rub her cheek against his chest—to feel the strength of him, to move her face up to the crook of his neck so that she could smell him again, as she had outside the restaurant.

The thought made a small shiver run through her. Her heart was racing, and the room felt much too hot. She desperately wanted to at least put her hand on his chest again—the brief touch during their kiss the other night was a tantalizing sample of how just how good that felt—but one hand was between her and his side, and the other was trapped in the job of balancing a beer she was not going to drink.

By the time Tom felt Liz shudder, he was already deep in his own struggle. She was soft and warm, and her hair smelled wonderful, and the minute he started thinking about their kiss the previous night, he was lost. His brain shut off. He realized he had been gently caressing her arm and paused for a moment to fully register the action. He began again but allowed the tips of his other fingers to trail along the inside of her lower arm as well.

She felt every nerve ending blazing at the contact point of each fingertip and was distantly surprised to find that each one of those nerve endings apparently ran directly to every possible erogenous zone. She felt her nipples contract, and a flood of moisture headed south in her body, sending another shiver rippling through her. *He's only touching my* arm. *I'm not going to make it.*

She gave up, closed her eyes, and firmly rubbed her cheek against his chest briefly, just for a moment, just to see how it felt. *God, he feels amazing.*

Tom had gritted his teeth with her second shuddcr, and his breath hissed in slightly when she rubbed against his chest. He was wearing loose cargo shorts, and there was already considerably less room in them than when he'd sat down a little while ago. He put his beer down on the side table and moved the bowl of popcorn.

As he gently took the beer from her right hand, she immediately moved it onto his chest, pressing in to feel the hardness of the muscles underneath his shirt. She could feel his heartbeat.

He removed his hand from her arm and lightly gripped her hip. His voice rasped, "Please tell me you're not watching this movie."

She grabbed a fistful of his t-shirt and said huskily, "I'm not sure I saw the title screen."

He moved quickly, saying, "Oh, thank God," as he pulled her to straddle his lap. Liz raked her fingers through his hair on her way to wrapping her arms around his neck, and he raised his head to kiss her parted lips. Tom held her with one arm angled up her back and the other across her hips. Their first kiss was an electric shock straight to his groin, and he flexed suddenly, pulling her against him tightly, pressing his firm erection to the seam of her jeans and thrusting his tongue into her mouth.

Liz moaned into his mouth as he pulled her into

him, and it was Tom's turn to groan when she ground herself briefly against the sizable bulge in his shorts. He ran his hands up her sides and under her shirt, cupping her breasts, and then reached behind to unclasp her bra. He moved his hands back around, stroking along her bare skin, and then pulled away from their kiss so he could watch her face as he ran his thumbs over her nipples.

The feeling was so intense she gasped out loud and grabbed his shoulder for support as her muscles jumped.

"Oh, God," she breathed, clearly trying to get her bearings.

Tom already felt his control slipping, and when Liz reacted so strongly just to him touching her nipples, his erection surged and made every effort to breach the restrictions of fabric. He could see she felt it, because she suddenly tightened her grip on his shoulder and looked at him with eyes almost feral in their intensity.

Her reactions were making him crazy. He was trying to remember there were reasons he shouldn't be doing this.

She shifted her hips against him, pressed and thrust along his length, and kissed him hard, pushing her tongue into his mouth. Tom pulled her in tight again as she bit at his lower lip, her fingers tangled in the hair at the back of his neck.

Liz was moving on his lap, making small rocking movements against his rock-hard erection. He shifted his hands down to her hips to hold her still in an effort to regain some measure of brain function but then pressed up into her, unable to stop seeking the heat and friction.

She gasped and moaned his name.

Tom. Not Micky.

It was just enough to pry through the lust.

He moved his hands up to her shoulders and in the greatest, and worst, act of willpower of his life gently pushed back from the kiss, saying, "Liz, I don't want to—"

Her eyes flew open, and she immediately backed toward his knees, saying, "Oh my God, Tom, I'm so sorry, I…"

He grabbed her wrists to keep her from moving further and croaked, "Stop! Stop. Let me finish." He looked at her, wanting her to understand. "I don't want to take advantage of you."

She blinked at him for a moment.

"Oh."

In a slightly strangled voice, he said, "I am about five seconds away from the point of no return. You are so fucking sexy," he continued, his voice getting lower and huskier, and his eyes dark and lusty, "and I am insanely turned on, and God, I want you. But we met like five minutes ago, and you're Paige's best friend. I don't want to take advantage of you."

Liz looked at him for a few seconds, breathing hard, and then asked, in the sexiest voice Tom had ever heard, "Can I take advantage of you?"

Tom stared at her, still holding her wrists, while her words filtered through to the part of his brain that could still process speech.

"Holy. Fuck. Yes."

Chapter Five

"You're wearing way too many clothes," she said from her position in the middle of the bed. He had already removed her shirt and bra.

Tom growled, a sound that sent shivers racing down her entire body. He climbed over her on the bed, and she sat up to kiss him, running her hands up under his shirt, finally touching his chest and back, pulling the shirt up over his head.

Liz pulled herself close to him, pressing her breasts to his chest, feeling the friction of his chest hair against her nipples, exploring the planes of his back with her hands, exploring the feel of his tongue with hers. She wanted to touch every part of him.

She moved her hands around to the front of his shorts, released the button, and pulled down the zipper. When she reached inside his boxer briefs and wrapped her hand around his hard shaft, he groaned and looked down at her with lust-filled eyes and a playfully wicked smile.

He gave her a shove back onto the bed, undid her

jeans, and quickly pulled them off along with her underwear before disposing of his own clothing. He moved back to hover over her, braced on his hands, looking down into her eyes.

Liz reached up with one hand to pull him down for a hard kiss while reaching down with the other to guide his hardness toward her entrance. She didn't want to wait, and they were both so ready.

The first pressure of him entering her was fantastic. He was a big guy, and everything about him was gorgeously proportional. And it had been such a long time—years. He was taking this part slowly, and it was amazing. She moaned and whispered, "Oh, God," getting lost in the sensation of his slow, shallow movements.

Tom put his head down near her ear, breathing her in, listening to her. He was taking things almost teasingly slow now they had actually begun, so she could get used to his size, and because it clearly turned her on. She shifted her left leg up over his hip, making more sounds of pleasure. He growled a little, enjoying what he was doing to her before they had even really started.

Liz was making small rocking motions with her hips as he moved further and further in with each small thrust; he was almost fully inside her now. With a final push, he pressed completely into her, grinding his pubic bone against her clit.

Liz gasped, clutched Tom, pressed her face into his neck, spasmed against him, and cried out, "Oh my God, Tom!" as the unexpected orgasm washed over her.

Tom froze in surprise, feeling her muscles

pulsing around him and hearing her call out his name in her climax. That she had orgasmed simply from him entering her caught him off guard, and he squeezed his eyes shut and dropped his head, not moving.

He felt Liz relax underneath him and heard her say quietly, "Holy crap." And then she shifted and pulsed around him one more time. She stroked his shoulder and said, "Are you okay?"

Tom gritted his teeth and growled, "I'm trying not to come. Don't move."

Another pulse, along with a gasp. She said, "Sorry about that, I can't control the aftershocks."

"Shit," he grumbled under his breath, twitching inside her. "Don't talk, either. Give me a minute."

She smiled and said, "I could add an extra nametag. The first one says, 'Hi, my name is Liz.'" She felt another twitch.

"Shut up."

"The next one is, 'Your name is Tom.'"

Another twitch. He growled again. "I'm serious."

"And then one that says, 'Think about baseball stats because they're really fucking boring.'"

He lifted his head and looked at her.

"They are!" she assured him. "Oh, wait, you were an econ major. Shit, if baseball stats make you really horny, that's not gonna help at all, is it?" Her eyes twinkled as she smiled at him.

Tom smiled, laughed, and said, "They do not make me horny. You, on the other hand..." His smile changed mood entirely, and he began moving inside her.

She moaned and dropped her head back onto the

pillow.

Tom moved in to kiss the hollow of her throat, then up under her ear, and then spoke into her ear, his breath vibrating the tiny nerve endings there. "You are making me crazy." He was slowly sliding in and out of her. "Feeling you come around me was unbelievable. I want to feel it again."

Her breath caught in a gasp, and she moved her leg up over his hip again, grinding against him.

He chuckled and moved his mouth to her other ear. "More than once. Tonight."

Liz caught his mouth with a kiss and grabbed his ass, pulling him as close to her as possible, trying to find more friction. Tom reached down and moved her leg on his hip even higher, pressing underneath her thigh, and then thrust deep and ground down hard.

She released the kiss to say, "Yes! Please! Don't stop!"

Tom repeated the deep thrust three more times, and she shouted her climax. He felt her clasping him in pulses, and she looked at him with eyes wide and smoky, and so sexy he felt it in his chest.

Liz put her hands on either side of his face and kissed him. Her voice was husky and low. "You are amazing. I want to watch you when you come. I want to feel you come inside me. I have an IUD, but if you want a condom and you have one, now is the time, because I have no intention of letting you go until I watch you have an earth-shattering orgasm."

She heard him say, "Christ," and then he was thrusting into her with a strength and fierceness that made her legs weak. She watched his face, listened to his breathing and the sounds he made, feeling the sensations building inside her again. She was moving her hips with him, and her sounds of pleasure were joining his.

It was becoming more and more difficult to keep her eyes open to watch his face, but he was almost there; she knew it. She was too.

Tom roared when he climaxed. There was no other word for the sound. It was primal, male, and utterly intoxicating. The sound triggered another orgasm for Liz, and they finished together.

He tried not to collapse directly on top of her and moved off to the side, hearing Liz groan as he slipped out of her.

She sighed. "That part always feels slightly wrong."

He pulled her to snuggle close into his shoulder. "That might be the most amazing sex I have ever experienced. And that is a compliment I do not give lightly." Tom looked down at her. "I have to know. Do you always come like that? At the beginning of sex?"

She chuckled, sounding happy, utterly satisfied, and slightly buzzed from the orgasm highs. "No, that was a first, and that was fantastic, by the way. Having three was new as well. Two, yes. Three? That was all you."

She ran her hands over his chest, emphasizing her words, humming contentedly. "Mmmmm. And I concur—possibly the best sex of my life." She looked up in his eyes and smiled. "Thank you."

It was his turn to chuckle. "My pleasure. Truly." The corner of his mouth turned up, and he put his hands behind his head and said, "All in a day's work for a fantasy, ma'am."

Liz laughed, and her eyes took on a twinkling look that was rapidly turning smoky. Tom already recognized the look and felt his heart jump. Other parts weren't quite ready to jump yet, but it wouldn't be too long.

"You do realize," she said, "that in a fantasy it's never just one time."

He pulled her in and kissed her, deeply and quite thoroughly. "It's a tough gig."

Chapter Six

Tom left Liz's place early in the morning, heading home to shower and change. There was no morning-after awkwardness, and they kissed goodbye at her door.

Liz got ready and went over to Chris and Paige's house for morning coffee. She and Paige were going to be heading a few miles south to the town of Occoquan to visit the art galleries, have lunch, and generally enjoy a quiet day wandering the pretty little historic area. That had been yesterday's plan before the zoo.

She had just started her first cup with Paige when Chris came out of the sliding glass doors, followed by Tom. Tom had not expected to see her and did not look entirely happy at the surprise. Liz was equally surprised by his arrival.

"Oh! Hi, Tom. I wasn't expecting to see you again so soon."

"Yeah, same here." He sounded a little guarded.

Paige spoke up. "It's our tradition. The week after the pool party is 'morning coffee with Liz' and

'Paige and Liz time' at our house." Tom's look softened a bit, but he still looked slightly ill at ease, almost suspicious. "Did you enjoy the zoo yesterday? Liz had just started to tell me about your visit there, but Lord knows she loves the place, so she'll probably tell me you loved all the animals just as much as she does."

Tom looked at Paige for a few seconds, trying to find some sort of innuendo or teasing involved in her line of questioning, but could find none. "I did enjoy it," he said, a bit cautiously, still searching Paige's face for signs that she was aware of their later activities. "I think the O-Line was my favorite, though. Watching orangutans swinging directly overhead is definitely not something you see every day."

Paige didn't blink at the mention of the name—the name of the zoo feature was a play on the naming of the lines of DC's Metro System—but Tom saw Liz's eyes go wide just for a moment in his peripheral vision. She had definitely caught his double entendre.

"Oh, I love that too! But I would not stand directly underneath. I don't trust an orangutan that far." Paige laughed. "So we're heading out to do something that Chris would hate. Do you guys have plans? Because I would love to force him to come along. We could convince him it's your burning desire to visit the little town of Occoquan."

"I'm standing right here, Paige."

Tom laughed and said, "I'm not sure there even is a plan. We'll probably just sit around and scratch ourselves. We are guys."

Paige grimaced. "Lord, that sounds about right. Hey, Chris, come help me find my spare set of car keys for next week before I forget about it again, okay? Liz, we can leave in just a second." Chris got up and followed her inside.

Tom sat down next to Liz, looked at her sideways, and said, "You didn't say anything." It was a statement, not a question.

"Neither did you," she pointed out. She sipped her coffee. "Should I have told Chris that I took advantage of his best friend five minutes after we met?" she asked, smiling around her coffee mug.

He smiled at her, looking completely relaxed for the first time since arriving.

"So," she asked, "are we okay, then?"

He chuckled. "I think that's supposed to be my line."

"Oh, sorry," she said. "Please, proceed."

Tom gave her a slightly exasperated look. She gestured for him to proceed. He laughed and said, "Are we okay, then?"

"Yes. Definitely."

Chris and Paige came walking back out, Chris holding his coffee cup. Seeing Tom laughing, he asked, "What are you two talking about?"

Liz once again inwardly thanked him. *Sweet, sweet man. Wait for it...*"I was just telling Tom about my reputation as an insatiable puck bunny."

Chris choked and spewed coffee. Tom gaped.

"No, really, ask around!"

Tom started laughing as Liz grabbed Paige's hand and ran off. She heard Chris saying, "God *damn it,* Liz!"

***

Tom watched the two of them heading off around the yard gate to Paige's car and heard Chris say, "Every time. Every *fucking* time," as he was trying to clean coffee off himself. "Well, shit. Come inside while I change my fucking shirt. *Again.*"

"So this is a thing?"

Chris glared at him, and Tom laughed and put up his hands. They continued walking, with Chris grumbling, and Tom realized this was actually the perfect opportunity to ask about Liz without being completely offensive.

"So I take it she's *not* an insatiable puck bunny?" He tried to sound funny, and he guessed it worked, because Chris answered without sounding pissed, but it was not necessarily an idle question.

She was confusing the hell out of him. If he was just one in a line of hockey players, that was fine, but he would like to know.

Chris's response was to laugh, look at Tom, and then laugh a lot harder at Tom's expression. "Holy shit, you're serious! Sorry, Micky, I sometimes forget you two just met. Hang on a minute, I'll be right back." Chris reappeared in a clean, coffee-less shirt a few seconds later and continued. "No, she is absolutely *not* a puck bunny. Insatiable or otherwise." He laughed again.

"Liz has a ton of friends—I'm sure you picked that up from the party—and knows a lot of the guys on the team just from being around. She and Zee are tight, but he's probably her closest other friend on the team besides me. She is a huge Guards fan. A hockey fan in general, yes, but she's been a Guards fan since long before I got here.

"Honestly, though, now that I'm thinking about it…shit, I'm not sure I've ever seen her with a serious boyfriend. Which I'm sure is why Paige went so batshit crazy when you rolled into town. I'm sorry about that again, Mick."

Tom said, "No, man, no problem. It's been fun."

"Paige just sees two people she cares about and wants them to care about each other. I told her to tone it down. I'm sure Liz told her that too. She's pretty levelheaded when it comes to stuff like that."

Tom chuckled. "It's all good, Becks. You know I love Paige. And Liz is great. I feel like she's already a really good friend." He stopped for a second and thought about it. "Shit, that's just fucking weird. I almost feel like I've known her for months, rather than a few days."

Chris slapped him on the shoulder and said, "Yup. She does that. I have no idea how. And it is fucking weird."

***

The girls had just gotten into Paige's car after Chris had spit his coffee. Paige turned to Liz. "Sometimes I think you are about ten years old."

"I know, right? I'm so much fun!"

"Oh, that's so not what I meant."

Liz just grinned at her.

Paige laughed as she started driving toward the highway. "Seriously, though, did you guys have a good time at the zoo yesterday?"

"I told you we did. Really. He is a smart and funny guy." She thought for a minute. "Hey, do you guys still have the extra room at the condo next week at Virginia Beach? Or did you find someone else to go with you?"

Paige replied excitedly. "No, we didn't find anyone else. Does this mean you can go after all?"

Liz said, "Ah, I wish. No, that's still not going to work. But I think you should ask Tom. He's never been."

They were sitting at a stoplight. Paige turned to her. "Oh, that's a great idea. Of course he's never been to Virginia Beach! Chris will have a blast."

Liz put her hand on Paige's arm. "No. Paige, he's never been to *any* beach. He's never been in the ocean."

"Get. Out." The car behind them honked to let her know the light had turned green, and Paige turned back to the road and continued on. "How did you find that out?"

"While we were walking around the zoo. It came up in conversation."

Paige smiled. Liz had a way of making people feel comfortable in conversations and ended up learning details like this. She had known Tom for days. Paige had known him for years.

"I know you guys don't go out and party like we all used to, but there must be some nightspots around there. I'm sure there would be plenty of lovely beach bunnies looking to meet a gorgeous hockey player. At least for the week." Liz raised and lowered her eyebrows at Paige, who had looked over at her briefly. "What?" Liz asked. The look

Paige had given her had bordered on sad. "What's wrong?"

"I had really hoped that you guys would hit it off."

"We did! He's great!"

Paige sighed. "That's not what I mean, Liz, and you know it."

Liz smiled and took one of Paige's hands. They were on the highway now, with straight driving for the next twenty minutes or so. "He just got here, Paige. He's barely unpacked his luggage, and I'm not sure the ink is dry on his contract yet. It's not reasonable to think he's going to want to get involved in a relationship the minute he gets here."

Paige glanced over and said, "You sound just like Chris."

"Occasionally even Chris says smart things."

"I just want you to be happy, Liz."

Liz sat up, stunned by the comment. "God, Paige—I feel like I need you to pull over to say this to you, I mean this so seriously—I am happier now than I have ever been in my entire life. These past few years have been the happiest I have ever had. I thought you knew that. How could you not know that?"

Paige said, "I know, I know. That's not what I mean. I mean I want you to share that with someone. I want you to be happy *with* someone. You don't have a Chris. You don't have a family." She drew a breath. "You know what I mean."

Liz smiled again. "I know. But that will either happen, or it won't. And you and Chris *are* my family. I *know* you know that. So please don't say I don't have one again, okay? Because that kinda stings."

"Shoot. You know I don't mean it that way."

"I do. And you know I love you like crazy. But you can't force it."

"I'm impatient. I want two people who I love to love each other. Is that too much to ask?"

Liz laughed out loud. "And you'd like it to happen in, say, two days. That should work out just fine. So are you gonna take Tom to the beach or not?"

"Oh, hell, yes. First of all, Chris will have such a great time. I can't wait to see that. Second, I will be off the hook for all the stuff that he likes to do that I don't want to. I can't see a downside to this situation. 'Sure, guys! Go ride go-karts! Nope, I don't mind. I'll just be sitting here on the beach reading my book.' That sounds like heaven!"

Liz thought for a minute and then said, "Will you take videos of Tom getting knocked on his ass in the ocean? Because that would be awesome."

"For you? Definitely."

Chapter Seven

The week that Chris, Paige, and Tom were at the beach was fantastic for them. As expected, Tom and Chris spent the entire week bonding, allowing Paige to spend the entire week relaxing.

"Liz, this has been ah-may-zing," she told her friend on the phone one evening. "They just left for some bar—I don't even know where. I've spent the entire afternoon in a lounge chair with a drink and a book, occasionally saying, 'Sure, honey, whatever you want.' You are a genius."

Liz laughed. "I have been trying to tell you that for years."

"Seriously, though, I haven't seen Chris this happy in a while. He and Micky always have so much fun together. Oh, I sent you a few more videos. None are as good as those first few, though. They were the absolute best."

One had been perfect. Paige had managed to capture that moment when Tom got a little too cocky with his new ability to manage the waves, got caught completely unprepared, and was knocked ass-over-teakettle. Chris had been right next to him when it had happened and had been laughing so hard it was amazing that neither of them had drowned.

"I had to watch that one, oh, about fifty times in a row," Liz said. "I made my boss watch it too. And then we showed it on the really big screen in the conference room."

She didn't mention how many times she had watched the videos Paige sent just to see Tom wearing board shorts. Sometimes she missed the entire point of the video the first or second time through because there were those broad shoulders, abs, a gorgeous back...or her vivid memory of what was under the board shorts...keeping her from being able to pay attention to anything but him.

Paige confided, "I sent it to their agent." Tom and Chris had the same agent. "She loved it, so she's going to see that it's released. It should be picked up on local social media soon. Something to the effect of 'New Guards Player Makes Waves at Virginia Beach.' Both of them would want to kill me if I did it myself. This way I can play dumb and say I was just sharing it with Janine for fun."

Liz grinned. "Perfect. You are an evil genius. Chris does not deserve you. I'll let you know when I see it hit the various Guards Facebook and Twitter stuff."

"Everything okay at the house?"

"Of course. I'm eating all your food and drinking all your beer. All is well."

Paige laughed. "See you in a few days."

***

On Saturday afternoon Liz was sitting by the pool, drinking water and reading a book, when the group got back from their trip. She had been house-sitting all week. It was an easy solution for all of them—Liz left her car parked at her apartment for the week and stayed at their house whenever they were gone for an extended time. She used one of their cars, had an entire house to herself, was able to use the pool, and they had the benefit of the house continually looking lived in, because it was.

She heard the car pull in and walked out front to meet them.

"We had such a great time!" Paige gushed, scurrying for the front door. "Let me get inside and pee before I die!"

Chris greeted her with a hug. "Hey, you! Thanks for watching the house."

"Anytime, sweetie, you know that. I'm always looking for a location for my next kegger."

"Ha, ha. But I am going to go check the liquor cabinet. I don't trust you that far." He grabbed a suitcase and started toward the house.

Tom got out of the car, stretched, and grinned at her.

"Hey, handsome," she said. "I wasn't sure I would see you. I thought they might drop you off at your place on the way home."

Tom watched Chris disappear into the house, and immediately put his arms around Liz, pulled her close, and delivered a bone-melting kiss. "I know the trip was your idea," he said, kissing her again deeply. "Thank you." Another kiss. "I missed you."

He let her go as suddenly as he had swept her up, and she stared at him, lips slightly parted, speechless, heart pounding, insides swirling. Just then Paige walked out the door chattering brightly about the wonderful time they had. Tom kept eye contact with Liz as he backed toward the front door, smiling, his eyes playful and flirty. Then he winked, laughed at her expression, and turned around to head inside the house.

Liz realized she had missed half of whatever Paige had just said. "I'm so sorry, Paige, what was that?"

Paige squinted at her suspiciously. "What's up with you?"

Liz went with the easiest answer. "I got totally distracted. I haven't seen fantasy boy there for more than a week. I need to build up my tolerance again to be able to focus when he's around. Gonna need more nametags."

Paige just said, "Oh, sweet Jesus. How often is this kind of thing going to happen?"

"How am I supposed to know? This is all new to me. It's not my fault he looks like that. And you brought him back all tanned. He definitely looks like he had fun, though. He and Chris both look like they had an amazing time."

"Oh God, they were like college kids. It was hilarious. I wish you could have been there to see it. You really would have loved it, Liz." She smiled at her friend. "You have to stay for dinner. We're just ordering pizza—forget cooking tonight—but I will make every embarrassing picture and video appear on the big TV and make the guys watch. They haven't seen any of them. You don't want to miss this."

Liz grinned. "I wouldn't miss it for the world." The video Paige had sent to their agent had hit social media two days ago and had been very well received, with lots of comments, shares and retweets.

*****

Liz thoroughly enjoyed the retelling of the beach stories, interspersed with the pictures and videos. She hadn't seen Chris this animated in a long time, and between the two guys playing off each other, she and Paige were breathless with laughter.

The news that the video had been released by their agent did not go as well, though. Chris was a little irritated but took it well. He had been through this with Paige and Janine before, and they were always right about this kind of thing. Good publicity is good publicity. Janine wouldn't release something that would hurt him; the team certainly wouldn't pick it up and put it on their news feed unless they liked it. Tom, however, was not happy, and was getting unhappier by the moment.

"Wait, what?" Tom was starting to look seriously angry. "What the fuck, Paige? Why the hell would you send that to her? And why would she release it?"

Paige was taken aback and was starting to look upset. She opened her mouth to reply, but Chris put his hand on her arm and quietly gestured over to the couch. Liz had reached out to Tom and took his hand to talk to him. Chris mouthed to Paige, "Just watch."

Tom turned to Liz when she took his hand and glared at her. She smiled at him. "She released it because it's perfect. It's completely relatable. Every person that has ever been to the beach has been knocked on their ass by a big wave. It's funny. It shows two big, handsome hockey players having fun at the beach.

"It draws people's attention to the sport in the middle of summer when most folks aren't thinking about hockey. Especially in DC—don't ask me why, but this is still a die-hard football town. Right now, a whole bunch of people that normally wouldn't care have been reminded that the Guardians have been making roster changes for next season.

"You wouldn't think twice if you were knocked over like that on the ice by another player. It would make a highlight reel that would be seen by people that were already hockey fans. This will be seen by a whole lot more people. It's good for you, Tom. And for the team. And for the sport, for that matter." She paused. "Plus, you look freaking hot in those board shorts, and I can guarantee you are now the object of many, many fantasies, not just mine." She ended speaking cheerfully and with a huge smile.

Tom stared at her for a minute, realizing his anger had evaporated, and then barked out a laugh. "I have no idea what the hell just happened. Is there some reason you're not in marketing?"

Chris leaned back, giving Paige a look that said, "See?" Paige just sat there, not quite sure what she had just witnessed.

Tom got up and said, "Well, on that note, I'm gonna hit the road. Thank you again, you guys. The week was amazing." He turned to Paige. "Sorry about that, Paige. Do me a favor and check with me first next time, please? I get a little touchy with that kind of thing. Clearly."

Paige got up, hugged him tight, and said, "Definitely. I'm so sorry, Micky! You know I didn't mean to upset you."

He squeezed her back, picking her up off her feet, said, "I know. You're just an idiot," and kissed her on the top of her head before putting her back on her feet.

She looked over to Chris. "Really? Nothing, Chris? He called me an idiot."

"If the shoe fits…"

Liz winced. "Ouch. Hey, Paige, can you give me a ride home? I took the rest of my stuff back to my apartment this morning, so it's just me."

Tom stopped on his way to the door and turned around. "I can take you."

"Are you sure? It's out of your way. You live in the other direction."

"I don't mind." He smiled at her, and his eyes had just the hint of a twinkle to them.

"Well, then, never mind, Paige. You're off the hook." She said quick goodbyes and walked out the front door with Tom.

After they left, Paige looked at Chris and asked, "How did you know?"

He shrugged. "It's what she does. I think maybe you've never noticed because when you two are together you're most often talking with each other. But I've seen her turn a conversation around like that quite a few times just because she's looking at things from a different perspective. She's an optimist and somehow makes that infectious. I don't understand it, but I knew it was going to happen tonight."

"How?" Paige pressed him. She was feeling oddly like she didn't know her best friend as well as she thought, and wanted to figure out what she was missing.

"Just the way she looked. She gets this look on her face, like she's about to say, 'But can't you see how wonderful this thing is?' It's hard to explain." He laughed. "But I knew there was no way Micky was going to stay mad."

***

When they got past the front window and into shadow, Tom put his arm around Liz. A few more steps and they were at his car. He turned and leaned against the door, pulled her to stand between his legs, and bent his head down for a kiss. It started softly, with their lips brushing together, but as soon as she brought her hand up and tangled her fingers in the hair at the back of his neck, Tom parted his lips and touched hers with his tongue. He put his arm around her waist, tilted his head, and deepened the kiss. He was moving slowly, exploring the inside of her mouth with his tongue, taking his time to do it properly.

His pulse was racing and he was already hard, but this time he had expected to react intensely to her, so he wasn't feeling frantic. She took a step closer, and he pulled her so she fit snugly against his body.

Liz's heart was beating out of her chest from the time his lips touched hers. By the time they were sliding tongues against each other, she just didn't want the moment to end. The gentle slowness of the kiss, the feel of his arms around her, the smell of him…she could have stood there all night, drowning in that kiss. When she stepped closer, and he pulled her tight to him, she could feel every inch of his arousal against her. She felt her heart skip, and blood flowing faster, her own arousal making her head spin. She gripped his hair just a little tighter and pressed harder into the kiss.

He growled. God, she already loved that sound. She broke off the kiss with difficulty and took a deep breath. She tried to speak quietly, but it came out a kind of croak. "We're still in their driveway."

"So we are." Tom looked down at her. "I was doing okay until that last minute, but now I'm feeling like it would take too long even to get to the backseat of my car. You're a minx." He kissed her quickly. And then again. And one more time.

"Shit. Get in so I can take you home before I'm not just kidding about that backseat thing."

Chapter Eight

Paige knocked on Liz's door, but judging by the bass coming through, there was no way she would be able to hear it. She used her key to let herself in, along with Chris and Tom. As she had expected, Liz was dancing around her apartment, singing along to "It's Raining Men" by The Weather Girls at the top of her lungs. When Liz saw the new arrivals, she danced over to them, pulling Chris and Tom in to join her, still singing, while they laughed at her. She was singing and flirting with both of them while Paige turned down the volume, shaking her head.

"Hey, guys. I really am almost ready. I just got distracted because that song simply demands both singing and dancing." She called to Paige as she went into her room to finish the last few things, "Speaking of which, Paige, when are we going dancing again? It's been forever."

"Too true. Soon. We'll figure out a time."

Tom had wandered over to look at Liz's computer, which was connected to her speaker system, and was checking out the playlist. The song had ended, and the next one had started—"You Shook Me All Night Long" by AC/DC. He started reading off artists. "Billy Joel, Disturbed, Bruno Mars, ZZ Top, Taylor Swift, Queen, Metallica, Elton John, Paul Simon, Imagine Dragons, Led Zeppelin, Black Eyed Peas…" He looked up as Liz came out of her room. "You realize that this reads like you're a schizophrenic, right?"

Laughing, she said, "I prefer the term, 'eclectic.' It's much nicer."

"There's another playlist here called 'Irish Folk Music' and a really large collection of classical music too." He stared at her with one eyebrow raised.

Chris said, "Don't try to understand her, Micky. It just leads to headaches." He had a small grin on his face. Even though Tom and Liz had shown no signs of being interested in anything beyond friendship, there was a definite difference in Tom when she was around. He seemed more relaxed and laughed more often. Chris wasn't sure what it was exactly. It might be just because Liz had a way of putting people at ease, but Chris suspected there was something more, and he enjoyed seeing his best friend happy.

Liz left last as they headed out the door for dinner, with Tom right in front of her, and she slipped her hand under his t-shirt, wrapped around to his front, and quickly dipped the tips of her fingers just under the waistband of his jeans before pulling her hand back to lock her door. Tom turned around and caught her eye. She gave him a playful wink, and he smiled.

***

A few days later, Tom took Liz to an early movie, finally following through on his original plan after their first dinner with Chris and Paige. They sat together in the dark theater, with his hand on the back of her neck, playing with her hair, and stroking up under her ear and down to her shoulder, and her hand on his leg, gently stroking from the inside of his knee to around mid-thigh. Later, neither one of them remembered much about what the movie was about.

They stopped by a local pizza place afterward and picked up dinner to go, heading back to her apartment. "Normally I would ask you what you thought of the movie, but honestly, I missed quite a bit of it, because I was having a hard time thinking past the nerve endings on the back of my neck."

He chuckled.

"So," she continued, looking across the table at Tom while eating a mouthful of pizza, "tell me about your family."

"Sure." He looked a little surprised. "What brought this up?"

"I figured enough time has passed." She smiled at his confused look. "I needed to wait long enough after taking advantage of you that first time. If I started asking really personal questions right away after that, it would have seemed very stalker-esque."

Tom chuckled. "So now you figured I've let my

guard down? Two can play that game. How about you tell me about your family?"

Liz laughed. "Absolutely. But you go first. I'm all ears."

Tom told Liz about his parents and siblings in Minnesota. He was the oldest, named after his father, who had grown up in eastern Canada. Liz laughed when he slipped into an imitation of his dad: "'For the love of all that's holy, Tommy, it's a sweater, not a jersey!'"

The next child was his brother, younger by two years, followed by three sisters, the youngest being only twenty-two years old and just out of college. "She got a full ride scholarship at UConn. She's brilliant," he bragged. His brother and one sister were married, and there was already one grandchild. "I don't get to see any of them very much, but Mom sends pictures of my niece. Alyssa is still too little to be skating yet."

Liz laughed and translated in her head that the baby wasn't old enough to walk. She was watching and listening, occasionally asking a prompting question to keep the information flowing. Tom was exuding joy talking about his family, and she was soaking it up like she was basking in the sun. It was wonderful.

After a while, Tom stopped and said, "Okay, enough. What about you?"

She smiled. "Not nearly as much fun. Parents deceased many years now. One was a heart attack, the other complications from long-term illness. One older brother, currently incarcerated for at least six more years for federal narcotics violations, among other things. We were never close to begin with; clearly less so now."

His face looked stricken, as she had expected. She reached across the table to take his hand.

"Please don't be sorry. You know my chosen family quite well. Chris and Paige are family to me. I've got a great life, Tom, and I'm really happy. I promise."

Tom looked at her closely. She was smiling, showing every sign of being completely serious.

"That's why you wanted me to go first."

She brightened, pleased that he understood. "Yes! You would have changed the way you told me about your family if you had heard my story first, and I would have missed out. I loved watching you talk about them. It's like I got to sneak in and share your joy." She paused. "Yikes, does that sound all stalker-y?"

Tom laughed. "No, it's not entirely creepy." He winked. "Just a little creepy."

"Joy is wonderful that way," she said with a slightly faraway look. "It doesn't diminish with sharing. If something wonderful happens for my friend, I can jump in and surf on their happiness. Nothing has been taken away from me. More happiness for them doesn't mean less for me. It's not like pie." She looked back at Tom, coming back into focus. She put her hands on the table, stood up, smiled, and said, "So do you want pie?"

Tom realized he was staring at her. Again. Because she had caught him completely by surprise. Again.

"Do you really feel that way? About happiness?"

She blinked. "Of course. Jealousy is a whole lot of work. It's much easier to mooch off the happiness of my friends if they've got extra floating around when I'm a little short. At heart I'm terribly lazy." She winked at him playfully.

"I have not noticed laziness," he said. His eyes were taking on a different look as he stood up and walked over to her. "So far, you have seemed very…industrious. Enthusiastic, even." He was standing over her, very close, looking down.

His height and size were intoxicating to Liz.

He ran his hand up her arm and then tilted her chin up to meet his gaze.

His blue eyes were gorgeous, thickly framed with dark lashes, and Liz felt her heart start to race just from looking at him. The corner of his mouth was curled up in a half smile, playful and sweet.

"I don't know how you do that to me," she whispered.

"Do what?" he asked, still smiling that half smile. He rubbed his thumb across her cheek.

"Make me forget everything with a look," she said, closing her eyes and turning her face toward his caress. She opened one eye to peek back up at him under her lashes and then closed it again and sighed.

Tom bent down and kissed her gently. And one kiss became two, and two became too many to count. Tom pulled back and chuckled deep in his chest. He cupped her face in his hands and said, "I don't know how you do that to me, Liz."

"Do what?" she asked, still smiling from their kisses.

74

"Make me forget everything with a kiss," he said. "I might as well be eighteen again whenever I touch you."

"Really?"

"Really. I intended to give you one quick kiss that first night." His voice got husky. "Just one. But I couldn't do it. One wasn't enough. One is never enough with you."

"I really hope you don't have any place you need to be real soon." She ran her hand slowly up the inside of his thigh.

He closed his eyes, and his voice was considerably lower when he said, "Me too, because I have no fucking idea about anything besides where your hand is right now."

"This hand?"

He growled as she squeezed gently.

"Or this hand?" She added her other hand and squeezed gently with that one.

He growled louder, put his head down, and spoke into her hair, breathing hard. "Do you want to go to the bedroom?"

She unbuttoned his shorts, and he heard the zipper. And then his breath caught as he heard her say, "No, I don't think so."

Liz pushed him gently backward until he was leaning against the counter. He was so gorgeous. Impossibly so. And she'd never had a good, proper look at all of him. It was time to change that. She pulled the t-shirt up as far as she could and let him finish taking it off and then ran her hands over his chest, through the soft hair, touching every beautifully defined muscle.

She brought her hands down his strong arms, and kissed and bit softly along his chest and stomach as she intertwined their fingers, and traced the trail of hair that began at his navel and ran down into his shorts.

She pushed his shorts down over his hips and to the floor and stood back to look at him. He was in boxer briefs, with his erection barely contained. She stepped forward again, sliding her fingers under the waistband of his underwear, and brushed against the tip of his hard cock.

He twitched and hissed in his breath as she ran her fingertips through the slick fluid already beading there.

Liz pulled the waistband away from his body so there would be room to release him and pushed the fabric down over his hips, kneeling down as she dragged his underwear to his feet, taking her time, gazing as she went.

His breathing was deep and measured, and when she looked back up to his face, she saw he was watching her carefully, hands gripping the edge of the counter.

"You look amazing," Liz said quietly as she leaned in and kissed and placed little bites at his hips while drawing one hand back up his inner thigh. Looking back up at him again, she cradled his scrotum in her palm, rolling her fingers gently, enjoying both the feel and the look on his face. She put her other hand flat on his abdomen, just under his navel, and moved down and then around until the skin between her thumb and forefinger was cradling the base of his shaft.

Tom made a groaning sound.

She slid that cradle upward the entire length of him, watching as she went, tilting her head as though simply looking on this part of him in wonder.

Reaching the head of his hard cock, she used her hand to spread his slickness over him, lubricating the top of his shaft, stroking and teasing, until Tom's knees shook. He took a gasping breath and moaned, "Oh, Christ, Liz. Please."

She looked up, met his eye, and kept eye contact as she took him in her mouth.

Tom wasn't sure he was going to live through this, much less continue to stand upright. He tried to hold himself still, allowing her to control everything, but after several minutes of receiving her oral attentions, he felt his hips begin shifting in rhythm with her movements and felt pressure building.

When he suddenly felt cool air rather than warm mouth, he was certain he wasn't going to live through it. His heart was pounding, and every nerve ending was screaming for release. He squeezed his eyes shut.

"Please, Liz." His voice was strained and rasping.

He felt her gently pull his right hand away from its death grip on the edge of the counter.

"Open your eyes." She was standing in front of him and had taken off her shirt and bra. Bare from the waist up, she was holding his hand in both of hers. Kneeling down in front of him, she brought his hand and carefully wrapped it around his erection. "Tom." Her voice was throaty, and her eyes were dark. "I want to watch. Please."

"Oh, God." He couldn't have stopped himself even if he had wanted to. "Oh, Liz." He wasn't going to last more than a few more strokes.

The sound he made at climax had become her favorite sound in the world from the very first time she heard it. It was the most deeply male sound she could have ever imagined. Tonight he yelled her name while making that sound; it had been erotic beyond reason. Watching the entire event had been exquisite. The fact that somewhere in the middle of talking with him she had realized—beyond doubt— that she was falling in love, had made the entire thing so much better. And so much worse.

Tom sank to the floor to sit with her, every part of him shaking. He stared at her for a few moments, breathing hard, at a loss for words. He put his head down on his knees, still breathing hard. She sat, arms crossed on her knees, chin resting on her arms, just watching him.

He finally looked up at her, and she smiled. He looked bewildered, and sleepy, and adorable. His voice was gravelly and rough.

"I don't even know what to say."

"Good or bad?"

"Good. Very, very good. I-need-to-sleep-on-your-floor good."

"My bed is more comfortable."

He smiled that smile and looked at Liz through half-lidded eyes. "Your bed seems really far away right now."

Chapter Nine

August passed by too quickly. Paige had to start worrying about school starting again at the end of August, and Chris and Tom both began thinking about training camp that would be starting in September.

Liz wanted to freeze time. She and Tom definitely enjoyed each other when they had the opportunity be alone, and there were a few more fun evenings with Chris and Paige, as well. She knew that as soon as training camp started, things would change; she figured she'd be lucky to see him once a month, if that.

A week before training camp started, Tom knocked on Liz's door one Friday evening to meet her—they had no serious plans, maybe a movie, maybe just time together. Hell, maybe just sex. The relationship was casual and still very secretive, so they didn't tend to go out much alone together, especially not where Tom might see teammates.

He wasn't sure why he was still keeping the fact that they were more than friends a secret. It had started that way, and he didn't feel like changing it. Liz didn't particularly seem to mind. It was definitely easier. No pressure or questions from friends or family about how things were going, what his plans were, when was he going to let them meet her.

He wouldn't have to deal with any specific shit in the locker room about his dating life, just the general shit about why he couldn't get laid. Which wouldn't bother him, because hey, what did they know, right? And he had to admit there was something intrinsically fun and sexy about a clandestine affair, especially seeing how much he could get away with when Chris and Paige were in the next room or even across the table at a restaurant.

He had a gut check when he thought too much about it—she deserved to be treated better than this, and he knew it—but then he figured she probably had her reasons for continuing the secrecy too. Liz did not strike him as the kind of person who let herself get walked over.

He heard her laughing and talking as she unbolted the door and opened it to let him in. She was talking on the phone—mostly listening and laughing, actually—and gave him a one-armed hug and quick kiss on the cheek as he came in the door. She walked to the fridge and grabbed him a beer and gestured to the couch, and they both sat down. Tom watched her and smiled. There was something about her that was lit from within and made her truly beautiful.

Finding a break in her conversation, she said,

"Hey, sweetie, I've got to go. You'll have to tell me more, though. I can't wait to hear it. So glad you're back in town! Yes, definitely. Okay, Sunday at three for coffee. See you then, Zee!" She hung up the phone, her face flushed with laughter, and turned to Tom. "Hey, handsome!" And then, "What's wrong?"

Tom's expression had changed into what now could only be described as a scowl. "That was Zee? What did he want?"

"He just got back in town from staying in Alberta for most of August. He always calls to tell me the dumb things he did with his brothers. They're all completely insane." She smiled, and then it faded somewhat. "Are you all right?"

The logical part of his brain was telling Tom that the way he was feeling was completely unreasonable.

The rest was full of jealousy and a level of possessiveness that was surprising even him.

"Apparently I'm not in the best of moods tonight. Maybe I should just head back out." He stood up.

Liz was so taken aback it took her a few seconds to process. She stood up. "Tom? Tom! Stop." She put a hand on his arm. He turned to look at her. She said, "Is this about the call from Zee?" He didn't respond. "We have been friends for years. You knew that the day I met you. There isn't anything else between us."

Tom's look softened a little bit, and he said, "I know." He still looked, well…off. And angry.

Liz sat back down on the couch and looked up at

him. "Okay," she sighed. "I don't know what has happened. You're clearly upset and want to leave. If it's possible to change your mind on that, I would very much like for you to stay." She smiled. "I have been looking forward to seeing you. I know you've got training camp starting soon, and I figure everything is going to change once the season starts." She looked startled for a moment, then said, "Oh, shit. Is that what this is about?"

Tom sat back down on the couch. The conversation had taken an unexpected turn, and he didn't know where this was going.

Liz smiled, but there was a sadness to it. "I figured this was a temporary deal. But even if we lose the 'benefits' part, I would really very much hate to lose the friendship. Are you okay with that?"

Now Tom just stared at her. She stared back.

He said, "I'm trying to figure out what the hell you're talking about."

She tilted her head, looking at him curiously. "Friends? With benefits? You and I?"

He slowly shook his head like he still didn't understand.

"Seriously?" She threw up her hands and said, "What the fuck? I feel like I'm in *The Twilight Zone.*" She took a deep breath and looked directly at him and said, very pointedly, "Tom. If you are ending the sex part of our relationship, I would still like to be friends." She added, "Please," afterward, with a smile.

Tom sat back on the couch, his angry look replaced by bewilderment. "Holy shit. I have never met someone I understand less than you." He sat up, leaned toward her, looking at her eyes. "You're completely serious."

"Yes. Although I'm starting to think this is what it feels like to go insane."

"It is." He moved, pulling her over to have her straddle his lap. "Why the hell would I ever give up sex with you, Liz? My God, woman, that idea is completely insane." He kissed her hard, trying to exorcise some of the personal demons lurking around in his brain, and held her close.

"I'm sorry about my mood. On my good days in the locker room Becks calls me a 'spiky bastard.' I must be starting early." He pushed her gently back and looked at her. "I don't want to miss out on time with you before the season starts."

Her heart was beating much too hard, and Liz could feel tears pricking her eyes.

Shit. I'm already in way too deep. This is going to hurt like hell when it ends. She leaned in and kissed him, feeling every part of him, immersing herself in his taste, his smell, his feel. *Totally worth it.*

***

The first two games of the season were home games, and Liz thoroughly enjoyed watching Tom play with the team on TV. She always watched games—if for some reason she couldn't watch, she listened to the play-by-play on the radio—but it was even more fun now that Number Forty was playing.

He was a hard-hitting defenseman, and she had always enjoyed the physicality of the game. A lot.

There was something about the intensity of the play. That was the part of football she enjoyed too, but hockey had a much faster pace and required so much more finesse and skill, in her opinion. And there was no denying that there was something inherently enthralling when the guys dropped the mitts and got into it. It wasn't just that they were fighting—she had zero interest in boxing or MMA, although she could appreciate the skill required there too.

It was the *passion.* Hockey had a pressure valve that allowed an outlet of testosterone-fueled game passion. She could pretend she didn't enjoy that part of it, but then her fantasy guy wouldn't specifically be an enforcer.

There weren't fights in every game, and there shouldn't be. That wasn't hockey, either. Sometimes the fights were strategic—she didn't understand all the nuances of the game in that way and didn't care to. It was just a damn fun game to watch. And it didn't hurt that Tom looked unbelievably hot in his uniform. Like, holy-shit-I-still-can't-believe-I'm-sleeping-with-him hot.

The next games were on the road, so Tom made sure to make time for some pre-road trip sex. He had smiled at her with that insanely charming smile, saying, "This has to last me for at least five days, Liz," as he undressed her. Their good-bye kiss lingered even longer than usual.

When he got back, he had a five-day growth of beard. Liz rasped her hand over his face, saying, "Mmm, very sexy. But I thought you guys did playoff beards or 'Mo-vember' mustaches. What's with the scruff?"

"The very first road trip I took when I was actually old enough to need to shave, I forgot my razor. So I grew a beard that season." He chuffed. "If you could call it a beard at that point. Although I guess for sixteen, it was pretty respectable. It just became a thing for me. First roadie of the season, I stop shaving. At the end of the season, the beard comes off." He looked directly at her. "Do you like it? I wasn't sure what you'd think."

"I love a nice beard." She ran her hands over his face. "I'll love it even more when it's long enough not to be scratchy. However," she added, "if you're looking for my input, I personally love a beard that's long enough to lie flat but still well trimmed. The ZZ Top look isn't my thing." He laughed, and she rubbed her cheek against his. "And until this comes in a little more, there will need to be adjustments as to certain…activities."

Tom's eyes got dark and sexy as he looked at her. "And now that you've said that, there is nothing in the world I want to do more than that certain…activity."

"Hey, I'm serious, you!" She laughed and pushed him away as he started to try to unbutton her jeans. "That's some formidable scratchiness on your face."

His smile was wicked, and he started unbuttoning her shirt, saying, "I'll tell you what. I will start at your neck." He breathed on her neck, kissing it very lightly, and ran the tip of his tongue from the skin behind her ear down to her shoulder.

She closed her eyes and shivered.

"And I will move down your body." Tom pushed her shirt away from her shoulder, trailing the tip of his tongue along her collarbone, breathing kisses on her skin, coming back across to the hollow of her throat. Her head was back, and she was breathing deeply, cheeks flushed.

Tom unhooked her front-clasped bra, pushing it off her shoulders along with her shirt, and then gently drew his hands up her sides.

"You can stop me any time you feel scratched." He trailed his tongue down toward her right breast, and she gasped and then moaned as he reached her nipple and gently pulled it into his mouth, swirling his tongue softly around her peak.

"If you don't feel any scratching…" he trailed his tongue across to her other breast, "…then I won't stop."

He flicked his tongue over her nipple, and she jumped.

He chuckled. "And I get to do whatever I want when I get there." He took her nipple in his mouth and swirled around with his tongue, sucking gently, enjoying her moans. "Deal?" He came back up to her face, looked into her eyes—pupils wide, softly unfocused. He whispered in her ear, "Do we have a deal, Liz?" as he stroked her nipples with his thumbs.

She turned to him, put her arms around his neck, and said, "Yes."

Chapter Ten

The season was well underway, and things had fallen into a kind of rhythm. To Liz, it felt oddly as if very little had changed, except for the addition of Tom. She and Paige spent some time together when the guys were away on road trips; that had always been true when it was just Chris traveling. Or Liz took that time to travel to see friends who were within a few hours' drive. When the team was in town, Paige spent most of her time with Chris, of course. Liz had never spent much time together with them as a couple during the season. Paige always invited her more often, but she didn't want to intrude on their time alone together when it was limited.

She saw Tom almost as much as if they were actually dating. Except they weren't. She hardly ever talked to him on the phone when they were away on road trips, because there was always a chance of being overheard by a teammate. She talked with Zee as much as she always did, but that wasn't necessarily something that made Tom happy, either. Not that she was willing to give up any of her friends for a relationship.

She knew this arrangement wouldn't last forever—at the very least, she knew very well it wasn't going to be healthy for her to stay in something like this over the long term. But she wasn't quite ready to give it up. Not yet.

She couldn't even put a name to the reasons she had for not telling, of all people, her best friend. Maybe just to have something that was only hers, just for a little while. Something utterly fantastical, even if it was ultimately impossible. A little bit of a secret fantasy to live in, for however long it lasted.

Sometimes reality was a little too much to bear, and right now with Tom, there was no need to deal with anyone else's expectations of what kind of relationship she "should" have. She didn't have to answer any questions: how much she liked him, did she think they were serious, had she met his family yet.

Tom's spiky moods were evident, especially after losses. He sometimes seemed to be waiting for her to either critique his game or artificially try to cheer him up by telling him he played well when he didn't. She would remind him she was a fan, not a coach or a player, and she had no place telling him how to play or how he had played. And that he should stop trying to pick a fight.

After one of these exchanges, she finally said, "Look, buddy, this is the only way I know how to cheer you up. And to shut you up, for that matter." She had grabbed him behind the neck with one hand to pull him down for a kiss and had drawn her other hand up between his legs to cup him until he hardened in her hand and forgot his anger entirely, along with everything else.

They had managed to navigate birthdays (his in September, hers in November) and the holidays without too much hassle. Birthdays were spent with Chris and Paige—no gifts, just dinner out paid for by the other three. Thanksgiving was with Chris and Paige, and Tom flew home to spend Christmas in Minnesota with his family.

Liz suggested it would be better to do something fun rather than exchange gifts, and Tom agreed, so they bought tickets to a local Cirque du Soleil show. That had been a fun evening out. It was almost possible to pretend they were really dating.

Liz smiled to herself, thinking about her impossible fantasy man. She was on her way to meet him at Chris and Paige's house, and the four of them were going to go out for dinner. It would be fun—they hadn't had a chance in a while for the four of them to spend time together. The team was on a three-game home stand, with two days in between games.

When Liz arrived, Tom and Chris were talking in the living room, and Tom was scowling. Chris was looking as exasperated as Tom was looking irritated.

"What's going on over there?" she asked Paige.

"I actually don't know," said Paige. "Some team stuff. As usual."

"Hey, Liz, come here for a second," Chris called, and she headed toward them.

"This is stupid, Becks. She'll hate this. She even

has a job where she's negotiated being able to wear jeans every day." Tom's scowl had deepened. There was a formal charity event, and he was being "asked" to attend with a few other players, including Chris, on behalf of the team. He detested these events. Anything to do with hockey—fan events, autograph signings, clinics—no problem, but these fancy dress things made his skin crawl. He didn't even know why.

"Just shut up for a minute, Micky, would you?" Chris said as Liz approached.

"Hi, guys, what's up?"

"I have a hypothetical question for you. Would you have any possible interest in going to a fancy charity ball with dinner and dancing?" Chris was looking at Liz and making a "shut the fuck up" motion to Tom with one hand.

Liz looked at Chris suspiciously. "This feels like a trick, Beckman. What's the catch?"

"No catch."

"Will I know anyone at this hypothetical event?" Liz was probing for the downside.

"Yes. At this hypothetical event, Paige and I would be there, along with this asshole." He gestured to Tom.

She folded her arms and squinted at him. "Do I get stuck being the bartender? Or picking up the tab for the booze?"

"Nope."

"Is there a downside I'm missing?"

Chris thought for a second. "There would be a few boring speeches."

"Do I have to listen to them? Will there be a quiz

afterward?"

Chris laughed. "No, no quiz."

"Okay, let me get this straight." Liz started to tick off the points to make sure she understood this hypothetical situation. "You are asking me if I would enjoy getting all dressed up to go out to dinner and dancing, with some of my very best friends, where I would have no responsibilities except to have fun and not disrupt some speeches. Seriously, am I missing something? Why would I not sign up for this immediately? This sounds like all the best parts of a really fun wedding without any old ladies telling me, 'Oh, you're so pretty, I'm sure you'll find someone soon, come over here and meet my sister's nephew, Wentworth, I'm sure he would date you.'"

Tom just stared. Chris laughed, as much at Tom's reaction as at her description.

"So is this just a hypothetical? Or is this a real thing, and the actual prank is that I'm not really invited? That would be just mean, Beckman. But I don't put it past you."

Chris laughed even harder. "It is a real thing. Actually, the one real downside is that you would have to go with this grouchy bastard." He clapped his hand on Tom's shoulder. "He hates these things." He walked off to get another beer and left the two of them alone.

Liz looked at Tom under her lashes questioningly. "Are you actually asking me to this? It's all right if you don't want to."

Tom started, as if surprised by her statement. "Of course I want to. Yes, I'm asking." He smiled.

"Okay, then. I would love to go." She brightened. "Yay! I get to go talk about dresses with Paige!" She practically skipped off to the kitchen.

Chris had returned with his beer and handed a new one to Tom, who was now watching Liz and Paige talk animatedly in the kitchen, presumably about dresses. Chris wrapped an arm around his friend's shoulder.

Tom said, "I have no idea what the fuck just happened."

"She just made something that you hate sound like fun. And now you kinda want to go, just because she's going to be there."

"Shit."

Chris clapped him on the shoulder again and laughed. "If I knew how she did that, I'd tell you."

Chapter Eleven

The charity ball was a week away. Paige needed to stop somewhere to drop something off for someone because someone else needed something or other—Liz had lost track of all of the reasons behind the various errands they were running. She was just tagging along, enjoying the day spending time with her friend, talking about things, window shopping when possible, drinking coffee almost always.

They pulled up outside a formal shop. "I'm meeting Chris here for a few minutes to make sure he doesn't screw something up with his tux. He would, you know." Liz laughed and walked inside with her. She sat down to wait while Paige fussed with Chris. While she was waiting, Tom walked out of the dressing room to the big mirrors, with an attendant working to make sure everything was properly fitted.

The earth stopped turning. Tom stood in a tuxedo, and Liz forgot how to breathe.

Paige walked by on her way toward the door.

93

"Okay, all set. Disaster averted." She was four steps further on before she noticed Liz wasn't following her.

Tom looked up into the mirror and saw Liz looking at him. He started in surprise, not expecting to see her there, and then just watched her. She hadn't realized he had seen her; she wasn't looking at his face. Yet.

Liz was taking in every inch of his six-foot-four inches. Slowly. Starting at his legs. The tux already fit beautifully, and where he was standing in front of the mirrors, she got a full view of both his back and front. She watched his strong hands adjusting the cuffs. By the time she had reached his immensely broad shoulders, she had started breathing again, a little faster than normal. Her eyes travelled up past his now-thick but well-trimmed dark beard, to his beautiful blue eyes. He was looking at her.

He waited until her gaze made it up to his eyes. Then he smiled that little half smile, his eyes darkly playful. Her face flooded with color, and her heart started beating wildly.

Paige was standing next to her by this point. She cleared her throat, and Liz turned to her, startled. "Shit. I did not count on him looking that good in a tux. I might need you to remind me to do simple things. Like breathe."

Tom watched her leave with Paige and chuckled to himself.

The evening might not be an entire loss.

***

Liz was enjoying getting ready. She might almost never wear a dress and makeup, but that didn't mean it wasn't fun to do it every once in a while. She just had no desire to take that kind of time every day. Because it happened so infrequently, Paige had decided they should make a whole big day of it, so she had made salon appointments for their hair and makeup. Later, they came back to Paige's house to finish getting ready.

Paige's dress was a deep red, and Liz was wearing more of a turquoise color. When she'd tried it on at the store, Paige had stopped her immediately.

"That's it. Don't try on anything else. Your eyes look amazing, and so does the rest of you."

Liz trusted Paige's judgment on these things, so that was that. The dress was long and satiny. It draped and clung in nice places but was not tight, and the neckline was low without showing any real cleavage. It was very classy, and Liz loved it. She wore three-inch heels. It was strange to think she was still going to be four inches shorter than her date. That was not something she was used to, and she loved that too.

Paige walked downstairs first, to an appreciative wolf whistle from her husband and applause from Tom. And then Liz descended. She was greeted by complete, stunned silence, which Chris broke.

"Holy shit, Liz."

Paige smiled and rolled her eyes.

Liz stood at the bottom of the staircase and just let them look.

Tom was completely speechless. He knew she

was going to look good. She always looked good. But this…he didn't know what to do. He wanted to walk up and kiss her and then take her back to her apartment. Or maybe take her right here. He definitely didn't want to share her with a room full of other guys from the team, not looking like this. Except—he wanted everyone to see him walk into the room with her on his arm, because there couldn't possibly be any woman more beautiful there. Liz looked him in the eye and winked.

He just said, "Fuck."

She laughed.

***

They had only been at the event for about a half hour before Tom began to remember how much he hated these things. Liz was a good distraction, but she could see he was already beginning to feel stressed and anxious. She slipped in next to him and took his hand.

"Hey, handsome."

He looked down at her, and his expression softened. He put his arm around her, and she walked him away from the group and over toward a quieter standing table. "You doing okay?"

He tried to ungrit his teeth. "I don't know why this shit bothers me so much." There were furrows forming in his brow. "There's no real reason for it."

"Hmmm. I was hoping that this dress would last as a distraction longer than this." She looked at him from under her lashes and used one finger to trace a pattern on the hand he was using to hold his drink.

The furrow had disappeared, and he gave her a smile that made her heart flutter.

"You're good, Williams. You're very good. You look stunning. But you did receive full and fair warning that I'm an asshole at these things."

"Very true. But I have made it my personal mission to figure out just what it will take for you to actually relax and have a good time. Because I definitely intend to have a good time tonight. I would love for you to, as well."

Tom grunted noncommittally, but his brow wasn't furrowed back up, so...small victories.

A few of his teammates were walking by just then, including Zee, who gave Tom a friendly slap on the back and stopped to say, "Hey, Micky! Nice to see you here. Why don't you introduce me to your lovely date?"

Zee turned and looked at Liz. She flashed him a smile and was rewarded with the most stunned, dumbstruck expression she had ever hoped to see on his face.

"I think you've already met her, Zee," Tom said. He had begun to get irritated when he heard Zee's voice, thinking the younger player was stopping by to flirt with Liz or give Tom a hard time, but seeing Zee's expression was deeply satisfying.

"Holy shit, Liz," Zee whispered and then gave her a bow. "I am well and truly speechless. You are lovely. Please save a dance for me." He turned to Tom. "I don't know how you scored this, Micky, but I am a jealous man."

Liz blinked as he walked away and said, almost to herself, "That might be the first time I have ever seen him behave like an adult. Will wonders never cease."

She turned back to Tom. His look made her heart beat a little faster. It was a little edgy, slightly primal.

He put his arm around Liz's waist and spoke into her ear. "He should be jealous. You are the most beautiful woman here, and you're sleeping with me."

Her heart was definitely racing now. "So I just thought of something that would help you relax and enjoy yourself more, that would last longer than seeing me in this dress."

Tom looked at her and smiled. "Really? Is it seeing you out of that dress? Because that's pretty much the only thing on my mind right now."

"Actually, it is."

Tom blinked. "Shit." He fidgeted and then said, "Vixen. It's a good thing tux coats cover as much as they do."

She took his hand and started leading him back over to the crowd.

"What are you doing?"

"Making you think of two things at once. I'm overloading your brain so you can't be grouchy."

He stopped and gaped at her. "If you were kidding about the other thing, I am absolutely going to be grouchy."

She laughed. "I was not kidding." She took hold of the lapel of his jacket and gently pulled him down so she could whisper in his ear. "I would never kid like that about sex with you. It's much too good. You know that." She let go of his jacket, but he didn't stand back up right away. "I'll be back in a few minutes. Go mingle, Tom." And she walked away.

Chris walked up to Tom at that point and pulled him into a conversation with some person or another he should be talking to. Liz watched from across the room with Paige for a few minutes.

"How are things going?" asked Paige.

"Great," Liz replied. "Zee was actually speechless when he saw me. I will forever have you pick my fancy clothing, Paige."

Paige laughed. "Like you wouldn't have done that anyway. But I meant with Micky. Chris has said he really can be in a foul mood at these things. I want to make sure you have a good time, even if he can't remain pleasant."

"Actually, so far so good. I promised to rescue him from the conversation he's currently having, though, so I'm going to go do that. And then I'm going to make him dance with me." She smiled and headed off.

The music was changing to a slow tune just as she slid up to the group and slipped her hand into Tom's. "I'm so sorry to interrupt. Would it be possible to steal my date away for a dance? I love this song." Tom stared down at her as if she had sprouted out of thin air. The "important person" he was talking to with Chris laughed indulgently.

"Of course. Mr. McCullin, you should never keep a lovely woman like that waiting if she wants to dance."

Liz slipped her arm through Tom's and led him toward the dance floor.

"How did you do that?" he asked in amazement.

"Feminine wiles," she replied. "Of course."

"Wait," he said, realizing she was seriously leading him to the dance floor. "I don't dance."

"Oh, sweetheart, you do now. That nice gentleman is watching you take me over to dance to this song that I love, and you are not going to disappoint either of us, are you?"

She turned to him, having maneuvered him onto the dance floor, to see he was looking irritable again. "Do you even like this song?"

She laughed lightly and stepped close to him, positioning them to dance together to the slow-moving beat. "I have no idea what it is. But I just brought you from talking with men about things that don't interest you to holding me close while I whisper to you about sex. Isn't that an improvement?"

Tom started to wonder if there was such a thing as mood whiplash. He looked down at her. "I hope you're not actually just teasing, Liz. Because as much as I enjoy you being playful, I don't think you understand just how much I hate these things. I'm starting to get a headache already, and I think we've only been here an hour. I still have to make it through dinner."

Liz looked up at him and saw the furrows in his brow. She reached up and stroked his beard with her hand for a moment. "I'm sorry. Just dance with me for a little while longer, and then I will explain my plan. And I will adjust my tactics." Her smile was sweet but not teasing, and Tom relaxed enough to make it through one song. She then guided him off

100

the dance floor and over to get a drink.

"I would like to get you alone," she said. She was speaking low and close to his ear to keep the conversation private. "Very much."

"That's just great. Where, exactly? Coat room? Classy, Liz." His hackles were definitely up.

She wasn't going to take the bait. She stepped back and looked at him. "We are standing in the ballroom of a hotel."

"And? I could take you home after this fucking thing just as easily."

"Think outside the box, McCullin." Tom looked at her sharply. He didn't remember her calling him by his surname before. "Is there a rule saying that the rooms can only be used at night?" She saw the light begin to dawn. "Or that they have to be slept in at all? What if I want to rent a room and, say, visit that room every hour or so for ten minutes?"

His eyes widened, then darkened, and then he stood close and positively loomed over her.

"So," she plucked an imaginary string off his sleeve and brushed his sleeve smooth, back to teasing now that he understood, "ask for the closest available room to this ballroom." She looked up into his eyes and said, "And then text me the room number."

He bent and spoke into her ear. "I want to see you sprawled across the bed."

"No."

He was startled by the strength of her refusal.

She turned and growled into his ear. "Up against the back of the door."

"Shit."

She turned and walked back into the crowd before he managed to restart his brain enough to turn and head to the front desk.

***

Tom: 403

She smiled as the text pinged on her screen.

Liz: I'm on my way.

Tom stared at the phone. An entire sentence, complete with punctuation. In a text. Who does that? And why? That must have taken several extra seconds that could have been spent on her way to the room. He tried not to pace.

The knock on the door was soft, and he opened the door and pulled her in. He closed the door by pushing her up against it while kissing her like a drowning man trying to breathe. He fumbled in her long skirt, trying to reach up underneath while still kissing her. She helped by pulling all the fabric up and away while he frantically pulled off her underwear and opened his pants.

Liz clung around his neck as he entered her in one hard thrust, gasping loudly at the incredible sensation. She wrapped one leg up around his hip as he began to thrust deep and hard, one hand braced against the door and the other holding her ass, trying to pull her into him even as he was trying to drive himself into her.

They didn't speak. There were growls and snarls,

grunts and panting, but nothing that qualified as speech. They didn't make love or even have sex.

They rutted wildly, up against the back of the hotel room door.

Liz felt the tension building and knew that she was going to come, soon, and very hard, and she could tell that Tom was almost there. The sound and feel of his orgasm triggered hers; he roared, and the sound she made might have qualified as a scream.

The entire encounter may have lasted all of three minutes. They stood, gasping and shaky. When Liz had caught her breath, she said, "Do you think you can make it for another hour in a good mood?"

Tom chuckled deep in his chest and said, "Yes." And then he kissed her and said, "You're a genius. Thank you. That was amazing."

"You're welcome. Zip up and head back. I will follow you in a few minutes. I have more repair work to do than you do. I'm glad Paige insisted I bring extra lipstick and such." She picked up her purse and underwear, both of which had been unceremoniously discarded on the floor. She caught his face in her hand and looked him in the eye, stroking his beard with her thumb.

"And yes, that was fucking amazing, Tom."

***

Tom had only been gone from the event about ten minutes or so. No one had noticed he had left; no one particularly noticed that he was back. And no one seemed to notice that anything was different, which seemed absurd to him. He felt like there must be an arrow-shaped neon sign saying "Just Got Laid" over his head, but apparently not. He chuckled to himself, thinking that maybe people would just misinterpret his look to think he had already been hitting the bar a little too hard.

Chris walked up to him just then, saying, "Hey, Mick. They're going to be seating for dinner in a few minutes. Paige has made sure that you and Liz are at our table." He looked strangely at Tom for a moment. "Holy crap, are you actually smiling? At a black-tie event?"

Tom surprised himself by briefly laughing out loud, saying, "Apparently the combination of a good bartender and a very nice date have been good for me."

"Speaking of which, where is Liz?"

Before he could answer, Tom felt Liz slide up next to him and take his hand. "I'm right here. Just back from the ladies' room."

Chris took her other hand, bowed formally, and kissed it. "My lady, I am duly impressed. I didn't think it was possible to see this bastard voluntarily smile at one of these events. He credits good booze and your company. Since I have seen him shit-faced drunk before, I know where the credit truly belongs."

Tom actually laughed along with Liz, drawing another small look of surprise from Chris.

"Anyway, dinner is about to start, and Paige sent me to find you two."

Chris walked toward the dining room, and they followed. Tom let go of Liz's hand and ran his hand up the back of her neck to put his arm around her.

He pulled her close and breathed her hair for a moment and then spoke quietly to her.

"I kinda do feel drunk. I don't think I've ever tried to get up and act totally normal right after sex before. It's like an amazing buzz. Except I just want to find a couch somewhere and kiss you."

Chapter Twelve

Dinner was quite nice and was followed by the requisite speeches. Tom's good mood started wearing off sometime between dinner and dessert, and Liz could feel him starting to tense again. She leaned in when the speeches started and said, "No quizzes after, remember?"

He tried to smile at Liz when she joked about the quizzes, but he was starting to feel trapped at the table. There was no way to get up and walk outside to get a breath of air without causing a disruption. He wasn't listening to the speeches, and the intermittent applause was jarring his nerves. Tom could feel himself getting…

What? What the fuck is the problem, anyway? Is this anxiety? Claustrophobia? Fear of goddamn tuxedos? Whatever it was, his brain translated it down into anger. And he was getting angry.

He hadn't realized his hand was clenched into a fist on his thigh until he felt Liz's hand move over it. And then past it, onto his thigh, near his knee. And then just on the inside of his knee. And she just left her hand there, moving her fingers slightly, caressing the inside of his knee lightly under the table, hidden by the tablecloth.

He unclenched his fist, shifted, and moved his arm around her shoulder, encouraging her to pull her chair closer to his so she could sit close by his side. She was still just gently caressing the inside of his knee, but that had been enough to shift the gears in his brain.

Now that they were sitting closer together, Liz took advantage and moved her hand slightly higher on the inside of Tom's leg. She was sitting close enough to him that she felt the slightest hitch in his breathing and smiled to herself. His arousal always excited her. That was the way it had always been for her. Knowing that she was turning him on was doing things for her too.

Tom turned his head to breathe into her hair for moment and kissed the top of her head.

***

Paige had been watching Liz deal with Tom off and on during the evening. It was fascinating, really. Ever since the evening after the beach trip when Chris had mentioned that Liz could diffuse Tom's anger, she had paid more attention than she used to when watching her friend interact with other people. She had been serious, though, about not wanting Liz's evening to be ruined by one of Tom's foul moods, so she had kept slightly more of an eye on their interactions than she might have otherwise.

Liz had been flirting with Tom. A lot. Which

was completely normal for her, especially under the circumstances. She was clearly going for distraction to try to keep him in a good mood, or at least out of a truly foul one. And Tom was clearly enjoying it and flirting in return. She had tried to relax and not worry about the two of them. Liz was more than capable of handling herself.

But now, watching them at dinner, she realized what had been nagging at her brain this whole evening. There was a comfort level between them that was beyond flirting. They weren't just flirting. They were acting like a couple, not just like they were on a date.

***

Tom felt her hand moving higher up his thigh. Pretty soon she was going to be meeting something other than his leg, and he wasn't sure how he felt about that. They were sitting in the middle of a room full of people, and Tom was not an exhibitionist by nature. Some flirting and play was one thing, but he didn't know how far Liz intended to take this; she was constantly surprising him, and this had the possibility of being way too far out of his comfort zone.

She moved her hand up another inch and grazed him. He jumped slightly, gripping her more tightly around the shoulders, and used the cover of applause to lean down and say, "That's not my thigh, sweetheart. I'm not sure you should do that again. I need to be able to walk out of here at some point."

Liz leaned up and breathed in his ear, "I'll be careful, I promise. Nothing that will run the risk of an embarrassing situation."

She started to reach for him again, and he held her wrist for a moment, looking at her. Her eyes were playful and smoky, and he wanted to let her do whatever she wanted. At the opportunity of more applause, he spoke again.

"I don't think you have any idea how careful you would need to be, and I don't think it's possible for you to be that careful." He leaned closer. "So you need to move your hand down a few inches, because you're making me crazy." He said it into her ear. His voice was low, and it rumbled through her while his breath stirred every nerve ending in her ear. And then, for good measure, he grazed his lips just under her ear. She was unable to stop the shiver. Tom chuckled.

***

The speeches were done. Finally. Liz excused herself to go to the restroom, and Paige went with her. She said, "You two seemed cozy. What's up, Liz?"

Liz smiled and said, "Hey, it's a date. I get to act the part. Since when would I turn down the excuse to flirt excessively with the best-looking guy I've ever met? How about you? Are you guys having fun?"

Paige looked at her, a little surprised that she wasn't sharing more information. "Sure. Chris is good at this kind of thing, and I've never minded."

"God knows you're perfect for this—you make gorgeous arm candy even when you're not trying. It's annoying, actually." Liz winked at her friend.

"Oh, please. Stop changing the subject." She caught Liz's eye in the mirror as they prepared to go back out to the guys. "What was going on at dinner?"

Cornered, Liz went with the easiest answer—the truth. Or at least part of it. "I had my hand on his knee under the table." Paige's eyebrows went up, and Liz looked a little sheepish. "It's possible that my judgment has been slightly impaired by the combination of alcohol and an excessively attractive man in a tuxedo. I'm having a lovely time, though. I'm so glad that Chris pestered Tom into this. I need to thank him again."

***

Liz and Paige came up to Tom and Chris, who were standing together waiting for them. Tom was saying, "I'm glad that part is over. I always feel like I'm trapped during the speeches. It makes me want to gnaw off a limb to get away."

Chris said, "Micky, you looked more relaxed than I've ever seen you at a formal event. I don't know what she's slipping into your drinks, but I'm going to ask Liz if I can get some for your water bottle in the locker room."

The girls had just arrived. Liz laughed. "Oh, Chris, you can't bottle this dress. And you wouldn't look nearly as good in it."

"And I feel the need for some brain bleach to get

rid of the image that caused. Yikes." Paige shuddered dramatically.

The four of them joked for a while longer, but Liz could see Tom was starting to lose his cool again. So much of what he was feeling showed on his face, and she wondered if he was at all aware when he started scowling.

They sat at a nearby high table to sip drinks. Liz wandered over to grab a new beer, and Paige and Chris began talking with some friends who stopped by the table. After a few moments, Liz returned to the table, put the beer in front of Tom, who was now fully scowling and looking annoyed, and had him lean down so that she could say something into his ear.

"I was just thinking that you look like a man in need of a blowjob. Meet me in five minutes." And then she walked off as if she was simply going to get a new drink for herself. There was a powerful surge to his groin, and his heart started beating faster. He turned to watch her walk away, completely taken by surprise yet again.

Paige happened to be watching from across the table. She was looking at Tom, noticing that he was starting to look irritable and unpleasant again. Just as she was wondering what, if anything, she should do or say, Liz walked up, handed him a beer, and whispered something to him. Whatever it was clearly stunned him enough to snap him out of his bad mood. He was now just watching Liz walk away, wide-eyed.

Paige spoke up. "Micky?"

He was still staring, but now his eyes were

looking less surprised and more…something else.

"Hey, Mick."

He turned with a start and looked at her, his mind clearly not fully at the table with them.

She thought about asking what Liz had said but decided to go with, "Are you doing okay? You looked pissed off a minute ago."

"No, I'm all right. Thanks for asking, though." Tom got up and started to walk toward the door. "I'm going to get some air for a few minutes."

***

Tom used his key to open the door to the room and found Liz waiting for him. It was her turn to drag him into the room. She kissed him, hard, while she was undoing his pants. They dropped to the floor, and she dropped down in front of him, wasting no time. "Oh God, Liz." Tom groaned. He was still just inside the doorway. So far they hadn't even made it all the way inside the room.

Liz thought for just a moment about moving so that he could sit on the bed or in the chair, but she had felt an urgency, a need to take him, and he was clearly feeling the same urgency based on his responses.

Tom had never felt an orgasm building this quickly from oral sex. The combination of the setting…and the secrecy…and how she had brought him here specifically for this…and how sexy and amazing she was…and the things she was now doing with her mouth…he was not going to last long at all. He had his hands resting gently on the top of her head, trying not to grip her hair, already moving his hips in time with her movements, already feeling the overwhelming pressure wave forming. He was breathing hard and fast, starting to lose himself.

"Oh God, Liz, I'm gonna come."

She responded by gripping his ass in both hands, and he twined his fingers through her hair and came apart for her for the second time that night.

He leaned his head back against the door and closed his eyes, laughing, as she stood back up, pulling his pants back up as she moved.

"Silk boxers. I hadn't even noticed the first time. Very sexy, McCullin." She dragged her hand over the silk and what was now underneath.

"Holy crap, I don't know if I can walk." He smiled at her, and her heart melted.

"I'm enjoying you looking sex-drunk in public," she said, winking at him. "You'd better go—at least be holding a real drink so it's believable."

He caught her around the waist and kissed her. "That was amazing." His voice was low, and he spoke slowly, sounding for all the world a little drunk. "I definitely want to return that favor sometime very soon."

Her breath caught, her heart sped up again, and she kissed him and pushed him away. "You have to go, because that is way too tempting right now. But don't worry, I won't forget. I've decided to keep score."

He laughed again and said, "Really? Now you're keeping score? I seem to recall a few times where there was a good three-to-one ratio in my favor…"

"That was before I started keeping score. My game, my rules," she said, teasing.

He put one hand along her jaw and up under her ear and kissed her. And then he smiled and said, "I don't know why I thought I would be able to kiss you just once this time," and kissed her again, and again.

She pushed him away again. "Go. I'll see you in a few minutes."

***

Once again, less than ten minutes had passed, and once again, he felt like he was wearing a sign that said, "Just Received Magnificent Blowjob." And yet, no one seemed to notice.

He wandered up to where Paige and Chris were talking with a few other folks and slipped into the circle of conversation, listening to the discussion with less than half his brain. Paige noticed him join in and also noticed he looked far more relaxed than he had all evening. Amazingly relaxed. Drunk relaxed. No, not drunk...

She narrowed her eyes for a moment and then shook her head. *Holy shit. He just got laid.* She didn't know whether to be excited for her friend, or concerned, or upset that Liz hadn't said anything. *This is definitely a strange turn of events.* She looked over at Chris, who was clearly oblivious.

Liz joined the circle a few minutes later, standing next to Tom, who put his arm around her and kissed the top of her head when she stood near him, pausing for a moment to close his eyes and breathe

114

in her hair.

Paige was quietly taking in all of this.

Oh, this has been going on for a while.

Chapter Thirteen

There were just a few more obligations as part of the evening, including photographs. Tom was even able to smile for them. Chris was amazed. "Okay, Micky. You know I don't usually do this, but shit— would you please ask her out for real? You're *smiling!* At a formal event!"

Tom bristled, and Chris sighed. "Fuck. Fine. Mick, I'm sorry. Your personal life is your own. You thorny bastard." He slapped Tom on the back. "Go find her. I just disrupted your groove, and now you're all grouchy again. Don't blame me, though, for trying to save you from yourself, you dumb fucker."

He walked off shaking his head, and Tom scowled after him.

***

Chris walked past Liz, saying, "I just pissed off your date. Sorry about that. Looks like you've got work to do."

116

She was surprised, wondering what could have happened between them in such a short period of time. They hadn't been talking alone for very long at all. Liz walked up to Tom, who was definitely looking angry, and put her hand in his.

"Not now, Liz."

"Yes, now." He looked at her and glared. She met his look without flinching. "I'm not sure what just happened between you and Chris, but I'm not willing to let this wreck a great evening between you and me." She stepped closer to him. "I'm willing to give you a little while to cool off if that will help. But I was not planning on leaving this evening without using the bed in that room." She stepped closer still. "I was really hoping it would be with you and not just by myself. I'm going to be naked in the middle of that bed in ten minutes."

He was still scowling, but much less so, and she definitely had his attention. All of his attention.

She pulled him down by his lapel and finally breathed in his ear, "I'll be starting by myself, but I really want you to join me." She blew gently in his ear, and it hit every nerve ending, finishing the short-circuiting of all his brain cells.

"Shit."

She walked away.

He didn't even remember why he was fucking angry. He knew that he was angry, or had been, but all the extra blood in his body had been diverted south. *When was the last time I had sex three times in the space of four hours?*

***

117

Chris walked up to Paige, exasperated, and told her what had happened. She looked over and saw Liz approaching Tom. She elbowed Chris and said, "Watch."

They watched the interaction, which took just a few minutes, and Chris just said, "Holy shit. Magical superpowers." Paige smirked a little. She was pretty sure what those magical superpowers actually were, but she wasn't going to say anything before talking with her friend. She needed answers, and the last thing she wanted to do was to accidentally start any rumors.

"I think he's crazy about her, Paige. He's just being a stubborn prick about it. I can't even imagine why."

"I don't know, hon." Paige sighed. "I'm glad they're having fun tonight, though." She kissed her husband. "It was a great idea to get them together for this."

***

She was waiting for him as promised, in the middle of the king-sized bed. Naked. And she had indeed started without him. When he walked in, he found her there, with one hand on her breast, teasingly circling her nipple, and the other between her legs, teasingly circling her clit, one leg bent at the knee. Her skin was flushed, and she was breathing hard. Her head was back on the pillows, lips parted, eyes closed.

He thought it was the most erotically beautiful scene he had ever laid eyes on, and it made his heart constrict in his chest at the same time as he hardened to iron.

She opened her eyes as she heard him growl and smiled as he walked toward her. But when he reached to start taking his clothes off, she said, "No, leave them on. Take me with your tux on, Tom." He shook his head in disbelief.

"Really?"

She was still moving her hands, slowly, teasingly. "Yes." She gasped, and he stared. "You can take the jacket off. Everything else stays on. You are so fucking handsome." There were occasional small gasps from her, as her hands were making just tiny motions which were, apparently, exquisitely effective.

He took off his jacket and undid the fly of his pants, releasing his erection. "I want to do that to you. What you're doing. The way you're touching yourself. I want to touch you like that."

"Next time, Tom, please, yes." She reached up and drew him down for a kiss with one hand and pulled him to enter her with the other. "Next time I want you to touch me like that all night." She moaned in pleasure as he pressed into her deeply. "I want you to not stop even if I beg you to."

He started moving, deep, steady, slowly. "I want you to tease me like that until I come and then keep teasing me until I come again." She moaned louder, moving under him, pushing the pace.

He was trying to go slower this time, but she had been driving this train all night, and he wasn't going to upset anything now.

She kissed him and looked at him. "I will, you

know. I will come just from teasing. Just from you touching me softly, gently, over and over." She was rocking her hips, forcing the pace.

He was already starting to lose rhythm; her voice, her words, were driving him crazy. He didn't realize that he could be so turned on from her talking to him during sex.

She was bucking and grinding under him by this point. Tom was just trying to hang on and not come before her. It was going to be a close call. This woman was driving him insane in every way possible.

"Tom," she breathed, groaning, "Tom, talk to me, please. Tell me when you're going to come. Your voice makes me crazy."

"Christ, Liz. Now. Oh God, now. I'm going to come now," and he buried his face in her neck and bellowed as she clamped around him in pulsing spasms.

When he could breathe again, he said against her neck, "I really don't know if I can walk this time."

She chuckled, saying, "Me, neither. That was a helluva thing, McCullin." She gave him a gentle shove. "But you've got a few more things you've got to do. So get up, and get back to your party thing. Whatever it is. I don't even know anymore."

He laughed at her. "Now you sound sex-drunk. I like it. We can be sex-drunk together."

"Excellent. Don't forget to zip up. Shit, I hope I don't put this dress on backward or something stupid like that."

She shoved Tom to get out the door, and he walked back for the final part of the event.

***

He had been gone only slightly longer this time, but he was now well and truly mellow. He was pretty sure he couldn't be more mellow if he tried. He found Chris and apologized for being an ass. Chris just stared at him and said, "How much have you been drinking, and where did you find the good stuff here?"

Liz returned, wearing her dress properly, but she had given up on her hair and had taken it down. It fell in waves below her shoulders, and Tom thought it was gorgeous.

He fulfilled all of his remaining team obligations. He danced with Liz—a slow dance where he just swayed and smelled her hair. But he stayed on the dance floor for the whole song. She had very nice-smelling hair.

At one point, near the end of the evening, he found himself trapped in a conversation with several people, including Chris, and started to feel the beginnings of anger and frustration building. It must have shown on his face, because Liz caught his eye, gave him a questioning look, raised an eyebrow, and held up four fingers in a kind of "Ready to go for it again, big guy?" signal.

Tom laughed out loud and then excused himself, explaining, "My date just threatened me. Apparently I look like I'm getting into a bad mood. I need to bow out and take my date home."

Chris gaped openly as if Tom had grown a second head right before his eyes.

Chapter Fourteen

Liz woke up to hear her phone ringing. She rolled over, away from Tom, who followed her movement sleepily to spoon behind her. Picking up the phone, she saw it was Paige calling and answered, concerned. It was unusual for Paige to call her early. Although, as she looked at the clock, she saw it wasn't actually early; they had just slept quite late this morning.

"Hey, Paige," she said, voice raspy from sleep, "Are you okay?"

"Everything is fine. Did I wake you? Wow, I'm sorry. I was sure you would be up already." She paused only briefly and said, "So are you alone?"

"Why wouldn't I be?" Liz was suddenly much more awake and slipped out of bed to take the phone call in the living room.

"I was wondering if Micky had left yet."

"Oh." Pause.

"How long, Liz?"

"What?" Her brain was trying to catch up to this conversation.

"How long have you been sleeping with him? It definitely didn't start last night. Days? Weeks?"

Liz sighed, sat down on the couch, and answered quietly, "Months."

Paige was silent for so long that Liz was afraid she had hung up.

"When did it start?"

"The night after we went to the zoo."

"Holy shit." Paige was well and truly shocked. "I don't even know what to say, Liz. Why didn't you tell me?" The last question was quiet and said with kindness and concern.

"I don't know, Paige. I really don't. Lots of reasons."

"Please just tell me he's not the one forcing secrecy. This all started right after you first met? Please, please say something to reassure me that this is not as creepy as it's sounding right now."

"No, no, Paige, I promise. This has been mutual. I'm not sure either one of us knows why. It just started quietly, and neither one of us talked about it, and then, well, we kept not saying anything." She smiled. "If it makes you feel any better, he was going to be a gentleman that first night and not take advantage of me because we had just met and I'm your best friend."

"So what happened with that?"

"I took advantage of him instead."

Paige barked out a laugh. "Really?" She laughed again. "Okay, now I'm torn between concern and an odd feeling of pride. Talk about double standards." Her tone became thoughtful again. "Is this a serious thing?"

"No. It's not that kind of relationship, or you would already know about it."

Paige felt her heart break a little for her friend and said, "Are you going to regret this?"

Liz smiled, loving her for knowing the right question to ask. "No. Definitely not."

"You're sure?"

"Absolutely. Not for one minute."

Paige sighed. "You know I love you."

"I do. We can get together later for coffee to talk, if you want to." She looked up as Tom wandered out of the bedroom, his rumpled hair and sleepy smile making her heart contract again.

"Yes. I'll text you. And Liz," Paige added, "I have to tell Chris. I didn't say anything last night. Not before I was sure. But I can't keep this from him. You know that."

It was Liz's turn to sigh. "I know. I will handle this end. Thanks for calling."

She turned to look at Tom, who asked, "Is everything all right?"

"Paige is fine. She was calling to ask me how long we have been sleeping together."

Tom stared at her and sat down at the other end of the couch. "Oh."

"That was pretty much my reaction." She smiled at him, and he gave a half smile back in return. "I did tell her. I'm a lousy liar."

"How'd she take it?"

"A little freaked out initially, but I reassured her that I was the one who stole your virtue in the first place, and I think that made her feel better." Tom chuckled, and Liz continued, "How *you* are taking this is a more important question to me. She's going to tell Chris. She won't keep something like this from him."

Tom looked thoughtful, almost perplexed, for a moment before answering. "It was bound to come out at some point." He really wasn't sure how he felt about this. There were emotions he couldn't name that were starting to swirl around in him. "How about you?"

"Actually, I think I'm okay. It was fun to keep you my personal fantasy for a while, but I'm starting to think trading that in for 'I'm dating a hockey player' might be a pretty good deal." She smiled at him, but his look had turned dark the moment she said the word "dating."

"Oh," she said. She sat up straighter on the couch. "Oh, shit. Okay, not dating. Got it." Her heart was fluttering wildly, and not in a good way, and she was suddenly feeling sick in the pit of her stomach.

Fuck, fuck, fuck, ask the hard question, ask it, ask it.

"So I guess I need more information about all of this." Deep breath. "Are we exclusive?"

Tom turned toward her so suddenly she almost jumped. He looked furious and all but yelled, "Why the fuck would you ask that?"

Liz lost her cool and yelled back, "Because I just learned that I'm good enough to fuck but not good enough to date, so I'm suddenly feeling really fucking insecure, that's why! Answer the goddamn question!" She stopped and took another deep breath, trying to calm down.

Tom had been so stunned by her outburst that he sat all the way back into the couch and was staring at her.

She tried to speak more calmly. "We have never discussed this. I have never asked, and you have never promised. I'm not looking to pick a fight over the answer; I just need to know where we stand." She took another breath. "Please."

Tom ran his hands through his hair, looking distraught. "Jesus, Liz." He turned toward her. "Yes, we are fucking exclusive." He got up and paced. "God damn it." He faced her, his voice rasping with emotion, volume rising, and said, "I can't believe how fucking angry I am, that you would think for *one minute* that I could be sleeping with someone else, and then have a night like last night with you. *God damn it,* Liz."

He stopped pacing, looked up at the ceiling for a moment, and turned to look her in the eyes. This was all going so wrong. *"You are not just someone I fuck,* and I'm trying not to put my fist through your goddamn wall because you even *thought* that for a second. I. Don't. Want. To. Share. You."

She stared at him as if he was completely alien and then barked out a sound that was half laugh. "I have no idea what the fuck is going on. How do I end up in these conversations with you, where I feel like I'm losing my mind?"

"What are you talking about?" He was still really angry.

"Explain to me how dating equals sharing. Isn't that the point of dating someone? That, then that person is with you, and not with other people, therefore you are *not* sharing them?" He sat back down. "Otherwise, isn't it then something else, like…swinging?" She laughed for a second and then said, "Shit, this isn't funny. I'm sorry. My brain has reached total overload."

Tom's lips turned up a little, and he said, "It's a little funny. I've definitely never asked anyone if they'd like to go out swinging." He looked at her. "Fuck."

"Yeah." Her chest hurt, and she felt tears pricking her eyes.

"You know I care about you."

"Oh, geez, I know. But thank you." She put her head back on the couch. "I'm sure you have your own reasons for the way we've done this. I think I just wanted to live in a fantasy for a little while." She turned to look at him. "No responsibilities. Well, not really. You know what I mean. No one asking questions. No one pushing for information. No expectations of what 'the relationship' should look like in week, or a month, or however long. No commitments."

Tom bristled sharply.

"That's not what I meant," she said hurriedly. "I meant no long-term commitments to the other person. Shit, that's still not coming out right." Looking for the right words, she added, "I have such a good time with you, and I don't want this to end, but I don't know how to handle this. Any insight would be really helpful." She smiled weakly.

"I don't know. I don't want this to end, either." He took a breath. "I meant…I don't want to share my relationship with you with the other guys on the team. It's one thing for Becks to know. I trust him. But work is work and personal is personal. I don't mix them, but you're friends with other guys on the team, and that makes it complicated."

Liz was surprised. "You don't hang out with your teammates outside of work?" Chris was friends with a lot of guys on the team. There was a camaraderie that was important to playing on a team, and she hadn't realized Tom didn't really socialize with his teammates. "What about your roommates?"

He looked at her rather darkly, as if she was judging him. "They're roommates. We share space. We're adult men; we don't interact besides grunting at each other in passing. And no, I don't usually hang out with my teammates. I work my ass off for the team; I practice, I train, I study, I grind. I will run drills as long as I'm asked to, and then I will go back and run drills more. And if my teammates want to practice more outside of work, I'm all in. I will be the first one on the ice and the last one off. But other than that, I don't need to hang out with them. The occasional beer after a big win is fine."

"But Chris…?"

"Becks is different. I've known him since USHL and college. He's like my brother."

Liz sighed. She looked over at Tom, at the furrows starting to creep into his brow, the scowl starting to take over his handsome face. She smiled a little wistfully, thinking about what she would have done just last night to take that look away from him.

"What?" Tom asked gruffly. Liz was looking at him with a slightly faraway look and a small smile.

"You're scowling."

He ran his hands through his hair and looked back over at her. His face was a little softer.

"I was thinking about how I would have made you stop scowling just last night," she said with a small sigh.

"I don't want to give this up." His voice was strained.

"I don't, either." She tilted her head. "How about a version of 'don't ask, don't tell'?"

He snorted. "Seriously?"

She shrugged. "I'm game if you are. I'm not going to lie to people if they ask, but I don't necessarily have to tell anyone, either. We can be 'casually seeing each other'…" she used air quotes, "…if you like. People saw us together last night. Someone is going to ask. Zee at the very least." Tom grimaced, and she smiled. "He's a good guy, Tom."

"If you say so."

"So what do you think?"

He took her hand, the first contact they had since she had gotten out of bed when Paige called.

"Okay. Let's do that."

She moved closer to him, and he tucked her against his chest and kissed the top of her head.

She let out the breath she hadn't realized she'd been holding and relaxed against him, listening to his heartbeat. *I wish this didn't feel like the beginning of the end.*

Tom felt her relax against him. Two things

happened simultaneously as he held her—something that was tangled in him uncoiled, and he felt calm, and something else in his chest twisted into a knot. It was confusing. Everything felt so right when he was with her.

And yet things were starting to go so very wrong.

Chapter Fifteen

Paige was waiting for her at Starbucks with two coffee cups in front of her. Liz saw the worry on her face and as she hugged Paige said, "I'm so sorry I didn't tell you."

As they sat down together, Paige said, "I suddenly don't know where to start. I guess, why?"

"I'm not entirely sure. We talked a little about it this morning. We hadn't actually talked about not talking about it before, if that makes any sense. I think it was an escape. I had a little secret fantasy life, with no expectations."

"No expectations?" Paige looked at her sadly. "Do you mean from me?"

She sighed. "Maybe a little. I'm sorry." Paige's eyes were slightly teary. "But also from me. Hey, a little credit for getting involved with someone again, though, right? I think it made it easier that it's with someone where it can't possibly work out in the long run."

Paige looked confused. "Why would you say that?"

"He's a fantasy, Paige. People don't end up with their fantasies." She was still getting confusion in return, so she tried to elaborate. "Look at it this way…say your friend introduces you to Channing Tatum." She picked one of Paige's favorite choices for eye-candy. "You hit it off, and there's chemistry, and he's interested in fooling around. If the universe sets that up for you, you say *'Yes,'* and you enjoy the hell out of it.

"In the meantime, you discover he's smart and funny, and you have a fantastic time together. That's awesome, but he's still Channing Tatum. And eventually he's still going to go back to his real life, and you're going to go back to yours. So you enjoy the hell out of it while it lasts, and you don't worry about the fact that it's not going to."

Paige looked surprised and rather upset. "Are you saying that you're somehow not in the same league as Micky, so it's okay to just play with this relationship like it doesn't mean anything?" she asked. "Do you care or not?"

Liz was shocked. "Of course I care. Too much. And this relationship means a lot. I'm not playing." She was hurt by the questions more than she realized. "Paige, do you really think I wouldn't care?"

"Why would it be impossible that he would care too?"

"He cares. He's a great guy. That doesn't mean it's going to last." She tried to steer the topic in a slightly different direction. "What did Chris say?"

Paige gave a short laugh. "He was surprised. Said something about not understanding Micky at all."

Liz smiled. "He is definitely confusing. Or maybe I should say interestingly complicated. Very smart. Very funny. Hard working. Deep feeling." At this last comment, Paige gave her a questioning look. "He loves his family. You should hear him talk about them; it's wonderful. There's a lot more to him than meets the eye." She smiled and raised her eyebrows, adding, "And what meets the eye is spectacular."

"Oh, for God's sake." Paige laughed but looked more closely at Liz after her last comments about Tom and put together all of the pieces she had from what she had seen and heard. She knew her friend very well. Reaching a hand across the table, she asked quietly, "Liz, are you in love with him?"

Everything in Liz's chest constricted at the question, and it showed on her face. She sighed and said quietly, "Yeah."

It was no use trying to deny it. Paige already knew.

"Are you going to tell him?"

"Maybe, eventually. I don't know. It's not that kind of relationship."

Paige tried one more time. "It's unfair to Micky to assume that he can't have feelings for you too."

"I know he cares."

"That's not what I mean."

Liz smiled and said, "Well, we'll see. Things have changed, and I'm not sure this relationship is going to survive the bright light of day as it stands." She explained the agreement that they had reached regarding continued non-sharing of the relationship.

Paige did not look at all happy by the end of the explanation. "And you're okay with this?"

"For now." Liz shrugged. "It was the compromise we reached. Neither one of us was willing to walk away. Not yet. So this is where we are."

Paige looked concerned and a bit sad, and Liz needed her to understand.

"No regrets, Paige. None. I promise. No matter how this ends." She stood up so she could hug her best friend until they both felt better.

Chapter Sixteen

Tom walked into the house he shared with two teammates and tossed his keys on the table. He was heading toward his room to get clean clothes to go take a shower when he heard the question. "Mick, is it true? Did you really go to that event with Liz last night?" He turned, startled to see Sven Andersson, another defenseman, standing in the hallway looking at him.

Tom was caught off guard. "Yeah. Why?"

"Just surprised. I guess I always assumed she was dating someone." He paused and raised an eyebrow. "Shit, is that why you only sleep here about half the time?"

Tom must have looked pissed off, because Sven raised his hands and backed off, saying, "Sorry, forget I asked." As he turned to walk away, he added, "Latest cable bill is on the fridge. And you got a package from Amazon."

Tom took a long shower, trying to convince himself this was not a big deal; he could handle this. He just needed to take it in stride. No problem.

Yeah, right. Because that's the way I always handle things.

***

At the next practice the first person that approached him was Zee. *Fuck.*

"Mick, I gotta know. How did you get her to go?"

Tom just looked at him. "I asked her." Technically, Chris had asked her for him, but Zee didn't need to know that.

"You just asked her. Really? That's it?"

"That's it." Tom's tone was not inviting more conversation on the matter.

"Huh." Tom was ready to walk away when Zee added, "So is this a thing? You two?"

"Why?" It came out sounding rather more threatening than Tom had intended.

Zee faced him without flinching and said, "Because if it's not, there's more than one guy that would be interested in that information."

Tom said curtly, "It's a thing." And walked away. *God damn it.*

***

After the initial flurry of interest in his personal life, including multiple inquiries as to whether Liz had a sister, things calmed down somewhat, and Tom was able to get back to his normal routine. Practice, game, practice, road game, practice…repeat as necessary.

There was an underlying pressure, though. A casual comment of "Hey, are you going to see Liz tonight? Tell her I said hi," was enough to make him clench his jaw. He was finding reasons to see her less, even though he always felt better when he was with her. She was no longer his secret escape.

It wasn't helping that he was in a bit of a playing slump. Nothing horrible. Most players had highs and lows throughout the season, and this was not the first time it had happened to him, but it was feeding his foul moods, which were becoming more and more common. The team was still having a good season, but right now they were having trouble putting more than two wins together back to back, and the stress was taking its toll.

Liz texted him while he was in the locker room one night after a particularly bad home loss. He had had an awful game. He had taken a few penalties, lost concentration, and gotten slammed into the boards hard enough that he knew he was going to have a great-looking bruise and, worst of all, missed a pass that resulted in a turnover and a score for Carolina. He was so pissed he had slammed his stick on the doorway overhead on his way into the locker room hard enough to snap it in half.

Liz: Are you coming over tonight?

Tom stared at the text for a full minute. Complete sentence, including punctuation.

He was so fucking angry. He should go see her; he hadn't seen her in days, and he missed her.

137

From behind him, Tom heard Zee start a phone call. "Hey. Did you see the game? Please tell me something funny happened to you today."

Tom saw red.

Tom: No

He didn't throw the phone across the room and was grateful that he wasn't actually strong enough to crush it with his hands.

Liz: Tomorrow? Please, Tom. I miss you.

She must have Zee on speaker, because she was texting him, and he knew she was talking with Zee. He could hear Zee's end of the conversation, and it felt like it was gnawing at his skull.

Tom: Maybe

Maybe he would feel better tomorrow.

Tom finished getting ready to leave in a silent, hot rage.

He sat in his car in the garage for at least five minutes, realizing that he was too angry to drive. *Fuck. Fuck. Fuck.* He looked over at his phone, arguing with himself, and finally sent another text.

Tom: R u awake

His phone rang almost immediately.

"I'm awake."

"Hey."

138

"Hi, handsome." She paused and then said quietly, "I think I have a bag of frozen peas for your shoulder." Another pause. "I'll look around, but I think I could find other things for the rest of you."

He felt the beginnings of a smile. "I'll be over soon." He paused a moment before adding, "I've missed you too."

"I'll scc you when you get here."

***

Liz greeted Tom at the door dressed for bed— wearing a very oversized t-shirt over her underwear. They didn't say anything. She wrapped her arms around his chest and held him for a moment. He tucked her under his chin and breathed in her hair and kissed the top of her head and felt the rightness that he always felt when she was in his arms.

She stepped back, took his hand, and pulled him gently into her bedroom. Sitting him on the edge of her bed, she took off his jacket and then his shirt and winced. The bruise was already forming, starting at the top of his left shoulder and spreading down his shoulder blade. It was going to be very colorful before it was done.

She touched it gently. "I wasn't kidding—I'll be right back," she said, walking to the kitchen and bringing back a bag of frozen peas. Instructing him to kick off his shoes and lie face down on the bed, she put the bag of peas on the bruise.

Then she climbed up and sat on him—on his rear, basically. He grunted. She responded playfully, "I'm not that heavy," and began massaging his lower back. Then he groaned.

She didn't have any oils so she had just gotten out her hand lotion and was using that. He was strong and muscular, but there was also incredible tightness, and she was able to lean into him with her weight to try to work out some of the knots that seemed to be all over, but especially in his neck and lower back. He made sounds of relief and pleasure as she worked on him. It felt so good to be touching him again.

When her hands and arms were too tired to keep massaging with any force, she simply stroked his back and neck. After a while, she took the peas from his shoulder and climbed off to put them back in the freezer for him to use again in the morning if he wanted to.

When she got back to the bedroom, she saw that Tom had fallen asleep and found an extra blanket to cover him up. She smiled as she took a moment to watch him sleeping, noting how much younger he looked in sleep despite the thick beard and how beautifully long his eyelashes were. Afraid to wake him, she carefully touched his hair, tucking some behind his ear, and then turned off the light and climbed onto the other side of the bed.

His body was warm, but he was sleeping on his stomach, which didn't make for easy cuddling, so she turned on her side and backed into him so she could feel his warmth and solid form at her back as she drifted off to sleep.

***

Liz woke in the morning to the wonderful sensation of being spooned. Tom was wrapped around her. He had apparently awoken during the night and taken off his jeans and socks, so she was surrounded by the heat coming from his warm skin.

When he realized she was awake, he rumbled, "Thank you," into her ear. "That was wonderful."

"You are very welcome." She relaxed into his arms and sighed. "I'm so glad you're here."

He had started nuzzling into her neck. The arm that was wrapped around her waist had started to wander around—his hand was currently on her hip. "I'm getting happier to be here every minute."

He pressed closer to her, and she started breathing faster. Liz could feel him getting aroused, could feel him growing against her. He started gently biting her neck where it met her shoulder.

He was getting harder. It excited her so much to feel him, knowing he was getting turned on by her. It was like a positive feedback loop. Feeling him getting a hard on was guaranteed to make her slick and ready. She pressed back and wriggled against him, and he chuckled and pulled her t-shirt off.

Tom slid his hand inside her panties to check and see if she was really getting turned on by this and found her hot and wet. He was now at full attention and took off her underwear first, then his own. Liz moved her top leg up and back over his hip, and he slid into her easily.

She gasped, and he growled softly and began to move. Slowly. There was no urgency. Tom held her around her waist, breathing in her scent under her ear, kissing her there softly, placing small bites on her shoulder as he stroked in and out of her smoothly, slowly.

Liz exposed her neck so he could have access to as much of her as possible to kiss. She held his arms around her and reveled in the feeling of his body sliding against hers, into hers.

He wanted this to last as long as possible. Tom kept the pace slow, and they moved together in a kind of timelessness. But eventually his soft kisses and bites changed to open-mouthed breathing against her neck, and his slow strokes turned into thrusts.

Tom held her tighter, driving into her faster and harder. Liz was gasping, and Tom was nearing the end. He pressed her over further so that she was more facing down on the bed and rode her, powerful and grinding, reaching under her to press and rub her clit while he shouted his orgasm and finished inside her. Liz jerked and cried out, and Tom felt her spasm around him. They both fell asleep again soon afterwards.

When they awoke, it was time for Tom to leave, so he could get to his place and then to the rink for practice.

"Thank you." Tom kissed her for the first time since arriving the night before. He stopped and then smiled, said, "Shit," and kept kissing her for a few more minutes.

"I'm so glad you came over." She held him tight.

"Me too." He breathed in her hair, kissed her on the top of her head, and left.

Chapter Seventeen

It would have been nice to think their time together that night had somehow changed things, helped to fix what had broken between them when their relationship had stopped being secret, but neither one of them seemed to be able to slow the unraveling.

Tom was still in a skating slump. He was frustrated, not playing well, getting less ice time, and taking bad penalties, including a nasty game misconduct. Part of him wanted to blame the relationship, even though he knew that wasn't really fair.

Except things were continuing to deteriorate between them, and it was getting to be a distraction.

His jealousy and suspicion were becoming an issue in a way that they never had been before. Never very happy with Liz's male friends, including ex-boyfriends, now it appeared to Liz that, with the exception of Chris, they all were categorized as threats. Even the married ones. It made no sense to her.

"Why do you stay in touch with them? I don't understand." They'd had this conversation more than once already.

"Tom, they were important in my life. These guys weren't one-night stands. Some were friends of mine before we dated, and we stayed friends after we broke up. I don't understand why that's an impossible concept. I liked the guys that I dated or I wouldn't have dated them in the first place."

"All of them? You're still *friends* with all of your ex-boyfriends?" The emphasis was quite obvious.

"Yes. I'm still *friends* with all of them." Liz was trying very hard not to fall into this and start arguing back, but it was becoming difficult to keep her cool. "It's not like there were that many. I'm closer to some than others. Some of them I just keep in touch with on Facebook; one or two I see in person. And for a few of them, I get along with their wives better, so we are the ones who keep in touch."

"Right."

"Okay, I've got to go to work. I know you're going to be gone for Columbus before I get back." She looked at him, at his scowl. "I don't want to leave like this." She touched his face and reached up to kiss him.

He didn't return the kiss immediately, but when she gently bit his lower lip, he bent his head down to hers, wrapped his arms around her, and they kissed goodbye like they meant it.

***

"So maybe you could stop by my office for a few minutes before you head to the rink for the game tomorrow?" Liz worked only a few metro stops or a short cab ride from the arena. Tom had never been to her office. Not once. No one she worked with knew anything about him. She looked over at him and saw he had bristled at the suggestion. "What? It wouldn't take long at all. We could grab a quick bite if you wanted, and you could meet Jason."

She had worked with her boss for more than eight years, and he had become a good friend. Tom and Jason would get along really well, if they ever met. And hell, Tom wouldn't even consider Jason a threat, unless he considered Jason's husband, Paul, a threat too. "Why do you look angry that I'm asking this?"

"I don't understand why you're suddenly making relationship demands."

Liz was stunned. "Relationship demands?" She had to consider that for a moment. "Really? Is that how you think of what I just asked? That it's a 'relationship demand?'" She looked at him, asking him seriously.

He just stared at her.

She said, "I guess if you consider me asking that you act like you're in some kind of relationship with me to be a 'relationship demand,' then yes, that's what's going on."

His staring now could be described more as glaring.

"I have friends that I care about, that care about me, that don't know anything about what's going on in my life. People you've never met and who you apparently have no interest in meeting."

"Yes, you have lots of friends. I'm aware." Heavy sarcasm.

"What's that supposed to mean?"

Tom gestured to her laptop, open to Facebook, sitting on the countertop. She was in the middle of a conversation with James, a friend from college, planning a trip to Richmond to visit him and his wife while Tom would be on a road trip with the team. "Another trip to visit another guy while I'm away. You don't even bother trying to hide it anymore."

"What? Hide? How? I don't understand. I'm not trying to hide anything. I'm going to see friends while you're away, so I can spend time with you when you're here. Would you rather I leave on a trip when you're here?"

"I'd rather you not travel around seeing other men." Tom was starting to raise his voice.

This was ramping up into a full-blown fight.

"I'm having lunch with him *and his wife*. I have much more in common with her than with him. And then she and I are seeing a show in Richmond. That's the whole reason for the trip. We both like the show, so we are going together."

"How about last month's trip to Pennsylvania to visit your ex-boyfriend who owns the gun range? Did you have him give you shooting lessons? I'll bet that was cozy. How close did he have to hold you to make sure you hit the target?" Now he was sounding venomous.

Liz was horrified. "He owns the range. His *wife* is the nationally ranked sharp shooter. So if anyone was going to teach me, it would be her. But I'm a pretty damn good shot, which you might know if you ever bothered to ask anything about me." She was getting angry enough to take some jabs herself, which she immediately regretted. She took a breath. "Sorry." Escalating this on her side wasn't going to help.

It was too late, though. Tom looked bitter and furious. It was almost like she was looking at a different person.

"I'm sorry, Tom. I didn't mean that." She spoke calmly, trying to explain herself. "You know my friends are important to me. I won't give them up because you're jealous."

He absolutely glared at her.

"There is nothing to be jealous of. They're just my friends. Nothing has changed in that regard since the day we met. I love my friends. I hug them. I want to spend time with them. But that's all."

Silence stretched between them. Liz was at a loss.

Tom finally spoke. "I need to take a break from this. From us." He was clearly still incredibly angry, but he wasn't yelling. His voice was strained.

"Oh." Her heart sank to somewhere near the floor.

"I need to focus on hockey." He wasn't looking directly at her. "We're coming up on the playoffs. I'm already in a slump." He looked her in the eye. "And this isn't helping."

She nodded. He was so angry. She still didn't understand that, but this she understood. He was a pro athlete.

"Is this a break?" she asked quietly, "Or the end?"

He looked away again. "I don't know."

"Okay."

He looked back at her again, jaw set, ready for a continuation of the fight, and found her just looking at him, eyes slightly too bright. She saw the slight shift in him, the subtle easing, as he realized there wasn't going to be a confrontation about this.

And then her phone rang on the counter. They both turned, and Zee's name popped up on the screen. Liz reached to turn the ringer off, and by the time she turned back, she could barely recognize him.

"Motherfucker!"

She had never, ever seen him this angry. He turned away from her and started toward the door.

Liz panicked. "Tom!" She grabbed his arm. *"Tom!"* She put herself in front of him at the door. "Please. Just give me a few minutes. Please. I just need a few minutes to tell you how I feel. Then you can leave. I swear I won't try to stop you. Please, *please.* You don't have to say anything. Just listen."

His jaw was set.

"Please."

"God damn it." He ran his hand over his face, glared, took a breath, and then turned and sat on the couch.

She sat down next to him. She was shaking slightly as she held his hands in hers and took a deep breath.

He didn't look at her.

"I love my friends," she started.

He shook his head, scowling, and started to get up, not interested in hearing the same thing again.

She gripped his hands tightly and said, "Please."

He sat, still not looking at her, but not leaving.

She took another breath. "But I am so very much in love with you." After that the words flowed from her easily, as if that phrase had been the one that had been painfully lodged high in her chest. "I don't want to taste another man's kiss on my lips; I don't want to feel another man's hands on my body; and I don't want another man in my bed. I am sorry if you have ever doubted that."

She held his hands gently for a moment more, took one more breath, and let them go.

Tom stood without a word, without looking at her, turned and walked toward the door. She didn't turn to watch him but winced as she heard the sound of his key to her apartment hitting the counter.

And then he walked out.

When the door shut behind him, Liz put her face in her hands and sobbed.

Chapter Eighteen

There was a home game the next night. Liz turned on the TV to watch and then turned it off, because it was painful to watch Tom play. And then turned it back on again, because it was more painful not to watch. She had been watching every Guards game she could for practically as long as she could remember.

It was not a pretty game. Even their goalie was having an off night, and the game was getting out of hand pretty early on, going into the first intermission with the Guardians down three-nothing. They rallied, but not enough to win, and the final score was a five-three loss. Ugly game. Tom played badly, but since a lot of the guys did, there was nothing in particular that would indicate his play was being affected by their breakup.

The phone rang, and she saw it was Zee calling. She should have expected it, after the shitty performance, but it still caught her unprepared, and she wasn't ready to be cheerful. But knowing that he would be much more concerned if she didn't answer the phone, she took the call.

"Hey, did you see that travesty?"

"I did. That wasn't pretty. I'm sorry."

"Please tell me you have something funny."

She paused. "Not so much. I'm sorry, sweetie. I should have been thinking about it during the game to come up with something, but I didn't." There was a long pause. "Zee?"

"Are you okay?"

"Yeah, I'm fine. Just been one of those days, you know? Even I have them once in a while." She tried to sound lighthearted, but it wasn't working, and she knew it.

"No. Sorry, that's not right. I'm coming over."

"No, Zee, wait, I…" The phone had disconnected. *"Shit."* She tried calling him back, but he didn't pick up, so she texted him.

Liz: I'm fine, really. Don't worry. You don't have to come over.

She got back:

Zee: shut up

Liz got up and at least went to put on clothes that looked like she wasn't depressed—Zee didn't need to see her sitting around in her pajamas—and washed her face and waited for him to get there.

***

Tom heard the call start. "Hey, did you see that

151

travesty?"

He should have known and expected it, but he hadn't thought this far. He hurried to get out of there, not wanting to hear more. He was already pissed off enough.

"Please tell me that you have something funny."

Shut the fuck up, you asshole.

"Are you okay?"

Every muscle tensed.

"No. Sorry, that's not right. I'm coming over."

Motherfucker.

"Motherfucker!" There was nothing in his immediate vicinity that he could punch without risking breaking his hand, and he wasn't so far gone as to ignore that.

He looked up to see Chris looking at him with concern. Chris had as shitty a game as everyone else, but Tom appeared to be the only guy at risk of harming himself or others.

Tom got himself out of the locker room as quickly as possible. It didn't make him feel any better to find out he was right. Zee was going over there tonight; God knows who it would be tomorrow.

Focus on work.

***

When she opened the door for him, Zee was standing there holding a small grocery bag. "I brought ice cream. Coffee flavor." Liz smiled as he walked in, but her face crumbled a bit, and he put the bag on the counter and pulled her into a hug.

"Do you want to talk about whatever it is?"

"Nope. Not even a little." Her voice broke, and he squeezed her tighter. "You don't have to do this, Zee."

"I had a shit day. Shut the fuck up and let me be a hero for a few minutes, okay?"

She laughed a little and returned his hug. "Thank you."

They sat on the couch for a while, eating ice cream and not talking about anything important.

"I'm feeling better. Ice cream is an amazing cure-all." Liz turned and looked at Zee. "Thank you, sweetie. Really. You were a hero tonight. Not just ice cream, but *coffee* ice cream." She put her hand over her heart.

He smiled. "You know you can talk to me, right? I mean, I know we're usually goofing around, but I've talked to you about serious things before. You're always there for me, Liz. Please, let me be there for you too."

Blinking a bit too much, eyes a bit bright, she said, "I know. This is just something I need to deal with on my own right now. Every once in a while I feel the need for a bit of a pity party. I've been overdue. I'll be okay in a few days, I promise. Thank you."

Zee hugged her with squashing force, making her laugh, and they said good night.

***

"Paige, I need to talk to you. Do you have a few minutes?"

"Sure, Liz, what's up?"

Liz had been dreading making this phone call, but after the way that her relationship with Tom had started in secrecy, she could not keep Paige in the dark that it had ended, or was at least on hiatus. "So Tom and I are taking a break."

"What? No! What happened? Are you all right?"

"I'll be all right. I'm really sad, but he needed to be focused on work, and things between us were becoming a distraction from that. With the playoffs coming up, it just wasn't the right time to try to keep something going."

"I'm so sorry. Shit! When did this happen?"

"Two days ago. I didn't want to wait to tell you, but I really didn't feel like talking about it yesterday. I don't know if he's even going to say anything to Chris. I'm sure he won't say anything to anyone else. The whole point of this is to eliminate distractions; bringing this up would negate that."

"So is this a break? Are you guys going to get back together after the playoffs?"

Liz paused before answering, and Paige heard her breathe in.

"He said he didn't know, but I don't think so." Her voice wavered, and Paige could tell she was starting to cry. "He's back to his life, and I'm back to mine. It was fun, though. And I don't regret it for a minute." Another pause. "But I'm really fucking sad right now, Paige."

Paige was crying too. "Damn it. Should I have Chris talk to Micky?"

"No!" Liz's response was immediate. "No, absolutely not. There's no way I want to screw

154

around with his career. They need to be focused on the playoffs." She laughed a little. "Not on whether I'm particularly weepy today. I'll be okay, Paige, I promise."

***

The end of the season was a disappointment. The Guardians had been unable to get out of the second round of the playoffs again, despite having excellent talent and coaching, and they were knocked out in Game Seven. It was difficult to swallow for the players, the coaches, and the fans. And the players had to deal with listening to, or trying to ignore, the inevitable media and fan complaints and insults.

Zee had been in touch with Liz often enough after the night he brought her ice cream to notice that Tom never seemed to be around or mentioned. Not that he had been often before, it had always been a weird relationship between the two of them, and he had never really understood what was going on or why Liz put up with it, for that matter. But after the season ended, Zee just asked her flat out one day. "So you're not with Micky anymore, are you." He said it more as a statement than a question.

Liz looked surprised at the topic but answered very simply, "No. We're not together."

Zee looked at her, waiting for more, then shook his head. "That's the night I came over. God damn it, Liz, why didn't you tell me?" He held up his hand. "Don't answer that. I know why you didn't tell me. And you were right not to, which pisses me off, just for the record."

155

Liz looked at him and smiled. They had been such good friends for so long.

Zee continued. "Okay, so to make up for that, let me set you up." Liz laughed out loud. "No, seriously!" He had a big grin on his face. "It will be fun."

"No! No, you are very sweet, Zee, but no. Thank you, though."

"Crap." He looked at her. "Are you sure? I've got a few in mind…"

"No!" She was still laughing. "But please believe me, I appreciate the offer. I'd just…rather not. Not yet. Not right now."

"Okay. But we are going out dancing. Tonight. Right now. Grab your stuff. We're going." She registered what he was saying with shock and then realized it sounded like a hell of a lot of fun, and fun was something that had been missing for a while.

"That sounds awesome. Give me five minutes." Zee's eyes went wide with shock. He had expected to have to cajole her, and possibly physically carry her out to his jeep, but this was much better.

They both called and texted a few friends and ended up with a small but boisterous group. There was drinking and dancing. Zee was her ride, so Liz had quite a few, and danced with everyone, and by herself, and with Zee, and with several other guys she knew, and several she didn't, and generally had a hell of a lot of fun.

It was nice to forget being lonely for a little while, and it was also nice to not worry about jealousy or anger from a guy who didn't even want to meet her friends. And yeah, the attention was gratifying. No doubt about it. Maybe she would have Zee set her up. *But that's probably a decision I should make sober.*

When Zee took her home, she hugged him fiercely, and thanked him. "You have no idea how much I needed that. Truly a hero tonight, Zee."

"You know I love you. I hate to see you sad." He squeezed her and then lightened up the mood. "Because if you're sad I've got no one to cheer me up. That's your job, woman. Get back to work, already!"

She laughed, kissed him on the cheek, and went into her apartment.

***

As Tom was rolling up to Chris's house, he saw Paige getting into the back of a Jeep Wrangler that had its top and sides off. The Jeep was facing away from him but looked familiar, and as he got closer, he recognized it as belonging to Zee. He was pulling up as they were pulling away.

The woman in the front seat with Zee, wearing shorts, with her feet propped up on the dashboard, her hair in a ponytail, and her head back in what appeared to be laughter, could only be Liz. It didn't appear anyone in the Jeep had noticed his arrival, and they were around the corner by the time he parked. He got a good look at Liz as the Jeep turned right, and his body reacted. His chest tightened, his gut tightened, and he started getting angry. He also felt a surge of arousal, which just fed the anger.

Chris was coming out the front door to meet him. Tom asked, "Where's Paige going with that idiot?"

Chris looked at him curiously. "Hey, Micky. Nice to see you too. And don't you mean, where are Paige and Liz going with that idiot?"

"Sure. Whatever."

Chris shook his head. "They're going to some festival or another. Folk Life, or some such nonsense. I have zero interest, but Paige and Liz like it, and apparently Zee thinks it's a great place to meet women." He laughed. "Which is probably true, because Paige and Liz like it and I have zero interest."

"Yeah, and if he doesn't meet someone, he's got Plan B in the car."

Chris looked surprised, wondering if he misheard, misunderstood, or if Tom was trying to make a joke. He decided to just let it go.

"So, ready to head to the batting cage?" Chris looked over at Tom and realized he was still looking off in the direction the Jeep had gone and had a scowl on his face. "Micky."

"Yeah." Tom turned. "I'm kinda not feeling it."

Chris shook his head again. "Okay, man, we gotta get you out of your head. Running?" Tom said no. "We could probably find some ice time."

"No, man, I'm sorry. I'm in a shit mood."

Smiling, Chris said, "I got it. Get in the car." Tom started to protest, and Chris said, "Shut the fuck up and get in the car."

When they pulled up outside of a boxing gym, Tom actually smiled. "Okay, Becks. That's a fucking good idea."

They spent the next several hours there, using the equipment, talking with the trainers and the boxers, and Tom spent a great deal of time taking out his frustration on a heavy bag. When they left, they were sweaty, tired, sore, and Tom was in a much better mood. "Man, there's nothing like beating the shit out of something to make a guy feel better. I might have to join that place."

"Yeah, it's pretty great gym. I have only been a few times, but it can definitely take the edge off." He turned to Tom. "You okay, Micky? I expect you to be tense as hell in the locker room during the season, but usually you're a pretty easy-going guy in the off season. This seems a little out of character."

Tom looked at him with furrowed eyebrows.

"I'm not trying to pry, man. Shit, if I was acting all weird and tense when I'm usually not, I hope you would ask me what the hell is going on."

Tom relaxed a little. "Sorry, Becks. Sometimes it just seems like same shit, different day, and it gets old, you know?"

Chris nodded. He really didn't understand what Tom was talking about but didn't want to pry any further. No use undoing all of the de-stressing they just did.

Chapter Nineteen

It was the time of year again for the pool party. Liz was there, talking with folks, being introduced by Chris and Paige to some of the new players that had already arrived in town. She hadn't heard from Tom since he had walked out of her apartment. After the season had ended, she thought maybe he would call. When he didn't, she briefly considered trying to contact him but decided to leave well enough alone. She had told him her feelings. There really wasn't a whole lot more to say beyond that. Maybe they would be able to be friends again, eventually.

Zee was already throwing kids in the water. Paige had just gone into the house to deal with food things, and Liz was watching the fun in the pool with a small smile on her face. She didn't see Tom walk up to her and was startled when he spoke.

"You're wearing a white t-shirt, so I guess he couldn't throw you in with all the kids around."

She spun around, and her breath caught, and her heart sped up. He was clean shaven, and she wanted to reach out and touch his cheek.

"Hi."

"So does that mean he just waits until the kids go home and then throws you in?" He sounded rather bitter.

Liz looked and felt confused and a little nervous. *Is he trying to make a joke?*

"How have you been?"

"Have you met the new trades yet?"

"A few of them."

"I was just wondering if you had picked out your consort for next season."

Liz recoiled as if he had slapped her. She was reeling and completely at a loss for words, totally blindsided. "I…" She simply didn't know what to do. "I'm sorry, I have someplace to be."

She walked toward the house, picked up her purse, and left. After she drove around the corner, she pulled over again and completely broke down, sobbing. She tried to pull herself together and texted Paige.

Liz: Sorry, got called into work. Crazy. Didn't see you and had to leave. Have fun!

She sat for a few more minutes to make sure she was okay to drive and then went back to her apartment.

It wasn't like her to run away like that. But then again, that interaction had been so…wrong. It had almost been scary, like there was a different person wearing the face of someone that she loved. She had seen him incredibly angry and never been afraid.

But this had shaken her and hurt her feelings beyond what she thought possible, and she felt awful.

Chapter Twenty

"I'm so bummed that Liz got called into work. I was hoping the four of us could hang out together for a little while." Paige joined Chris and Tom in the kitchen. The party had ended, and the three of them were lingering. "It must be a big project; I don't remember Jason ever calling her in on a weekend before."

"It's probably just as well," Tom said. He sounded gruff.

"Really? Damn. I was hoping you guys were friends. Micky, can I ask what happened between the two of you? You seemed really happy. And I know that she would want to be friends with you still."

"Yeah, well, that would be part of the problem, wouldn't it? It's really easy to get sick of all of the old boyfriends and other guys," he said brusquely.

Chris and Paige both looked confused. "Other guys?" asked Paige. "You mean like Zee? Or friends from college? I'm not trying to be a pain in the ass, Micky, I just don't understand. Are there

163

guys I don't know about? This doesn't sound like her."

Tom bristled. "Oh, please. Don't play dumb. You know she's got men everywhere. Every time we went on a road trip, she was seeing someone else." He started pacing.

Chris looked questioningly at Paige. Her eyes were wide, and she shook her head, saying quietly to him, "There hasn't been anyone since Jimmy."

Tom said, "Great, who the fuck is Jimmy? That's a new one I hadn't heard of yet."

Paige started feeling ill. She asked quietly, "Did you talk to Liz about this?"

"Of course I did," he said, bitterness creeping into his voice. "She gave me the usual crap about how important her friends are in her life, how she still gets together with old boyfriends *and their wives and families,* and how she's very open with her affection. And when I got up to leave, she asked me to stay just long enough to tell her feelings, and then the real crap started. When she was done, I just walked out."

Chris's mouth hung slightly open in shock. Paige was starting to look like she was going to cry and almost whispered, "What did she say?"

"Some bullshit about being in love and not wanting to be with anyone else."

Chris and Paige just stared at him, momentarily at a total loss for words.

Tom went on without looking at his friends, "I mean damn, Becks, how many other guys on the team has she been with, anyway?"

Chris stood up so suddenly the chair fell over.

The noise startled Tom from his irritable pacing, and he turned to look as his friend. Chris took a controlled breath, shut his eyes, and said in a quiet, dangerous voice, "Did it ever occur to you that she meant every word?"

Tom looked at him like he had lost his mind. "What? No. Of course not. It was bullshit."

Chris's voice rose and continued rising. "So you're telling me that it never *once* occurred to you that she might have meant *Every. Single. Fucking. Word?*" By the end of the sentence, he was shouting, fists clenched at his sides, staring daggers at his best friend.

Tom took a step backward. "What the fuck are you talking about? No! No one talks like that!"

Chris was truly yelling now. *"Liz does, you arrogant, pig-headed asshole! She is not Michelle!"*

Tom stopped in shock at the name, feeling the force of it almost like a physical blow. He looked around him—Chris looked uncomfortably ready to come over the kitchen table and take a swing at him for real, and Paige...*holy shit, Paige looks like she's going to cry. What the hell is going on?*

"No! No. No, that's not possible." He looked from Chris to Paige and back again, his face practically begging one of them to join his denial.

"God damn it, Micky, *I* was the one that set you up with her. Would I do that to you?" Chris was still yelling and still really pissed, but the danger of physical violence was mostly gone—the look on Tom's face was telling him an awful lot. "She's one of my favorite people in the world, you fucking unbelievable bastard!"

Paige glared at Tom and asked, "Micky, what did you say to her after that?"

In a rather smaller voice than earlier, Tom said, "What do you mean?"

"After that! After. After you left. After you walked out of her apartment. That was, what? More than two months ago? I know she didn't call you. Do you know why she didn't call, by the way? Because you're a professional athlete, you jackass. And you were heading into the playoffs. And she didn't want to mess with your head. Do you know the side of the story I heard?" She had barely paused to take a breath at this point.

"She told me you guys were taking a break, that you needed to focus on work. That she wasn't sure how long it would last, or if you would get back together or not. That she missed you, and that she was sad, but that she wasn't going to interfere in your work. *You fucking prick! Did you even call her once? Did you contact her even one time before you saw her today?"*

Tom sank into one of the chairs, looking at Chris. "Shit. Oh, shit." His hands had started shaking.

Paige felt tears prick at her eyes for her friend, and with the growing realization that Liz hadn't been called into work, she rasped out, "Micky? What did you say to her today?"

Tom looked up at her and shook his head.

"What. Did. You. Say."

He croaked as he admitted, "I asked her which of the new trades she had picked out for next season."

"Jesus Christ, Mick," Chris said, and Paige

slapped Tom so hard even Chris winced. She stormed out of the room and out the front door. They heard her car, and Chris knew she was on her way to Liz's apartment and wouldn't be back for hours.

He turned to look at Tom, sitting crumpled at his kitchen table, looking utterly defeated. His face was completely stricken, ashen except for the red palm print left by Paige.

"God damn it, Micky." Chris's voice was rough with emotion. "You can be an ass, but I have never, ever seen you be cruel before. Ever. Not even to Michelle, and she fucking deserved it." His voice got a little quieter, almost like he was talking to himself. "Jesus, I never would have suggested you guys get together in the first place."

Tom looked completely devastated, and Chris knew this was totally out of character for his best friend, this man who was as close to him as a brother. "I had no idea you were still this fucked up over Michelle. Why didn't you say something?"

"I don't know. I thought…I don't know. Shit. *Shit.*" He felt sick.

Chris stood leaning against the kitchen counter, watching the emotions play across Tom's face. He was clearly trying to unravel some of the mess in his head, and Chris wasn't sure what to do.

Events of the last weeks before the breakup were playing through Tom's brain, but the worst part was the memory of the last words Liz said to him before he had turned and walked out on her. He remembered exactly what she had said—every word, every turn of phrase, the sound her voice,

167

everything.

Not the generalized line he had fed to Chris and Paige when they had asked.

But up until now, each time he'd thought of it, he had used it as proof of just how absurdly low she was willing to stoop to hurt him. Now the words were playing on a loop in his head. He gripped the edge of the table for about thirty seconds before standing up and walking down the hallway to the bathroom.

The undeniable sound of retching was startling and unexpected. Chris almost walked down the hall to ask if Tom was all right but thought better of it. He was obviously not all right. After a few minutes, Chris got a glass of ice water, a few aspirin, and a cold Coke, put them on the table where Tom had been sitting, and returned to his spot leaning against the counter.

Tom emerged about five minutes later, looking pale and tired. He sat down at the table without speaking, took the aspirin, drank most of the water, and held the cold can of soda against his forehead.

"I don't get it, Micky. I know you've dated other women since Michelle. What the hell went so wrong here?"

"I don't know." He looked exhausted.

"Did any of those relationships get serious at all?"

"No." Tom opened the Coke and started drinking, hoping the sugar and caffeine would help him start to feel human again, holding the cold can to his head between drinks.

"Did you love any of them?"

Tom visibly stiffened, feeling ill again.

Chris was startled by his reaction. "Oh shit, Micky. That's it." The look on Tom's face was the most confused mix of raw emotions he had ever seen. "Jesus, you didn't even know, did you?"

Tom gave up and walked back down the hallway.

By the time he returned a few minutes later, Chris had refilled his glass of ice water. Tom sat and folded his arms on the table, resting his head on his arms. With his eyes closed, he asked, "Is this fucked up beyond repair?"

Chris looked at him, thinking, weighing the options. "I don't know, Micky, but it's worth trying." He sighed. "You managed to be an utter dick to one of the nicest people I have ever met. You are lucky I love you, my brother." He sat down next to Tom, put his hand on Tom's shoulder, and leaned in closer. "And here's the really bad news— the *only* way this has a chance is if Paige agrees to help."

Tom didn't even raise his head. "Fuck."

Chapter Twenty-One

Liz heard the key unlocking her apartment and knew Paige was coming to see her. She was the only person who had a key since Tom had returned his. And the only reason she would be letting herself in was if she knew what had happened. Liz didn't get off the couch or even bother looking around.

Paige hugged her, and Liz cried, letting the dam break on how badly Tom's comments had hurt her. "I'm so sorry, Liz. I can't believe he did that. That's not the Micky I know. I swear."

"I know. I think that's what freaked me out. It felt like it was someone I had never met." Her face screwed up a bit as she tried to keep from crying more. "And I had really hoped we could be friends again. I feel so stupid, Paige."

"No. No, something is wrong with him, I swear it. Not that I think that's any excuse for treating you that way, but you had every reason to think he would act like a human and not like a total asshole. There's no reason for you to feel stupid, Liz. You

didn't do anything wrong." With a wry smile, she added, "If it makes you feel any better, I slapped him. Really hard. Like, my hand is still burning from it."

Liz looked at her for a few moments, and then the corner of her mouth turned up a little. "Yeah, that does make me feel a little better. It shouldn't, but it does."

Paige got up and made them both some coffee, and Liz got up to splash cold water on her face. When she came back, she simply said, "I had forgotten how much this shit hurts." After thinking for a moment, she added, "Although, to be fair, I've never had someone I dated be vicious before. Much less someone I loved." Tears were threatening again. "Shit." She turned to Paige and said, "I seriously don't even understand."

"I am so angry." Paige had tears pricking her eyes. "That doesn't even cover it. Furious. Outraged. Wrathful." Liz smiled at her English teacher friend. "I don't even think I can look at him again."

"Paige." Liz hugged her friend. "Thank you, but you know that's not the right answer, either."

"Don't." Paige was trying not to cry. "Don't make it seem like I'm being unreasonable. My best friend was just treated like shit by my husband's best friend, who is also someone I thought was my friend." Liz just looked at her. "God damn it. Stop looking at me like that."

"Please, Paige, don't make me be the one to argue on his behalf. Not today. I'm not up for it." Liz sighed. "You know how I feel about this kind of thing."

"Why can't you just be normal and demand people choose sides?" Paige realized she sounded ridiculous even as she was saying it and laughed darkly. "You're a pain in the ass. You know that?"

"I do." Liz smiled at her friend. "Thank you. I love you." She hugged Paige tightly. "Let's drink coffee and talk about anything except idiot assholes, okay?"

Paige sighed. "Okay." They sat back down on the couch. "So when are we going dancing again?"

***

"You didn't see his face, Paige."

"I didn't want to see it. I still don't. Maybe not ever again." Paige was trying not to raise her voice at her husband. "I have never been so…so…*furious*." Her voice caught as she added, "And devastated."

Chris took her in his arms. "I know, baby. Me too."

"It's just not fair, Chris." She had tears in her eyes. "I know you love him, but I wouldn't have even met you without Liz. So, if there's a choice that has to be made here, in my book she wins. Especially after the way he treated her."

The look he gave her was stunned. "No, Paige." He took her by the shoulders and made her look him in the eyes. "No. I am not giving up on my best friend because of this. I'm telling you, you didn't see his face. He *knows.*" Her brow was furrowed, so he added, "Besides, you know perfectly well Liz

172

would be pissed off if you made me give up my best friend because of her. Or even if you and Micky stopped being friends because of something that happened between the two of them. You know that's the way she thinks, crazy as that is."

Paige softened. "She's wrong about that. I can disown anyone I want."

"He wants to talk to you."

"Yeah, well, I want him to…to…I don't even know. I'm still so angry."

Chris held her again. "Will you just talk to him? Please, baby?"

She made a non-committal noise against his shirt.

He started to pet her hair. "He was such a mess after you left here. I have never seen him like that. When he realized what he had done…" He paused and looked at Paige again. "He didn't know, Paige. I saw it on his face as he figured out he was in love with her."

"I don't care."

"You do."

"I don't want to!" She practically yelled it. "I don't want to feel bad for him, Chris! I just found out how badly he hurt Liz. I don't want to have any sympathy for him! How do I know he's even sincere? The Micky I know would never have done that!"

Chris smiled. "Yeah, I told him the same thing. And then I saw the Micky I know—when he realized, it made him sick. Literally sick. That kind of regret is hard to fake."

Paige looked at him. "Really?"

"Really. Multiple times."

Paige closed her eyes. "God damn it." Chris smiled and hugged her close.

"Thank you, baby."

"I haven't agreed to anything."

"But you'll talk to him."

"Shit."

***

Tom approached their house with something akin to fear. Paige was more than a foot shorter than him, but he was afraid to face her wrath in this. It's difficult to feel confident when he knew he was completely in the wrong.

His devastation must have shown in his face, because Paige's resolve to stay furious at him wavered, and she allowed him to pull her into a crushing hug. "I'm so sorry, Paige. I'm so sorry."

"I'm not the one you should be apologizing to. I'm not the one who's been crying over this. I'm not the one you treated like shit."

He winced as if she had slapped him again, and she was fine with that. It was taking a lot of willpower to resist the urge to say incredibly hurtful things to him. Part of her wanted to be absolutely vicious, to see if she could find the words that would make him look just as shattered as Liz had.

But that wouldn't help, and she knew it. And Liz wouldn't want her to, and she knew that too, damn it.

"I know." He put her down. "I want to apologize. God, I want to erase this and start over." He closed his eyes and took a deep breath. "But I think a chance at an apology is probably the best I can hope for. I don't think I'll even get that chance without your help, though. Please."

"Sit down. I'm listening." She pointed at him. "I'm not promising anything. But I'm listening."

Chapter Twenty-Two

It had taken a while, but Paige had convinced Liz that getting out to a party would be good for her. It would be a small crowd, rooftop, music, bar, some dancing. Nothing formal, wear jeans and a cute shirt. It was some friends Paige knew from school, so not a team event, which would make things easier. No chance of running into Tom or having to answer questions from teammates about whether or not they were still an item.

She took a cab to the hotel, figuring she would be drinking enough not to want to drive, and texted Paige when she arrived. Paige responded that they were already on the roof, and she should come up in the elevator.

Liz got off the elevator at the rooftop, a little surprised that she didn't hear music or other party noise. When the doors opened, there was a podium in front of her, with a handwritten note, large enough to read from a distance. She recognized the handwriting immediately as belonging to Paige.

Liz, I'm so sorry for the set-up.

Please just give him a chance and listen.

You know I love you like crazy.

—Paige

The bottom of her stomach suddenly dropped out, and there was a slight roar in her ears. She turned to her left and saw the rooftop lounge area, the bar empty. One table had a white table cloth and an ice bucket with what appeared to be several beers. Standing next to the table, dressed in his full tuxedo, was Tom. She turned back toward the elevator.

"Liz, please, just listen. You don't have to say anything." She stopped, and he continued. "Please. Just give me a little while. If you want to leave after that, I won't try to stop you."

He saw her shoulders sink as he reflected her words back to her.

She turned toward him. "I will stay and listen. Because I trust Paige—not you."

They sat down at the table, and he began.

"I was engaged. I had known her in high school, and we started dating my sophomore year of college. I asked her to marry me as soon as I graduated. We got a place together when I started playing in the AHL.

"I can be a jealous guy." He chanced a look at Liz across the table. "I don't know if you had noticed that at all."

Liz was sitting still and quiet. She was listening, but her face was neutral, registering as close to a blank as he had ever seen from her. At this comment she allowed a small flicker through.

She's definitely listening. "Michelle was a beautiful girl and drew a lot of attention and comments wherever she went. She loved the attention. I would get insecure and jealous. She would tell me I was being ridiculous. Nothing uncommon.

"One night after one of these arguments—'I think you're cheating,' 'You're imagining things,'—she put her arms around me, looked up, and said, 'Tommy, I had a huge crush on you even back in high school. You know I love you. I don't ever want to sleep with another man.'"

Liz winced visibly, recognizing her own words to him, knowing that this story ended badly.

Tom continued. "My brother, Joe, was in town to see me play the next night, and the two of us were going out for drinks after the game. We were supposed to be out for hours celebrating—it was Joe's birthday—but I told him I wanted to go back and apologize and make up with Michelle properly.

"I heard them before I saw them," he said, his voice sounding strained now. "I actually thought she was watching porn." He paused and then continued. "I was really getting turned on thinking I would walk in on her taking care of herself in that big bed, and we would have amazing make-up sex." His voice was choked and rough; he had never told anyone these ugly details.

Somehow he felt like Liz deserved his raw,

unvarnished truth.

"I was hard and horny and opened the door to see her getting fucked from behind by another man. In our bed. And I knew the guy." He took a deep breath and looked at Liz. "I had no idea what to do. There were too many conflicting signals for my brain to accept at the same time. What I remember for sure is that I punched a hole through the bedroom door, walked out, and slammed the front door hard enough that shit fell off the walls. I know I called Joe, because he kept me from ending up in jail. I almost turned around to go back and kill the guy."

Tom stopped talking and pushed back his chair and stood, his heart suddenly racing. Liz had stood up and started moving. *No, please, I'm not done. I didn't tell her the important part.*

He moved around the table, and his voice was strangled, panicked, as he started to say, "Liz, wait, please, I—" but he stopped, because she had moved around the table to him and put her arms around his chest in a hug.

She had done it because he was her friend, or at least had been once, and he had told her something awful, and she would have hugged any of her friends who told her that. She would have hugged a stranger who had told her news like that. It was the right thing to do, even if it was him.

Tom held her close very gently and breathed in the scent of her hair. He was almost afraid to touch her, afraid to move. It seemed impossible that she could be here after he had treated her so badly, acted like such an asshole. He felt a knot in his chest that seemed far too large to fit. She could still walk away; the fact she hadn't yet seemed like a minor miracle.

He heard a muffled voice from his chest. "You're such a fucking bastard."

"Yes," he agreed. He took a chance and began to pet her hair. The knot in his chest wasn't getting any smaller. "And an incredible idiot."

There was a brief pause, and then he heard, "Yes."

He took a deep breath, pulled her just a little tighter, and said, "And I love you, Liz."

She went completely still in his arms. The knot in his chest made his voice catch, but he forced himself to keep talking, because this next part was the hardest.

But it was the most important of all.

He was glad he was holding her, rather than looking at her for this. If he had been looking her in the eye, he wasn't sure he would have been able to follow through.

One more deep breath. "I am so sorry. You don't deserve the way I treated you, and I don't deserve another chance. In a moment I'm going to let you go." His voice broke a bit, and he felt her flinch. "If I have screwed this up beyond fixing, I hope you will eventually still be willing to consider me a friend. In time. But regardless, I want you to know—I love you. I think I have for a long time now." He tightened his hold on her one more time, kissed the top of her head, and let her go.

Except she didn't let go. Liz tightened her arms around his chest. Tom stood stock still for a moment, not believing.

He croaked, "Liz?" He was afraid to touch her.

"Shut up." After a few more seconds of unmoving shock on his part, she added, "Oh, for God's sake, Tom, will you please hold me?"

He wrapped his arms around her so tightly she thought she might not be able to breathe. And then he lifted her off her feet. It felt wonderful.

Tom put her back down and stepped back, looking at her with wonder. "Thank you."

Liz sighed. "We have a lot more talking to do. Have a seat."

They sat back down, and Liz looked at Tom thoughtfully. He felt like he was not quite attached to the ground and was fairly certain there was a ridiculous grin on his face.

She took a deep breath. "I'm assuming Chris and Paige gave you some basic information?"

Tom nodded. "No specifics, though."

Liz gave a wry smile. "As you can imagine, it's not the first topic of conversation I'm looking to bring up with someone I'm dating. Or not dating. Or whatever it was that we were doing. 'Dead fiancé' isn't particularly romantic." She looked down and swallowed hard.

"Jimmy was a great guy, and I loved him very much. The accident was awful. And it was a complete accident. The worst part was we had been fighting for a few days before it happened. Not even really fighting, just grousing at each other, not being particularly loving and nice, you know what I mean. We were being bitchy, and he left my place. It was late, it was rainy. Two cars, a bolt of lightning, and a downed tree. No one was drinking, no one was texting, no one was speeding. Both were wearing seatbelts. No mistakes. Two drivers, two totaled cars—one walked away and the other one was dead. I didn't even have anyone to be mad at. Except myself, because he left my place without us really saying we loved each other that night." Her voice caught, and her eyes teared up, even after all this time. "Geez, still." She wiped at her eyes.

"So, lots of therapy. Lots and lots of therapy." She laughed at his surprised expression. "Actually, it's the best thing I ever did for myself, and I wish I had done it a lot sooner—you remember the rest of my family history, right? It helped. Immensely. Perspective is a beautiful thing. It helped me realize things about myself. What I believe, what I want, what prices I'm willing to pay.

"For instance, regret is too high a price for me to pay for anything. I will swim through an ocean of embarrassment or rejection to avoid regret." She smiled at him. "If I had been honest with you, I would have told you I loved you a lot sooner. I knew a lot sooner. But that night, you were so angry, and you were about to walk out my door not knowing how I felt. I couldn't live with that regret again. I panicked. I had to tell you."

Tom whispered, "Shit." He thought for a minute. "I don't think it would have made a difference if you had told me sooner, although I wish like hell I could say it would have. I had no idea how hard I was trying to prove to myself that you were just like Michelle. When I couldn't find betrayals I had to invent them." He chuckled and looked at her. "They were really tough to invent. Even I wasn't really believing them. Certainly no one else would."

"Our brains are strange and wondrous places. It's quite amazing how far we can go down a random rabbit hole." She looked across the table at him. "And thank you."

"Seriously? What on earth for? Whatever it is, you are very welcome, sweetheart."

Liz smiled. "I kind of handed you the perfect opportunity to turn this whole thing around and blame me—if I had just been honest with you sooner about how I felt, we could have avoided this whole mess. But you didn't. You owned your part, that it would have happened anyway. Thank you for that."

She shifted gears, back to the business at hand. "Right, a few more things. If we are going to try to do this, you and me," she gestured back and forth across the table, "it has to be for real, Tom."

He thought his heart was going to leap right out of his chest. "Yes." It came out slightly more than a croak. But only slightly.

"People will know we're together. If you're near enough, I'm going to be touching you. About half the time, it will be deliberate, because I love touching you," she smiled, and he thought his heart was going to explode, "but the other half will be unconscious, because that's who I am. It took a force of will to not do that this whole time. I had to consciously sit or stand far enough away that I didn't accidentally just hold your hand or have my hand on your knee all the time. Are you okay with that?"

Tom stood up and moved to the chair next to her, rather than across from her. He took her hand and said, "Oh God, yes. Please, Liz. I don't want you to be a secret. And I can't think of anything better than you randomly touching me. Shit. That sounds fucking amazing."

A glazed look came over his face, and she laughed in spite of herself.

"Okay, keep paying attention."

They had both started to relax. It was wonderful. Tom grabbed two beers from the ice bucket and opened them, putting one in front of her and taking a drink from the other.

"I'm a pain in the ass," she continued. "I laugh too loud and I talk too much. I overshare, and although I try to respect the boundaries of others, that doesn't mean I always succeed. I've got very little shame—as I said before, I'll swim through an ocean of embarrassment to avoid regret, so I've lost a lot of perspective on what constitutes an embarrassing situation for other people." She looked him in the eye.

"I'm not feminine."

Tom interrupted. "Correction. You're not girly. You are incredibly feminine." His voice dropped some, and he smiled at her around the mouth of his beer bottle.

She smiled, feeling her insides flip around a little. "Okay, I'll take that. I'm not girly. I have a deep personal relationship with profanity. In the right setting, I will cheerfully swear like a sailor. While I do strive for situational awareness—I hope to never accidentally drop a 'motherfucking

184

cocksucker' at a funeral, for instance—as you know, I will sometimes have an f-bomb appear where it shouldn't."

Tom barked out a laugh. Things were starting to get interesting. "I'm beginning to see why you feel so comfortable around hockey players."

"Yeah, well, there are other things. But you get the idea." She paused and watched him start to take a big swig of his beer. Unable to resist the timing, she said, "Like, I can belch the alphabet."

He choked a bit but recovered. "Bullshit."

She laughed and said, "You're right, I never made it past 'F.'" He looked at her suspiciously, trying to decide if she was kidding, and then took another drink.

"But I can absolutely belch on command."

He spat out his beer to the sound of her laughing. "Fuck." He cleaned himself up and looked over at her. "You can't."

"I can. Not girly. Not even a little bit."

"Prove it."

So she did, not entirely sure how he would react. He looked at her for a minute and said, "Do you know how much money I could make from my teammates with this kind of knowledge?"

She threw back her head and laughed, and it might have been the most wonderful sound Tom had ever heard.

"But seriously, Tom. I'm not set up to be good pro-athlete arm candy. That's just not who I am. I need to know that you've thought this through, and you accept all that."

He stood up, pulled her to her feet, and pulled

her in close to him. "You're perfect."

"I'm not perfect; no one is. But I am serious."

"I am too. I don't need girly arm candy, Liz. I need you." He stopped for a moment and looked at her. "Although I have seen you when you try to be arm candy and its un-fucking-believable, so there's that too." She smiled at him. "So are we okay?"

She snuggled close into him, resting her cheek against his chest so that she could hear his heart beating.

"No, Tom, we're not okay. Not yet. But we might be."

"I'll take it." He chuckled, a deep, warm sound. "God, I never would have believed I could be so happy to have someone tell me that we are not okay."

Chapter Twenty-Three

"By the way, why the tux?"

Tom smiled down at her. "I was hoping it would buy me a few extra seconds to convince you to stay so I could talk to you. I was desperate. Did it make a difference?"

It was her turn to chuckle. "It didn't hurt," she admitted.

Tom was holding her in his arms again. She wasn't leaving. She was giving him another chance. She knew he loved her. All was right in the world, and he was finally relaxing.

Well, almost every part of him was relaxing.

There appeared to be one part of his body that was beginning to notice he was holding Liz in his arms again. That she wasn't leaving. That she was giving him another chance. That part certainly knew he loved her and was becoming interested in showing her just how much.

Liz felt him twitch against her hip, and it made her jump just slightly. It also awoke a bunch of nerve endings she was not expecting to use any time

187

soon. He twitched again, and her breathing hitched, and her heart sped up some.

"I'm trying to ignore this, but it's becoming difficult," she said, trying to sound casual. But her voice had gotten husky, and her tone caused a new surge. She swore quietly but colorfully, and Tom smiled.

His voice was low and rumbled through his chest. "Apparently, when I stopped being scared you were going to leave, I started noticing you were staying." He paused. "You're distracting." He took a deep breath. "I could step away from you, but only if you want me to."

"No!" The strength of her response caused another, impressive surge, and she gripped the front of his shirt. "No. Don't you dare. Don't move." She was breathing hard, and blood was singing through her veins. "There is nothing that turns me on more than feeling you get hard because of me."

"Shit." That was it. He was at full attention.

She leaned her forehead against his chest and then looked up at him. He took a chance and leaned down to kiss her. She reached up to stroke her hand over his smooth cheek, and he moved his tongue to her lips. The kiss was deep and perfect, and he made it last.

God, I have missed kissing her.

Liz put her arms around his neck and deepened the kiss, becoming almost demanding.

Tom crouched down slightly, put his hands on her ass, and lifted her. He sat her on the edge of the table, stood between her legs, and pressed against her, enjoying the small sounds she made as he began to move his hips slowly, rocking his erection against the seam of her jeans, moving his tongue against hers in time with his hips.

She gasped her way out of the kiss, and he moved to her neck, dragging his open lips along her skin more than actually kissing her, his breath hot against her as he brought his mouth up next to her ear, kissing the sensitive skin underneath.

Her muscles were tense, and she made a desperate sound and grabbed his ass with both hands, trying to grind him against her with more force. Tom complied and moved against her deeper and harder. When he heard the sound she made in response, he moved his head back to look at her— eyes wild, breathing so hard and fast.

Tom knew that look, knew her body. He gripped her tighter and in a voice now husky with desire asked, "Could you come like this?" as he ground against her again.

Her eyes squeezed shut, and she made a breathy gasping sound before saying, "Oh God, yes."

Tom started in earnest, grinding himself against her, kissing her deeply, stroking his tongue into her in time with his hips. He could think of nothing better than to bring her to orgasm right here, right now. She was gasping between his kisses, making small sounds as she felt the pressure building. She started moving with him, pressing back against him, increasing the friction, making the pressure of his hardness touch her exactly where she needed it to.

As her movements were increasing, Tom was starting to feel slightly out of control. The silk fabric of the boxers he always wore under his tux was adding a layer of sensation to this that was beginning to fray him at the edges. He slowed down to try to get his bearings, but Liz tightened her hands on him and pleaded, "Oh God, don't stop. Tom, please."

He pushed against her further so that she was partially reclined on the table and grabbed her under one thigh, changing the angle of pressure and continuing to grind against her. Her movements became almost frantic against him, and she climaxed suddenly, shouting wordlessly, as the spasms rocked her.

At the first sound of her orgasm, Tom's movements shifted from grinding to his own frantic thrusting, as if there were no clothing between them, and a few seconds later he shouted his own powerful orgasm.

Liz sat on the edge of the table, leaning back on her elbows, gasping for air. Tom had his hands on either side of her on the table, his head hanging down, his face obscured by his hair, breathing heavily.

His voice was low and shaky, and he said with a small chuckle, "I think I was sixteen the last time that happened." He started to push himself up and away from her, but she stopped him.

"Wait, please. Just for a minute. Just look at me."

He brought his head up and smiled at her and asked, "What?"

Her voice was sexy and sweet, and she said, "I want to remember this. The way you look, the way you sound, everything. I think this is one of the most erotic experiences I've ever had."

Tom tilted his head slightly, looking amused, and asked, "Because I acted like a horny sixteen year old?"

She laughed low, making his chest contract. "No, sweetheart." Another heart contraction. "Because you are *not* sixteen." She stroked his cheek again. "Because you are so very much a grown man. And because you just completely lost control…for me."

He kissed her slow and deep. *"Because* of you, Liz. It's always because of you."

It was her turn to feel her heart twist in her chest.

"I plan to keep this memory saved for when you are on long road trips, and I'm missing you terribly." She reached up and kissed him sweetly. "And now I'm hoping for your sake that you have a change of clothes with you."

"As a matter of fact, I do." He kissed her on the bridge of her nose and helped her down from the table. Her eyes got wide for a moment as she tried to figure out whether her legs were going to work. "I got a room for tonight."

"Really." She looked at him. "That was a confident move, McCullin."

"No." He laughed, and she looked confused. "Actually, I figured the odds were that you would leave. After that I was going to go to the hotel bar and drink until I couldn't stand. The room was for me. I was trying to be responsible. I figured even my roommates wouldn't want me home at that point. Better to sleep it off here."

She winced. "Oh."

He kissed the top of her head and whispered into

191

her hair, "I'm so glad you stayed."

She smiled at him, and it was the most beautiful thing he had ever seen.

Steering him toward the elevator, Liz said, "Okay, then, let's go get you into clean clothes. I can't say from experience, but I imagine that's just gotta feel weird."

Tom laughed, put his arm around her, and walked her to his room.

Chapter Twenty-Four

Liz curled up in the room's one comfortable chair, tucking one leg under her and propping her other foot on the seat, and called Paige, who picked up almost before the phone rang.

"Please don't be mad. How did it go? Are you mad? Are you still there? Is he still there? Did you leave? Where are you? Are you all right? Did you listen to him? Did he tell you? About everything? I'm so sorry, Liz! I'm dying! Please tell me what happened!"

"Oh my God, Paige, breathe."

"I'm breathing."

"You weren't."

"Tell me!"

"I'm still here. He's still here. And I'm very, very *not* mad at you." Liz heard her friend exhale in relief.

"Thank you. I'm still really angry at him on your behalf, just to be clear."

"Thanks."

"Hey, let me talk to Micky for a second."

193

"He's just taking a quick shower; he should be out in a minute," Liz said without thinking. *Shit.*

"What? Liz, where are you? Exactly?"

"Um, someplace with a shower?"

"Are you kidding me, Liz? Are you in a room at the hotel?"

"…maybe?"

"I don't know whether to laugh or yell at you."

Liz laughed at her friend and said, "Well, to be fair, he…" She trailed off. Tom walked out of the bathroom, wet hair slightly tousled, one small towel over his shoulder, another towel tucked around his hips. Liz stared and whispered in a small voice, "Holy crap."

Paige was talking on the other end, "Liz. Liz! What's going…wait. Did he just get out of the shower? He did, didn't he? Damn it."

Tom looked over and smiled, asking, "Is that Paige?"

Liz just kept staring, letting her eyes flow over Tom's body as he walked over to her. They lingered on his broad chest, small water droplets still clinging to some of the soft hair, and tracing down to his toned abs, and the angles of his hips, lingering again on the trail of hair that dipped down underneath the towel.

Tom took the phone out of her hand, looked at it briefly, and said, "Hi, Paige, and thank you."

"Let me guess: You're standing there in a towel, and she has lost the power of speech. Do I need to send more nametags?"

He laughed and said, "No, don't send extra nametags. I'm kinda liking her at a loss for words.

This is new." He took a step to the side to dodge a half-hearted swat from Liz.

Paige said, "Micky?"

"Yeah?"

She hesitated a moment and then said quietly, "Tom?"

He blinked, surprised, not sure he had ever heard Paige use his given name before. Pausing a moment in understanding, he replied, "I promise, Paige. I swear." He heard the call disconnect and tossed the phone on the bed.

Liz uncurled from the chair, stood up, and stretched. "You need to get dressed, handsome. And not out here, much as I would love that view."

"You sure about that?" Tom asked playfully, with a hand poised at the knot of the towel.

She gave him a small smile. "I'm sure. As much as I enjoyed our rooftop interlude," she closed her eyes for a moment, "and I cannot stress enough how much I enjoyed that," she looked back at him again, "this is going to take me some time. The last few months have been rough. The last few days have been…" Her voice wavered slightly, and her brows creased together for a moment.

She took a deep breath, opened her eyes too wide, blinked a few too many times, and said quickly with a half laugh, "Well, they've just sucked ass." And then added, "Fuck," under her breath, wiping away the stray tears that had snuck out.

Tom had an aching knot in his chest that felt too large to fit in his body. He was next to her in one stride, wrapped his arms around her, kissed her on the top of her head, murmuring, "I'm so sorry."

She pushed at his chest. "Clothes first. Then comforting."

He grabbed his duffle bag and headed to the bathroom to get changed. With his hand on the doorknob, he turned to look at her, his face suddenly anxious. "Please be here when I get out."

She smiled, looking tired. "I will be here. I promise."

He came out from the bathroom less than two minutes later, wearing jeans and just finishing pulling a t-shirt over his head. "Okay to comfort now?" he asked.

"Definitely."

Liz walked over and leaned against his chest with a sigh, wrapping her arms around his back. Tom put his arms around her, tucking her head under his chin, stroking her hair and back. "I am so sorry, Liz," he said.

"I know," she mumbled against his chest.

"I have to keep saying it. I don't want you to think I'm taking this second chance for granted. Not for a minute. I don't deserve this." His arms tightened around her, and it was his turn to blink a few too many times.

He heard, "Well, you are a bastard," from somewhere around the middle of his chest.

He kissed the top of her head and said, "Yes, definitely. And an idiot."

She pulled her head back and looked up at him. "Yes."

Loosening his arms from around her, he cupped her face with both of his large hands, looked into her blue eyes, slightly brighter than usual from tears, and said, "And I love you, Liz." He kissed her very gently on the lips, then on the forehead, and pulled her back into his chest to hold her for a few more minutes.

After a while, she sighed and stepped back from him. He loosened his arms and asked, "Can I drive you home? I know you took a cab here." He started gathering his things, getting ready to leave.

"I'd like that. You may even walk me to my door," she said with a smile.

He stopped to tuck a stray lock of hair behind her ear and gave her a little lopsided grin. "Would a good night kiss be pushing my luck?"

"You may kiss me goodnight on my doorstep," she replied with a small smile. "I believe that will be safe."

He raised his eyebrows. "Do you not remember our first kiss? I felt like I was eighteen and about to lose my mind, and I had barely touched you."

"Of course I remember. That's why I said on my doorstep. Under no circumstances are you to come inside my apartment tonight. In fact, I might have to institute some sort of 'six inches of space between us' rule."

He grinned and turned to follow her out the door. As she got to the hallway, he bent his head down to say quietly into her ear, "Six inches wouldn't be enough."

Chapter Twenty-Five

Throughout the rest of July and most of August, they dated. Really dated. He came to her office and they went to lunch. He met her friends. Tom picked her up at her apartment and they went out—to the movies, to dinner, to look at the monuments, to a concert at Wolf Trap, to museums. And of course, out with Chris and Paige for double dates. For real.

And they talked, finally, about everything. All the topics they had instinctively avoided, or mostly avoided, as being too personal during the entire first year they had known each other. There were so many things Liz would have naturally talked about with any of her other friends that just…hadn't seemed to ever come up in conversation with Tom before, either because they felt somehow out of place in their relationship or because they were too busy doing other things with their time together to worry about talking.

And after their dates, Tom walked her to her apartment door, and they kissed goodnight. They only kissed. They stood slightly apart, one of his hands tangled in her hair, the other on her hip, one of her hands on his chest, the other around his back, or maybe touching the hair at the back of his neck, and they kissed. A lot. Long, slow, deep kisses that neither one wanted to end, that left both of them with racing pulses and bodies flooded with desire.

Liz hadn't been ready for him to be back in her bed, not yet, no matter how much her body would protest otherwise, and Tom was not going to push her. He spent a great deal of time in those weeks becoming intimately reacquainted with his right hand.

They were nearing the end of the summer off-season and the beginning of training camp. Tom walked Liz to her door, helping her finish the last of the ice cream cone they had shared while walking in one of the local parks. The sharing of the cone had become messy, and flirty, with licking involved, and they were both laughing. Tom grabbed her hand, held it still, stole the last bite of cone, and licked the ice cream from her palm, then placed a kiss in the middle of her palm and looked at her.

Her eyes were dancing with laughter, and she said, "Seriously? The very last bite of cone? You're a creep."

He licked her finger. "I like ice cream." He licked another finger. "Always have. I can't believe we haven't had this conversation before." He licked a third finger more slowly, becoming less playful. "I can't be trusted around ice cream."

Looking at her hand for a moment, he turned it over palm side down and then moved his thumb to gently press apart her middle and ring fingers. With a sexy little half smile on his face, and the most enticing bedroom eyes she could imagine, he kissed her on the side of her ring finger, by her nail, and slowly and gently ran his tongue up between her fingers until his tongue was nestled where her fingers joined her hand. He kissed her there, with a tiny bit of suction, and a completely unnecessary flick of his tongue that made her jump and gasp.

"Your hands are sticky." Her voice sounded distant even to her.

He kissed the inside of her wrist, where he felt her pulse with his lips and tongue. "Yes."

"You could come in and wash up."

Tom looked up from her wrist with surprise and said, "Are you sure, Liz?" He could suddenly feel hear his own pulse thundering in his ears. He was pushing the teasing and playing tonight but hadn't even hoped that she would invite him in. They both knew where things would end up once he walked through that door.

She stepped closer to him, got up on her toes, put her arms around his shoulders, pressed her face into his neck, and breathed him in. "God, you smell so good. Did I ever tell you, that very first night, when we were on my couch, and you were going to 'not take advantage of me,' all I could think was if I don't have sex with this guy I'm going to regret it for the rest of my life? Come inside, Tom."

Chapter Twenty-Six

The players came off the ice and back into the locker room after practice, sweaty and joking around. They had just finished the first full week of training camp. It was good to be back to work again after the off season, and spirits were high. All was well in Tom's world; this did not go unnoticed by his teammates.

"Hey, Mick," he heard from across the room. It was one of their centers. "I noticed that you tied your skates *and* used the right end of the stick today. You must be getting laid."

"Fuck you too!" he yelled back as he took off his skates.

The team's top goalie swatted him in the back of the head as he walked toward the showers. "You actually look like you remember how to skate again. Definitely getting laid. Finally get your head out of your ass?"

"Seriously?" Tom said, getting up to stow his gear and head for the showers. "Are there no rookies around here for you guys to screw with?"

201

A heavy Russian accent from the other side of him called out, "Don't mess with him too much. He's back together with Liz."

Tom turned around and looked at the big right-winger, who was also team captain. "Out of curiosity, what would make you say that?" A chorus of good-natured ah-ha's, see-I-told-you's, and a few whistles followed his question.

The big Russian said, "You are better with her. Better player. Better person. You are skating good, you are smiling, you are with her." He shrugged and walked past Tom.

Chris briefly caught Tom's eye, grinning. Tom shook his head, grabbed his phone, and sent a quick text.

Tom: B at playr door

***

As requested, Liz was waiting for Tom outside the players' entrance after practice. His request had been surprising—she had been waiting at her car. Tom had ridden to practice with Chris so Liz and Tom could go out.

When the players started coming out, a few of them nudged each other and laughed after waving and saying hi. The waving and greeting was normal, as she knew a lot of them; the nudging not so much. When Tom came out, he dropped his gear bag, put his hands on either side of her face, and began to kiss her quite thoroughly.

Enthusiastic cheers, whistles, and catcalls came

from his teammates. He moved his arms around her waist and picked her up, and she put her arms around his neck. He put her back down on her feet but continued the kiss. The cheers turned to laughter and shouts of "Get a room!" with a few calls of things like "You can do better, Liz!" thrown in. By the time he had put her feet back on the ground, Tom had stopped listening to his teammates, lost in his inability to kiss her enough.

She laughed and smiled when he finally let her go. "I guess the cat's out of the bag, huh?"

"You're not a secret. *We* are not a secret. I didn't intend for us to be, but in a fascinating turn of events, my teammates all decided that we must be together because, apparently, if I'm happy and skating well, it means I'm getting laid. By you."

Her eyes got wide. "Seriously?"

"Seriously. I believe the exact quote was, 'You are skating good, you are smiling, you are with her,'" he said in his best Russian imitation.

"I could pretend I'm not pleased, but that would be such a lie," she said as they walked hand in hand to her car. There was still an occasional hoot as a latecomer filtered out of the practice rink. "But I'm glad you're skating well. And I'm glad we get a little time tonight. It's going to be hard to give you back to the team for the season."

"Whoa, whoa, not so fast. According to my teammates, I'm going to have to get laid on a very regular basis to keep up my on-ice performance. This is important for my career, Liz."

"Oh, well, that's different, of course. Anything for your career, sweetheart." They got to her car, and she turned to face him, stepped close, pressed her hand firmly into his crotch, and whispered, "You know how much I love watching you play."

Chapter Twenty-Seven

Tom had a sudden thought. "What are you going to wear?"

"Gotta 'Rock the Red!'" she said cheerfully, grabbing him around the waist and looking up at him. "I'm so excited, hon. *God,* I can't wait for this game. Freaking Pittsburgh." It was the first game of the year against their arch-rivals, at home, and Tom had gotten her a ticket to sit with the other wives and girlfriends. He knew she would love being there, and it would be the first time for her to be his "official" date.

"Yes, but what exactly?"

She said, "Well, my home jersey is one of Chris's." Tom's jaw set. "Sorry," she said, smiling, remembering his family traditions. *"'Sweater.'"*

"No," he said. "God damn it." Liz was taken aback by the vehemence of his response. "Becks' wife can wear his fucking sweater. I don't want you wearing anyone else's sweater, *ever."*

She was surprised by how upset he was.

"I have an away sweater with no number or

name. I can wear that one."

"No! Fuck. You can't sit with the other WAGs and not be wearing my number!" He started pacing around her apartment.

"Tom." She caught up with him. "Tom." She put her hand on his arm. "Tom!" He finally stopped and looked at her. "It's okay. There's a couple of things we can do about this. I'm going to list them. You tell me what works, all right? Because you're kind of freaking me out, so I need to figure this out in my head before we go any further. I will handle this however you want."

Tom looked at her, blue eyes stormy.

Her heart skipped and not in a good way. He wasn't just upset, he was angry, and she didn't understand. This felt like a fight. She had been to home games before while he had been playing in DC, but since their relationship had been a secret, she had never been sitting with the wives and girlfriends. And he had certainly never asked her what she was wearing to the game; he never saw her while she was there.

Tom looked pissed, and anxiety flooded her system. There was no way she was going to let him leave for the rink like this. She took a deep breath.

"Here are options. Whatever choice helps you play tonight, Tom. This is your *job.* I will be fine. *Got it?"*

He met her eyes, scowled, but agreed.

"Choice one, I stay home—shut up while I run through the choices," she interrupted his angry protest. "Choice two, I go to the game, no sweater. Choice three, and here's where you are reminded that you are dating a genius," she said, trying to sound a little lighter, "I just go a little early and hit the team store and get one of yours to wear…shit, why are you still looking angry?" She had really hoped she could diffuse the situation by giving him a way out and then using humor. But if anything, he looked more pissed off than before.

She took a deep breath, trying to calm herself. His anger was upsetting, but it was clear there was something more going on here. This wasn't actually about her. She took another deep breath.

"Tom," she said calmly and softly, "please. What's wrong?"

His shoulders were tense, and he was staring over her head, giving off a vibe of I-want-to-put-my-fist-through-a-wall. "I am *so fucking angry* I haven't given you my sweater already!" If it was possible to yell and growl at the same time, that was the sound.

Her heart started beating again. He was still glowering, looking angry, but her mouth twitched upward at one corner. This was something she could work with.

"Okay. I'll make you a deal," she said. He looked down at her and made a visible effort to unclench his fists and relax his shoulders. "I'm going to go to the team store before the game and buy your sweater like a star-struck fan, which, to be fair, I am. I think I'll even ask you for your autograph. Probably on my boob." The corner of his mouth twitched. "By the way, you are not allowed to sign other boobs. Only mine." She continued. "However, as you know, I do keep score between

207

us, and I'm thinking…this new potentially autographed sweater of mine will be worth…" She thought for a moment. "Three? Three."

Tom's eyebrows unfurrowed a bit, and he squinted sideways at her. She moved closer to him.

"So now, McCullin, you are going to go to the rink, and you are going to take all that anger I just saw, and you are going to use it where it actually makes sense and knock some Puffins on their asses. You guys are going to win. In regulation. Do *not* let those fuckers push this game into OT."

She was right up in front of him and poked a finger in his chest. He tried not to smile but felt one slipping through.

"Because I've just decided this very minute that I'm taking a cab to the game, and you're driving me home. If you guys win in regulation? You're getting laid in the backseat of your car before we even leave the garage."

That was it. He knew he was smiling at her, and he could see her eyes sparkle. There was humor there, but there was also an underlying heat in them that promised she meant exactly what she said. He pulled her in for a deep, hard kiss.

"I promise," he said, biting her gently on her neck under her right ear, "that I will not let those fuckers…" He bit her with slightly more pressure where her neck met her shoulder and was rewarded with a small gasp. He pushed the neck of her shirt away from her collarbone and pressed a kiss there before continuing, "…push the game into overtime." He switched sides and moved up, grating his still-new beard along her jaw and cheek. "And after the game I will make you come so hard…" he bit her gently under her left ear before finishing with a growling whisper, "…while I am fucking you in the backseat of my car."

Liz was breathing hard. Tom looked at her and made a very masculine sound of satisfaction. Pupils dilated, breasts rising and falling rapidly, lips slightly parted, and skin flushed from where the V-neck of her shirt began all the way to her cheekbones, more so where he had rasped it with his beard. He put his right hand at the back of her neck and pulled her to him for one last hard kiss and said, "I will see you after the game."

***

Tom got to the rink about ten minutes earlier than usual and sought out the Equipment Manager, Tony, who was in the middle of the nine thousand tasks that happen behind the scenes for every game.

"Hey, Tony, I've got a favor to ask. I need to get a game-worn sweater."

"Mr. McCullin." Tony always used "Mr." with the players, but it was just his way. He was actually not too much older than Tom and very friendly with all the players. "I can certainly arrange that."

"Yeah, well, it's a bigger favor than that…"

Tony looked at him and raised an eyebrow. "How soon?" Tom looked sheepish. "Seriously? You're killin' me, Smalls." He sighed. "You need it cleaned after?"

"Nope."

"All right. Sometimes jerseys get damaged in the

laundry and I have to arrange for replacements. It happens. Too bad it happened to yours tonight after the game." He shook his head.

"I owe you, Tony. Big. This is important." Tom was grinning.

"You're my kid's favorite player. A picture with him and we'll call it even."

Tom looked surprised. "I'm not really, am I? Shit, Tony, for this, I'll take him out on the ice sometime."

"He would flip. Yes, you are. What can I say, Mr. McCullin? The kid loves a good hockey fight."

Tom laughed. "We can figure a good day for him to come to practice or something like that." He headed into the locker room to start getting ready as the other players were beginning to arrive. "Thank you. You're the best."

Tony shook his head, smiling.

Chapter Twenty-Eight

It was a tight game. It was almost always a tight game with Pittsburgh. The two teams had a long-standing and bitter rivalry, and the Puffins had knocked the Guardians out of the playoffs more than once. In a row. Liz hated them. But the games were always great.

Paige wasn't there, so this was a complete solo flight for Liz in the world of hockey girlfriend-ness. Sitting with the wives and girlfriends was fun, but different. As a real die-hard hockey fan, she was not necessarily in like company among the other women in the group. Many of them, like Paige, had not known anything at all about hockey before meeting their hockey player significant other. But, Liz was Liz, and she was there to watch the game. She knew that she was going to jump and yell and high-five people nearby like she always did, no matter where she was sitting.

Not arm candy, Tom, she thought to herself. *Hope you don't hear about it too much from other players, but you can't say I didn't warn you.*

211

She felt a bit self-conscious at first, wearing her brand new "McCULLIN—40" red home sweater, but soon felt more at home. After all, most of these were people she knew. Some better than others, of course, but almost all were familiar faces. And the ones who weren't familiar were most likely feeling more lost than she was, as they were probably connected with the newer players this season who'd just been traded in or drafted or called up from the minors.

She greeted folks she knew, and then did what she always did and introduced herself to the people she didn't. If they were new, well, so was she. If they weren't new, then she should probably learn who they were.

She had learned long ago that the best way for her to deal with a new situation was to just admit she was completely lost. She chuckled to herself, thinking she should really just have a permanent nametag made that said, "Hi, my name is Liz. I have no idea what I'm doing." That would definitely save time.

They did win, in regulation, but as with so many games against the Puffins, the last few minutes of the game were an insane flurry of activity, with Pittsburgh pulling their goaltender to try to make up the one goal deficit to send the game into overtime. The six-on-five was intense—the Guards' goaltender was one of the best in the league, and he showed it, but the Guards' defense also did an amazing job of shutting the Puffins down.

The icing on the cake was the empty net goal sent in by Tom in the last five seconds of the game.

Liz was pretty sure she had lost her voice, but who could tell with everyone else in the arena screaming too? Maybe she just couldn't hear herself.

***

She waited outside the players' entrance with several other people for the press conferences to be finished and the guys to come out. When she saw Tom, Liz launched herself at him and jumped into his arms, croaking, "That was amazing!" Apparently she had lost her voice a little. He laughed and swung her in a circle and then put her down and looked at her. And saw what she was wearing.

She saw his brows knit together, and his eyes got a little stormy. She looked at him questioningly. He put his hand behind her neck and kissed her, hard, and said, "We won. In regulation."

Her smile got sultry, and she said, "You most certainly did. And with style, Tom."

He took her hand, turned, and led her away to the garage. His car was further away from where he would normally park, and by a wall. He had been looking for some semblance of privacy when picking a parking spot this afternoon. Tom pushed Liz against the side of his car and started kissing her, deep and hard, biting at her lower lip. He put his knee between her legs and pressed them apart, pushing himself against her, and was rewarded with a small gasp. He opened the back door of his car, threw his bag in, climbed in, pulled her in after him, and shut the door.

213

"Take off your jeans and underwear. Now." He was growling his instructions, and Liz complied. He was taking charge, and it was doing things to her insides.

She started to pull off the jersey, but he stopped her, saying, *"No.* Leave that on," as he pulled her to him for another bruising kiss, and then pulled her onto him to straddle his lap. His jeans and underwear were down to his knees, so when she straddled him, his erection was directly at her slit. Liz rubbed against him just for a moment, her wet arousal slick against his hard cock.

Tom growled louder, his eyes getting darker by the minute. "No teasing." He was holding her by the back of the neck. "Not tonight." He kissed her hard again, his tongue probing the inside of her mouth while he lifted her and fitted her onto his shaft. He pressed upward, hard, as he pulled her down, and her gasp mixed with another low growl from Tom as they slid together.

Liz was already breathing hard, so turned on, already moving, desperate to feel more of him. He had his hands on her hips, moving her, pushing her against him faster and harder. She had her hands clutched into the fabric of his shirt at his chest and shoulders, breathing fast, saying "oh," with every breath, every word getting slightly higher pitched, adding his name, adding "yes," until she reached a gasping, crashing climax riding on him, calling out his name.

Tom grabbed her hips and ground himself into her one more time and then moved her to the seat next to him. Liz waited for him to follow, expecting

214

that they were just changing positions, but he gripped the back of the seat in front of him and just sat there, looking at the floor, breathing hard. And then started to pull up his jeans.

"Tom? What are you doing?"

"I'm buying back that fucking *jersey.*" He managed to make the last word sound like part of the profanity.

She stared, watching him attempt what seemed like the impossible task of fitting himself back into his jeans while fully erect. It was surreal. When he finished, she said, "That might be the single most astounding act of willpower I have ever seen."

He finally turned and looked at her and then closed his eyes. "For God's sake get dressed, and get in the front seat." He sounded like he was talking through gritted teeth.

She did, and he started the car to get them out of the garage and on their way to her apartment. When she reached out to touch his leg, he grabbed her wrist. "Don't touch me. I will wreck the fucking car trying to get out of the garage." His growling voice did such things to her.

She turned in her seat to watch him drive. Once they were out of the garage and on the main roads, she reached out again, asking, "Can I touch you yet?"

Her hand touched his upper thigh, and he jerked and said, *"No. Fuck."*

The trip to her apartment took far less time than it usually did. She had no idea how fast he was driving, but it was impressive.

He parked the car, turned, and pulled her by the

back of the neck for another searing kiss. She grabbed his upper thigh and raked her nails into his jeans.

Tom grabbed his bag out of the back of the car; by the time he got to her door she had it unlocked and open. He pushed her inside, kicking the door closed with his foot, and claimed her mouth again. Pulling her into her bedroom, he ordered, "Take off your jeans and underwear and lie down on the bed." Her smile at him was pure sex as she did what he asked.

Grabbing one of her ankles, he pulled her to the edge of the bed, knelt down on the floor, and started kissing and biting his way up the inside of her thigh.

"Oh, holy shit." Liz had not been expecting this. Every nerve ending in her entire body pinged to attention; the anticipation was already causing pulses mimicking tiny orgasms. As he got closer to her center, Tom moved more slowly. The bites were gentler, and then there were only kisses, and licks, and tongue flicks. He pressed her legs further apart, lifted them over his shoulders, and licked slowly from her entrance all the way up to her clit.

He stopped there, not moving, and then flicked his tongue once.

Liz was already falling apart, her hands tangled in the bedclothes, her head thrown back. He pressed into her, teasing, flicking, sliding, sucking, kissing, until she arched her back and yelled out her climax.

And then, when she tried to push him away, because the feeling was too sensitive, too overwhelming, too much, he wouldn't let her go. He held her hips and made her ride his tongue through her climax, and then kept her in place, teasing and flicking and sucking until she came again, soon after, this time with a scream.

Liz lay back on the bed, feeling wrung out, but in the best way. She looked up at Tom, now standing next to the bed, and saw his eyes, hard and fierce.

"Now taking that fucking thing off."

She sat up and then got to her knees—she had almost forgotten the jersey she was wearing that had started this whole thing. She pulled it over her head and tossed it to the end of the bed.

"Now take off the rest."

She smiled, and took off her t-shirt and bra, kneeling naked before him.

Tom crouched down, reached into the bag he had brought with him from the rink, and pulled out the red sweater he had worn during the game. Liz sank from her knees to sit on the bed. He held it up, front facing her.

"This is my sweater, Liz. This can't be bought. I *earned* this." His voice was deep, and there was raw emotion in it. Passion. He turned it around to his name and number. *"This. My* name, Liz. *My* number." He tossed it at her as he stood up again.

"Put it on." It was a growled order. She did as he asked, kneeling on the bed again.

It was huge on her, made to fit over pads on his six-foot-four frame. She rolled the sleeves up so her hands were free. It was damp with his sweat from playing a full game. It smelled like him, and it was making her heart race again.

He had not intended for this to happen this way, but he was feeling feral. Wild. On the edge of control. Tom got on the bed, on his knees behind Liz, looking at his name on her body.

"My name, Liz." He took her hair in his hand and came up close to her ear and rasped out, "Don't *ever* wear another man's name again."

Her heart was beating out of her chest.

Tom turned her, put his hand behind her neck, tilting her head to look in her eyes, and growled, "Are you afraid of me?" He looked and sounded on the edge of violence.

"No." She was breathing hard, and her eyes were slightly wild, too.

"Good. Don't ever be scared of me, Liz." He sounded savage. Tom turned her back around. He stripped off his clothing, put his knee between her knees, and moved them apart.

"My sweater. *My* name."

He put his other knee between her legs and pressed in the other direction. *"My* number."

He took her hand and put it on the headboard as he pressed himself inside of her, enjoying her gasp. *"My name,* Liz." He started moving, sliding in and out of her. "Say it."

"Tom!"

"McCullin!"

"Oh, God," she panted, "McCullin!"

"Yes. *My* name." He was slowly starting to increase the speed of his thrusts into her. "Say it again, Liz."

"McCullin! Tom McCullin. Oh, yes."

He wrapped his hand into her hair at the back of her neck, already starting to feel the pressure building at the base of his spine, sliding in and out, feeling her hot slickness tight around him.

"You're *mine,* Liz." He bowed his head, starting to pant. "You wear *my* name. *My name,* Liz." He was speeding up; the headboard was starting to thump against the wall with the force of their coupling.

His thrusts were deep and powerful. *"My* name. *My* number. You wear *my* sweater." He was starting to lose rhythm. "You're *mine. Say it."*

"Oh, God, Tom, I'm yours!"

"Say my name again!" He was so close. "Say it!"

"McCullin!" She was gasping for air. *"Tom."* A few more seconds passed, and then Liz screamed, *"Micky!"*

Tom grabbed her hips and thrust into her one last time, holding on and grinding against her as he ejaculated, shouting as he claimed her in this primitive ritual, feeling each surge as if they were coming from his toes.

He rested his forehead on her back, one arm on the headboard, the other curled around her body, trying to catch his breath. He had skated a full game and then participated in multiple sex acts. His legs just weren't going to hold him anymore. Not after that.

He pulled Liz down with him in a controlled collapse onto the bed, into a spooning position. All of his muscles were shaking. From exertion, from exhaustion…and now that he was coming back to his right mind, from concern.

"Liz," he spoke into her hair, his voice rough, his chest tight, "are we okay?"

"Hmmm?" After her fourth orgasm of the

evening, she wasn't sure she could connect two words together, but this sounded important, so she tried to swim to the surface. "What?"

He turned her over to look at her. "Are we okay?"

She smiled, in a sweet, sleepy way, and said, "Yes. I'm yours. Sleep."

She rolled back over to snuggle into his arms again, and they both fell asleep.

***

The next morning, she woke before him and spent some time just watching him sleep. When he woke and saw her watching him, he smiled. "Good morning, beautiful."

"Good morning." She winked at him and added, "Micky."

He chuckled. "I love that you call me Tom. I hear Micky enough in the locker room." He looked at her from half-lidded eyes. "But I'd be very happy to hear it from you once in a while like last night." He smiled. "That was fucking amazing."

"Yes, it was." She looked at him for a second and said, "Just to be clear, so you won't worry about this, please remember that part of my fantasy specifically included that my six-foot-four defenseman is an enforcer." Her voice got very husky suddenly, and she drew patterns with her fingers on his chest. "A little rough can be very, very sexy, Tom."

"Shit." He growled. "I didn't think it would be possible to get hard again for at least a day after last

220

night."

She laughed and winked again.

"Consider it my contribution to your cardio training."

He chuckled.

"So I guess I'm going to need a new away sweater too." She raised and lowered her eyebrows suggestively, and he laughed.

"Yes, you will. In all seriousness, though, all the other sweaters need to go. Today, Liz." She looked at him in surprise, seeing that there was no hint of joking. "Give them away, I don't care. But they need to be out of your apartment today."

"Not just the Beckman one?" She was a little confused.

"No. All of them."

"Realizing I probably shouldn't even ask…even the one I just bought yesterday that does, in fact, have your name on it?"

He looked at her, eyes getting dark and stormy again, and said, "Yes, that one. You don't own that one anymore—I do. Get rid of it." She looked at him, meeting his angry eyes with her curious ones, and he softened, shaking his head. He took a deep breath. "It's important to me."

"Clearly," she said. "I'm happy to do this for you. I am curious, though."

"It's hard to explain. It's just a thing I've done since I've been playing and been old enough to be interested in girls. I think some other guys do it too—Becks used to, but I don't know if he still did when he met Paige or if it was just when we were kids—but my girlfriend has to have my gear. From me. Not from anyone else. And certainly not that she had to go buy for herself because I fucking forgot to take care of her before a game." His face had a small scowl. "It doesn't matter that your away sweater is blank. It's not from me. Everything not from me has to go." He pulled her to him. She was still wearing his game sweater from the night before.

"This is the one that mattered the most, Liz. I will get you regular ones that fit better." He smiled at her, and his voice got low, "Although you could wear nothing but this all day every day and I would be a happy man."

She laughed, and his body reacted. "I will get you a home, and an away, that are mine. From me." He kissed her. And then kissed her again. "I have no idea what I was going to say next."

He kissed her again, moving so she was lying back on the pillow. "I think I was going to ask you if you were getting wet."

Kissing, moving next to her. "Because I am so hard."

Kiss, tongues. "And if you're not wet, I could help you with that."

His hand was between her legs, stroking her very gently, and she gasped and moaned. He dipped his finger to her entrance to find that she was indeed starting to get wet, and brought the moisture up to lubricate his slow, gentle movements around her clit. Her face was already flushed.

"I remember watching you at the hotel, when you were lying on the bed touching yourself. I told you I wanted to touch you like that." He dipped his finger down again to pick up more lubrication and continued his slow, gentle, teasing motions. "You said you could come from this. Just from teasing." He continued his slow movements and leaned to her ear, breathing against her. "Is that true?"

"Yes." Her voice was breathy.

He shifted, making his movements smaller, and she whimpered.

"You said to not stop even if you begged." Dip down, press in a little, back up with more slickness. "You said to tease you until you had an orgasm and then not stop teasing you until you had another one."

She was panting. "Yes. Oh, yes."

He dropped his voice low and rumbled in her ear. "You said my voice drives you crazy," and then he flicked directly over her clit once. She jerked as if she had been given an electric shock.

"So," he said into her ear, shifting back to the tiny movements he had seen her making in the hotel room, "I'm going to talk to you while I touch you and see if I can make you come so hard you see stars."

He was right next to her clit, his slick fingertip making very small movements, sliding against her, brushing against her, teasing. Her heart was pounding, and he continued to alternate his light, teasing movements with dipping to rewet his fingers.

"You make me crazy, Liz." His deep voice vibrated through her body. "I have never wanted anyone the way I want you."

Her face was so hot. She tried to move to press

223

harder against his hand, but he kept moving away to keep his touch maddeningly light.

"I want to be inside you."

She was moving her hips, bucking against his hand, but he continued to only allow her to have the lightest of touches.

"I want to grind into you again and again."

It was torment. It was exquisite. She was moving her hips as if he were riding her.

"I want to feel your body grip mine when you come."

She cried out. And spasmed. And gripped every part of his body she could get her hands on as she came apart in his arms.

Tom smiled against her, deeply satisfied with her reaction; she was panting and pushing at his arms to let her go. He moved, sitting up, pulling her into his lap. He wrapped his left arm around her and trapped both of her arms to stop them from moving and kept his right hand exactly where it had been, still moving.

"No, stop." She squirmed. "Don't." She was trying to get away, trying to stop the sensations, which were overwhelming. "It's too much. Stop."

"You said not to stop even if you begged me to." Tom's voice was low and rasping in her ear.

She was still struggling against him, panting.

"I'm taking you at your word on that this time, Liz."

She wasn't struggling against him now so much as drowning in the sensations.

"After this, we will need a safe word if we are going to play like this. I won't ever go past you saying no again."

Her back was arched, and every muscle in her body felt strung tight like a bow string.

"But, sweetheart, now that I know you enjoy getting a little rough…"

She was gasping, the pressure was building, and his words were pushing her beyond what she thought was possible for her to handle.

"…sometimes, I'm going to just want to hold you down and take you hard and fast."

The second orgasm was unbelievable, clenching every muscle in her body, repeatedly. When she started to be able to move again, she opened her eyes, looking at Tom. He looked deeply pleased.

"Hold me down and take me hard and fast." Her voice was rough from panting and vocalizing. His look changed immediately, and he held her down, and took her. Tom held her hands pressed into the bed over her head and entered her in one thrust, driving into her with a ferocity that surprised even him. Then he rode her body hard and fast, seeking only his own pleasure, losing himself in the sensation of pounding into her, until he reached his release, and finally found himself back in his own body and mind again.

***

"I don't know how you do that to me."

He was mumbling into a pillow. They were sprawled across the bed in a strange tangle of limbs and sheets, too exhausted to figure out which body parts belonged to each of them.

"Me?" she chuckled, although that seemed like far too much effort. "You started this. This is all on you." She sighed. "I feel boneless. Languid."

His turn to chuckle. "Me too." He paused. "I think I'm going back to sleep." Another pause. This time his voice sounded more slurred. "I don't think I have a choice about that." And then finally, "I love you, Liz," followed by light snoring.

She smiled and then fell asleep too.

Chapter Twenty-Nine

"This is going to be our longest road trip of the season. I'm finding it a little hard to believe I'm not going to see you for ten days." They were sitting together on her couch, Liz cuddled next to him with his arm around her. Tom was going to have to leave soon. "I'm going to miss you." He pulled her into him closer.

"I will miss you too. At least I get to see you on TV, though." She smiled at him. "I have told you how insanely hot you look in your gear, right?"

Tom chuckled. "Once or twice." He kissed the top of her head. "But God knows I love hearing it. So please don't stop."

"You look freaking hot playing hockey. Like, lick the TV screen hot." He laughed out loud and stood up, pulling her with him.

"Shit, I don't want to leave." He smiled and touched her face gently, his gaze getting more serious as he looked at her.

"What's wrong, sweetheart?"

"Do you remember what you said to me, you

know, that night, here, before I…left?" Tom asked her. His tone was now serious too, and she looked at him closely. By his tone and manner, she understood what he was talking about.

"Yes, of course," she replied, waiting quietly for him to continue.

Tom hesitated a moment and then looked slightly away from her eyes. With a small hitch in his voice, and something Liz could only label shyness, he asked softly, "Would you say it to me again? I would like to have a memory of those words that doesn't end with me walking out on you."

Liz was glad he wasn't looking her in the eye in that moment, because she was afraid he would take the look of her fighting tears the wrong way. The sweetness of his request tore her heart. She said nothing but took his hand and pulled him back down to sit as they had been sitting that night. She turned toward him, but instead of holding his hands in hers, she gently took his face in her hands and stroked his beard with her thumbs.

She spoke softly, with a small smile on her face. "I am so very deeply in love with you." She placed a gentle kiss on his lips. "Yours is the only kiss I want to taste on my lips." She kissed him again tenderly. "Yours are the only hands I want to feel on my body…" another soft kiss, "…and you are the only man I want in my bed, Tom." She finished with a kiss that lingered only slightly longer but was still soft and sweet.

Tom stood up again, bringing her with him, and pulled her to him in a gentle embrace. He murmured into her hair, "You changed it."

She smiled against his chest. "I did."

He shifted back and kissed her softly. "It's better."

"I'm glad." Liz smiled at him, checked the clock, and said, "I think we have just enough time left for you to kiss me goodbye properly." Tom smiled his heart-stopping smile and kissed her, dipping her down for a moment to make her laugh, and then bringing her back up to take his time to kiss her enough to last them for ten days.

When he let her go, she said, "Go win some games, sweetheart."

"Fuck, yeah." Tom grabbed her ass for a moment. She laughed, and he walked out her door, making his "just scored a goal" gesture.

***

They were finally on the bus, heading toward the hotel in one of the cities on their long road trip. The game had gone into overtime and then to a shootout. They had won, so Tom was in a good mood, but everything had seemed to run longer than usual—post-game interviews, et cetera. It was late, but he knew Liz would still be awake, waiting for him to call.

She picked up on the second ring. Her voice was husky, and it made his chest tighten. "Hey, handsome," she said. "I've been missing you."

"You too. Anything going on? You sound…"

She chuckled, low and throaty. Tom squeezed his eyes shut and put his head back against the

229

headrest. "I wouldn't have answered the phone for anyone except you," she said. "I'm sitting on the couch, thinking about the night on the hotel rooftop…" Her voice was breathless, and she gasped out a small sound.

He realized with a start what she must be doing, where her hand must be. She had told him the night on the hotel rooftop was going to be the memory to keep her warm while he was gone on long roadies, but this was new.

"Christ, Liz," he breathed. He had gone from calm to fully, painfully erect in heartbeats, sitting in the middle of a bus crowded with his teammates.

"Should I tell you more?" she teased.

"No!" he said, much louder than he intended.

His seatmate hit him on the shoulder, saying, "What the hell, Micky?" Other voices protested in general, and from a few seats back, he heard, "Shut, it, Mick!"

Tom turned to the window, lowered his voice to a whisper, and said again, "No! I'm on the *bus,* for chrissakes."

Liz laughed suddenly, breaking the mood. "Oh, sweetheart, I'm so sorry. I thought you'd be in the hotel by now."

Tom put his head back against the seat again. "Everything ran late. We're not going to be there for at least another twenty minutes." He lowered his voice again. "But either way, I was definitely not expecting *that.*"

"Well," she said, trying for a moment to shift back to sultry, "I just can't seem to get you off my mind." His groin pulsed again, and he swore softly.

Liz laughed again. "I'm gonna hang up the phone before I do any damage," she said. "I love you."

"Love you too."

***

Liz hung up the phone. The giggles became snorts of laughter. She almost felt bad about how hard she was laughing, but seriously—her first ever attempt at phone sex, and it turned out he was sitting on the team bus instead of in his hotel room?

The sensual mood was gone, temporarily at least, but it was worth it for the laugh. She had needed that.

***

About five minutes later, Tom's phone vibrated with a text message.

Liz: I JUST stopped laughing. Seriously. Call me when you're at the hotel and I'll make it up to you. I promise.

He smiled and shook his head, still amazed that she bothered to text in full sentences with proper grammar.

Tom: K

He added a heart emoji. He hit send, knowing

she would smile and shake her head at the shortcuts.

***

Liz picked up the phone and heard Tom's deep voice rumble on the other end. "Hey, gorgeous. I'm in the hotel room. Rooming with Zee. He's in the bathroom right now, so I've got a few minutes to talk. What the hell was that? Not that I'm actually complaining."

"Well, hello, handsome," she said. Her voice was playful and low, and somehow it felt like she was breathing directly into his left ear. "I know you're tired, but I suspect you might also still be somewhat aroused by our earlier conversation. I know I am."

Shit. "Well, I am now," he growled. He ran his right hand through his hair. "Zee is going to be out here any minute, Liz. This is *not* helping me."

"Just trust me. All you have to do is listen. I've never done this before, so, as usual, I'm just gonna wing this."

Tom put his hand over his eyes. He was tired, and he had already been somewhere between half-mast and rock hard for the past half hour because of the woman on the other end of the phone.

"Okay."

"You do what you need to do. Just listen, right? I'm just going to talk to you. Just hold the phone to your ear. Get changed. When Zee gets out of the bathroom, go in and brush your teeth, get ready for bed…and your phone is waterproof, right?"

"Yeah?"

"So if you should end up wanting to get in the

shower for a few minutes…"

"I showered at the arena."

"I know, sweetheart. I'm just saying. The shower makes some extra noise, and you won't have to let go of the phone. Just in case."

"Okay."

Tom started getting his stuff together one handed, holding the phone to his ear. He really was tired.

"Tom," she breathed, "I am not going to tease you. Maybe some other time, but right now I just want to tell you what I would do if I were there with you. Because I miss you like hell, and I want you so badly. I'm picturing you wearing jeans, because God, you look good in jeans."

She made a small humming sound. "Mmm. Okay, you're in jeans. I would stand in front of you and undo the button to make more room. And since this is my fantasy, they're button-fly, so I would undo, say, two buttons."

She was trying to find a good pace, a rhythm. Talking slowly, but not too slowly, her voice sexy and low—that wasn't difficult, because she had her eyes closed, picturing everything she was saying.

"And then I would move my right hand around to your back and down inside your jeans to grab your ass cheek. Because your ass is amazing. Have I told you that your ass is amazing?"

Zee came out of the bathroom.

"Micky." Receiving no response, he repeated, *"Mick."*

Tom realized he had been standing, staring out the window, holding the phone in one hand and his toothbrush in the other.

Tom turned around, looking slightly glazed. "What?"

"Bathroom is free. Is that Liz? Tell her I said hi, and good night."

"Tell Zee I said good night, Tom," said Liz.

"She said good night." His voice was a little distant.

Zee laughed. "Don't suppose I could hear that from her, maybe in a really sexy voice? It's a long road trip, and it's definitely not the same coming from you."

"What?" Tom blinked, hearing Liz laughing on the other end of the line. "No. *No!* Definitely not."

Tom went into the bathroom and closed the door, hearing Zee laugh from the other side.

"We're alone."

"Oh, good. Start brushing your teeth, sweetheart. I'm gonna move this right along, because even in this little fantasy of mine, it's late, and you're tired, and I really, *really* want to get you off.

"I was two buttons down with my right hand on your ass. My left hand would come up to open the rest of the buttons on your jeans, and I would reach down inside those cute boxer briefs to cup my hand around your balls."

She could hear the water running, the sounds of him brushing his teeth, and the sound of him breathing hard, but beyond that he was just listening, which was exactly what she wanted.

"I'd spend just a minute or two rolling your balls in my fingers, just because I love that feeling, but then I would shift my hand up where I really want to be, right at the base of your hard cock."

Tom made a small sound, and Liz smiled a little, knowing that he was surprised and turned on by her language.

"I would keep my thumb and forefinger curled snug around the base of your shaft and let my pinky slide up the underside, right to that little indentation under the head, right there, and then back down. And then, because there's just no time to mess around tonight, I would reach back down with my left hand to play with your balls again, while I let go of your ass with my right hand to bring it around to the front to grip the rock-hard shaft of your cock."

He was breathing hard, unable to stop small, sexy sounds escaping through the phone line.

Her voice was husky. "It feels amazing in my hand, Tom. The skin is like velvet, and it's so damn hard underneath. I would rub my thumb all over the head of your cock, spreading the slickness there. You know that it would be so slippery already. I'd rub my thumb through all that wet precum, all around."

She heard the shower turn on.

Tom knelt down in the tub with the water at his back, because he didn't trust his legs to hold him any longer. He was breathing hard, completely lost in this, in what she was saying to him, in what she was doing to him just with her voice.

"So I would start stroking you, moving my hand along your hard shaft, and I know you're thinking 'handjob' because hey, phone sex. But this is my fantasy, Tom, so I would kneel down in front of you and pull your clothing down far enough to be able to get my tongue to run up the entire length of the underside of your big, hard cock, from the base all the way up to the tip."

She heard a soft groan and a gasp for air.

"And then I would take your cock into my mouth, still holding and stroking your shaft with my right hand, and cupping and rolling your heavy balls with my left hand, and I would swirl my tongue around the head of your cock. Once. Twice. Three times."

Another gasp and a whisper, "Shit."

"And then I would flatten my tongue against the underside of your shaft and press you against the roof of my mouth, and I would suck."

A quiet strangled groan, one of her favorite sounds. He was just on the edge.

"Hard."

She heard him start to come, gasping, trying to stay quiet.

"And then I would swallow."

There was a loud clatter as the phone dropped into the tub. Tom put his left hand on the back wall of the shower stall to keep from falling over as the spasms of his orgasm tore through him one after the other. After a few deep breaths, he picked the phone back up. "Sorry," he said, his breath ragged and his voice thick.

"Don't be," she said, smiling to herself, still sounding sultry. "I suspect that a dropped phone is the highest form of praise in phone sex. Sweetheart, before you pass out in the bathroom, rinse what needs to be rinsed, dry off, and get in bed."

"'Kay," he said, starting to sound drunk with

sleep and sex.

She heard the shower turn off, shuffling sounds of what she assumed were towels, a minute or two of random noises of doors and lights and fabric, and finally a deep, contented, masculine sigh, followed by steady breathing and a very familiar light snoring.

She smiled and hung up the phone.

Chapter Thirty

Tom opened his eyes the next morning, slightly confused to see the corner of his phone directly in front of his face. He was under the covers sprawled across the bed diagonally, on his stomach, with one arm holding the pillow under his head. He heard Zee head into the bathroom, then say, "Jesus, Mick. What the fuck? Did you go out drinking after I went to bed?"

Tom closed his eyes again and mumbled, "What the fuck are you talking about?"

"I see enough of your underwear in the locker room, asshole. I do not need this greeting me in the morning."

Something draped over Tom's face. He snatched it off and sat up. "What the hell, Zee?" he said, throwing the underwear back toward his teammate.

"They're yours, man. I'm just giving them back." Tom was then hit in the face with a pair of jeans, followed by a shirt and some balled-up socks. He started to get up and return fire but stopped very suddenly when he realized he was not currently wearing anything under the covers.

Zee took one look at his face and said, "Seriously? Commando? Fuck, Mick, you used to be one of the good roommates. It was way too late to go out. Really, dude, were you drunk?"

"No, man, I was just way more tired than I thought, apparently. I don't really even remember going to bed." He ran his hand through his hair. He was definitely starting to remember and was really hoping not to accidentally give that away. What were the odds that Zee would drop this conversation?

"I crashed and fell asleep right after talking to you. You wouldn't let me say goodnight to Liz. Then you went into the bathroom, and I passed out." He got a grin on his face that Tom did not like. "You were on the phone with Liz when you went into the bathroom." He started to laugh. "Holy shit, Micky!" His laughter was building. "I can't fucking believe it! Phone sex? I didn't think you had it in you." Zee looked at Tom's face and started laughing even harder. "And Liz? Yeah, okay, never mind…her, I can see, but you?"

At the mention of Liz, Tom saw red. "Shut the fuck up about her, Zee. Don't go talking about this. You've got no right to say shit about her like that."

Zee stopped laughing and squared off. "Really, Mick? Don't act like you don't know the stuff people catch shit about. If you've never been on the receiving end of something like this, then you're way overdue. And Liz has been one of my best friends a hell of a lot longer than you have even *known* her. She knows what goes on. She called you *in your hotel room,* jackass. It was a calculated risk. If I called her about this right now, she would pretend that she has no idea what I'm talking about, but she would laugh.

"She would *laugh* about it, Mick. And she wouldn't be angry at you, even if you told everyone in the locker room, you fucking asshole. Every guy in the world would be jealous of that. And there are one or two guys on this team who would give their left nut for her to look at them the way she looks at you. So shut the fuck up and quit whining, Nancy." He stormed out the door.

Tom sat back against the headboard, stunned by the rebuke.

***

As Tom was eating breakfast, his small hope that Zee had shown restraint was dashed as he heard the offhand comment, "Kids and their sexting these days," from one of the tables.

"Hey, Micky, what kind of data plan have you got?"

"So, Mick, talked to Liz lately?"

There were only a few comments during breakfast. Things picked up in the locker room during morning skate, and it was getting under Tom's skin.

But the stuff Zee had said was worse, because Zee was right. Everything he said had been right on, and Tom was struggling with that on multiple levels. Zee was a much younger guy, so Tom should know better than Zee how to handle himself in the locker room. And yet, experience had shown that Tom had spent most of his career on the fringe of the group, even though his coaches and captains had repeatedly encouraged him to take on more of a leadership role. Chris had always referred to him as a spiky bastard when it came to locker room banter. With the exception of Chris, he kept his teammates at arm's length when it came to anything personal.

He made a conscious, somewhat uncomfortable decision before heading to the rink that afternoon. He would try to ease up, to let the comments roll off his back. Maybe even join in? *Fuck, not sure I can go that far.*

The Guards hadn't been playing badly lately, but they had not been playing as well as they could. This was a really good team, with top talent, but they were playing tight, and their recent wins had been more from exceptional goaltending and a little puck luck than from great on-ice play. They were playing tonight against a top-tier Blackbirds team in Chicago. This could get ugly real fast if they weren't on top of their game, and they always played better when they were more relaxed.

The smack talk had started immediately in the locker room, with Zee leading the charge. Tom had known that the game time locker room was going to be the worst and that there would be no holds barred on what was being said about him. Sure enough, there were darts being thrown from all over.

Tom was just letting things go, not reacting, but then one of the youngest guys, a player who had just been called up from Washington's AHL affiliate team for the road trip, walked by him and said, "Hey, Micky, I heard your girl is into some really kinky shit."

Tom heard Zee say behind him, "Oh, fuck." It was one thing to say shit about Tom…it was something else entirely to be saying things about Liz, and Zee knew it.

"Don't believe everything you hear," Tom responded. He looked up at the young player. "Zee likes to exaggerate things." He looked over at Zee. "Like size. Or so I hear." There were a few whoops, and Zee looked briefly shocked that Tom was engaging in banter and not looking to kill someone.

Zee narrowed his eyes, took a chance, and responded, "Really, Mick? You trying to deny your late-night phone call from your girl?"

"Nope. Just saying there was nothing kinky involved. Not my style. Or hers." He looked over at Zee, took a deep breath, stepped way the hell out of his own comfort zone, and said, "Unless you consider phone sex itself to be kinky."

Whoops, catcalls, and "Holy shits" rang out. The younger AHL call up who had started the whole thing said, "So, was it good?"

Tom called over the noise, "Hey, Zee, the kid here wants to know if it was good."

Zee laughed and yelled, "He forgot his fucking clothes afterward!"

Tom looked at the player and said, "I forgot my fucking clothes." He raised his voice a bit, and said, "It was so fucking good I forgot my fucking clothes." The locker room exploded with cheering, whistles, foot stomps, and the like.

Tom stood up and held up his hand, requesting a

moment of silence. "If we could please win in regulation tonight, that would be great, because I have to make a phone call as soon as possible after the game." This was greeted by laughter and even louder cheering.

Tom sat back down and finished getting ready. He was repeatedly cuffed and slapped on the back and shoved in the shoulder. He got knowing looks from the captain and both assistant captains, and he smiled to himself.

I'll be damned.

***

Liz was watching the game at home. The local announcers, who were so much more fun than the national ones because they knew the guys so well, spent quite a bit of time commenting on how much better the team was playing tonight.

"I don't know what was said in the locker room, but these guys just came out looking loose and ready to play. They are skating tonight like they're enjoying themselves."

"I agree! And there's an awful lot of chirping going on. They seem to be trying to get under the skin of the Blackbirds players. It looks like it might be working too."

"Yeah, we might just be having a fight or two tonight if Chicago can't get their guys to settle down and ignore our boys out there."

It was a great game, and there were two fights, including one near the end of the third period. Chicago was down and frustrated, and Tom managed to goad a player into starting a fight with him.

"That was an unusual move for McCullin! Normally we see him going after guys in more of an enforcer role, but he just pestered Wilkins into dropping the mittens and coming after him. They both got the fighting major, but Wilkins also got a two-minute minor for instigating, so the Guards will get a power play here to hopefully put this one away. That was a nice pull for Micky there."

"Oh, yeah, check out McCullin, look at the grin on his face! He's still chirping away, heading off the ice to the locker room. He's chirping at the whole Blackbirds bench. The Guards are just having fun out there tonight. That's just great to see. I hope they can keep this up. This is what they've been missing for a while now."

***

The phone rang not too long after the game ended, and she answered it and practically yelled, "That game was awesome! Holy crap, Tom!"

Cheers and whistles greeted her, and she heard Zee's voice, not Tom's. "Hey, Liz!"

"Oh God, Zee. Do I even want to know why you've got Tom's phone? Are you in the locker room?"

A few more whistles, a lot of laughter, and one or two calls of "Hi, Liz!" in the background, prompted her to ask, "Am I on speakerphone?"

"Yes! You're on speakerphone! In the locker room! Micky is no longer allowed to have private access to his phone…" She started to hear scuffling noises, more laughter, "…because he can't be trusted with it…" More scuffling, Zee laughing, and the sound of Tom's deep voice suddenly joining the conversation.

"…what the fuck are you doing? Is that my phone?" Scuffle, laughter.

Liz had already started laughing.

"Seriously, Zee? How old are you? Give me the phone." The sounds of large guys thudding against equipment, more laughter.

"You can't be trusted! No private phone calls for you, Mick. All calls must be public." Zee sounded like Tom probably had him in a headlock, based on his strangled voice. "Liz, tell Micky you would hate it if he killed me."

"Christ, is she on the phone? Are you fucking kidding me?" Tom stopped long enough to realize he could hear Liz laughing through the phone line. "God damn it, Zee." He was not sure how to deal with this—his immediate instinct was to get royally pissed off, but that would fuck up everything he had been trying to do today. This was getting farther and farther from his comfort zone.

Why the fuck couldn't Zee have just left this alone?

Liz said, "Hey, Tom," and all the guys said, "Oooooooh, Tooooom," as if they were, indeed, ten years old. She continued. "Zee, sweetie, give him the phone."

"No fucking way. I know what went on last night, Liz. He has lost solo phone privileges."

Tom tightened his headlock on Zee and closed

his eyes, considering for a moment whether someone was going to have to physically remove him from the locker room to keep him from causing actual injury to the other player.

Liz was caught off guard, not prepared for this turn in the conversation. Recovering quickly, she said sweetly, "I'm quite sure I have no idea what you're talking about, Zee. But what I am sure is—I have known you for a really long time, and I have enough dirt on you to bury you up to your neck. So hand the phone to Tom, please. Thank you!" She said the last words brightly, as if there was no doubt he would comply with her request.

The other guys in the locker room laughed and cheered at her victory as Zee handed the phone to Tom. He released Zee and took the phone off speaker. "Hey."

"Are you okay? That game was all kinds of amazing, and you were awesome, but I'm getting the feeling there's an awful lot going on behind the scenes right now."

"Are you angry?"

She paused. "At what? What happened?"

Tom moved toward the side of the room to get a little privacy. "Zee figured out what went on last night. And told the locker room."

She snorted a little. "No, I'm not mad. I am curious, though. What do you mean, 'figured out?'"

"Are you laughing?"

She snorted again. "No." A giggle snuck through. "Not quite." Another giggle. "Seriously, how did he figure it out?"

He started smiling, he couldn't help himself, and

said sheepishly, "I left all my clothes lying in the bathroom and crawled into bed naked."

"Holy shit!" She started laughing so hard she couldn't breathe. "Oh my God, I'm sorry." She started laughing again. "I'm sure that wasn't funny for you, but holy shit!" More laughter. Tom started walking back to the group of guys. "Oh, sweetheart," she said between gasps of air, "is it bad that part of me is really fucking proud of myself?"

That was enough to make Tom laugh out loud. "I'll call you later." He looked around, raised his voice exaggeratedly, and said, *"When I'm alone."* This earned him more laughter and cheers from the other players. "Oh," he said to Liz, lowering his voice again, "I'm going to be buying button-fly jeans before I get home. Several pairs."

After he disconnected, he looked at Zee and said, "You win. She's laughing so hard she might have some sort of aneurysm."

Zee smiled and hit him on the shoulder on his way to the showers.

"You win, man. She's your girl."

Chapter Thirty-One

The win in Chicago was a big one for the Guards, and they were riding pretty high. They were staying overnight rather than rolling out immediately, so guys from the team were congregating at the hotel bar to celebrate.

Tom would normally skip this but joined the group, hanging out with Chris and a few of the other, older players, watching the younger guys acting ridiculous. It always seemed amazing to him that there were a few guys on the team who still weren't old enough to drink.

He elbowed Chris. "Were we ever that young and stupid, Becks?"

Chris laughed and said, "You obviously killed all the brain cells that would allow you to remember just how young and stupid we used to be." He looked over at his friend. "By the way, nice job today, Micky." He took a drink of his beer and turned back to watching the younger players. "And I don't just mean on the ice."

"Yeah, well. Apparently even I can learn to

loosen up."

"Who would have thought it?"

"Shut the fuck up."

Chris slapped him on the back and walked over to get another beer, and Tom made his way over to where Zee was standing slightly apart from a group of other guys. "Hey, Zee."

"Mick."

"Thanks. You were right, and I needed to hear it." He paused and then asked, "So are you one of those guys?"

Zee looked at him questioningly. "One of what guys?"

"One of the guys who would give his left nut."

Zee stiffened and took a half step away from him.

Tom said, "What?"

"You've got a wicked right hook, Micky. I'm trying to be ready if you're planning to take a swing at me."

"I'm not." He looked at Zee briefly and then turned to look at the room. "She loves you, you know. If it helps any, I'm pretty sure you're on a short list of people she would die for."

Zee looked closely at Tom. "Are you?" His voice had an edge of bitterness.

"I don't think so. Not yet, at least."

Surprising himself, Zee said viciously, "Good. Earn it." And then stalked off.

"Shit." That hadn't gone terribly well. Although, to be fair, he probably should have left well enough alone and walked away after saying thank you.

He walked out of the bar and toward his room,

feeling less social. On the way, he called Liz. "Hey, did I wake you?"

"Hey, handsome. No, I'm still up. Did the guys let you use the phone by yourself, or do you have an audience?"

Tom smiled. "I'm alone. But Liz? Call Zee. I think he could use talking to a friend right now." There was a long pause. "Are you there?"

"I'm here." Another pause. "You're managing to surprise me quite a bit today, Tom." She sighed. "Damn, I didn't think it was possible to miss you more, but I just want to kiss you right now."

He laughed. "Don't start. That's how we ended up here in the first place." He stopped walking and stood in the hallway for a moment. "I'm kidding about that. I definitely want to do that again. But not tonight. Give him a call, Liz." His voice got low and deep and rumbled through the phone. "I love you. I'll call you tomorrow, okay?"

"I love you too." She paused and then said quietly, "I'm yours, Tom."

His heart contracted in his chest, and he smiled, putting the phone in his pocket.

It's been a helluva day, McCullin, he said to himself and started toward his room.

***

Zee looked at the phone and wondered for a moment if he should answer it.

"Hey."

"Hey, sweetie. How's things?"

"Just great. We won, right? Great night."

250

Oh, something was definitely not right. "I call bullshit. What's up?" No answer. "Normally I would tell you something funny that happened to me today, but you already know what that was."

Zee caught himself smiling in spite of himself.

"So that's not going to work. And when I sounded like shit but said I was fine, you just got in your car and came to my apartment with ice cream. Since you're in Chicago and I'm in DC, that's out too." She sighed dramatically, and Zee smiled a little more. "So I'm afraid you're going to have to use your words this time."

He closed his eyes, smile fading. They had been friends for a long time. Really good friends. He just needed to say it. "Why him?"

"Why who?"

"Mick. Why him, Liz?"

She was surprised by the question and had no immediate response.

"All this time I've known you, if you had been interested in dating a hockey player, you could have had your pick of a bunch of guys on the team." If she had been surprised before, she was now approaching shocked. "So why now? And why the fuck did you pick the one guy in the locker room who has no sense of humor? A whole team full of fun guys, and you're dating the one angry, humorless, fun-hating, soul-sucking…"

Her eyebrows were climbing into her hairline.

"…hot-tempered, cranky…" He was starting to run out of things to add, "…bug-eyed, worm-headed…" He had resorted to quoting their shared favorite movie *Christmas Vacation,* and she started

251

laughing. "…snake-licking, dog-kissing, son of a bitch."

"Man, when I asked you to use your words, I wasn't expecting you to actually do it."

"I'm serious, Liz. I don't get it. Why him?"

Liz took a breath and tried to think this through. "The simple answer is that we were set up by Chris and Paige. He's Chris's best friend and Paige is mine, but we had never met until he was traded here. Chris thought we'd get along; Paige jumped at the idea. We hit it off. Believe it or not, he does have a really great sense of humor. Apparently just not at work." She paused. "Do you really think I would date someone who didn't make me laugh on a very regular basis?"

Zee was quiet for a moment before answering, "I find your logic irritating."

She smiled. "Beyond that it was chemistry. I know that sounds dumb," she added as she heard Zee scoff, "but what can I say? I'm just a walking bundle of hormones."

"Oh, Jesus, Liz!" Zee started laughing, which was exactly what she had wanted.

"I don't know what to tell you. I was a mess when I met him. I kept blushing."

"Bullshit."

"I swear. Ask Chris."

He laughed harder.

"When I went to say goodbye after the pool party, I noticed he had long eyelashes, almost tripped, and then shook his hand instead of giving him a hug. Chris thought I had completely lost my mind."

Now he was really laughing. "A *handshake? You?*"

"I know, right? Nothing at all awkward about that. Especially when he had literally just watched me hug every single other person at the party."

Zee finished laughing. "I'm glad you called, Liz. Thanks."

She considered for a moment before saying, "Would you believe it if I told you that Tom asked me to?"

He stiffened. "No. What did he tell you?"

"That you needed to talk to a friend. That's all, Zee. No details. You know I'd tell you."

She would. He knew that. What the fuck. Might as well go for broke here. "Why not me?"

"Why not you what?"

"Fuck, Liz, you don't make this easy. Why not me? We've been friends for years. If you're suddenly willing to date a hockey player, why not me?"

She was so shocked she thought she would drop the phone. "Holy shit."

"That's not really the kind of response that builds a guy's ego."

"I'm sorry. That's not what I meant. I just…I mean…what the hell?" She laughed. "I'm going to treat this like you're not just fucking with me—if you are, consider it your most brilliant prank ever— but honestly…" She let her breath out. "I'm six years older than you. That alone meant I automatically sorted you into the unavailable-to-me category when we met.

"You're one of my best friends, Zee. I love you

253

like crazy, like you're family. You know that. You mean as much to me as Paige and Chris, and that's the highest praise I've got. But even if we were closer in age, there isn't any chemistry between us, not really, and I think you know that too. If something were going to happen, it would have by now. Or at the very least you would have said something. I don't think we would even be having this conversation if I were dating someone you liked."

He didn't answer for a moment and then said, "Your logic is really fucking annoying." Another pause and then, "That doesn't mean I never thought about it."

"I have boobs. You're a guy. I think I might actually be offended if it didn't cross your mind at least once in the years we've known each other," she teased.

"That's not what I meant and you know it." *What the hell, the conversation has gone this far.* "Have you really never thought about it?"

"Shit, Zee." She took a deep breath. "Of course I have. I'm not going to pretend the thought never crossed my mind. But that doesn't change all the other things I just said, and you know that." He grunted. She tried to lighten the mood some. "And besides, I can't control where my mind wanders off to when I'm sleeping."

"Wait, you've *dreamed* about me? Now things are getting interesting." He started to take the bait.

She knew he would. "Don't get too excited. I've dreamed about other guys on the team too."

"Really. Now I do need to know more."

"Well," she continued, "you're quite a bit younger than I am, but older guys can be very sexy too. There's a certain older gentleman on the coaching staff who is quite handsome…" She purposely trailed off.

"No."

"Oh, yes. Grey hair…"

"Stop talking."

"Van Dyke beard…"

"For the love of God, stop talking." Liz laughed, and Zee said, "I will never be able to remove that image from my brain. I hate you."

"I know. That's why we're such good friends."

"Holy shit. It's like you put an evil time bomb in my head for the next time I see him at practice. Fuck. I don't even know how to handle that."

Liz got serious again. "Do you know how much I want to see you happy with someone? Honestly, Zee, at the next fan event, you have to get your picture taken playing with the kids. And if you can get a picture of you holding a baby, even better. Ovaries will explode all over the DC metro area." He laughed out loud. "You're a really good-looking guy. And that is purely objective. You are exceptionally easy on the eyes."

"Well, now I might be blushing."

"Pics or it didn't happen." She paused. "So are we okay? Or are things going to be insanely weird between us? I don't want that."

"We're okay. I love you too, Liz." He paused. "Hey, so, can I get you to say good night to me in a really sexy voice? Just once? I'm still feeling slightly bitter, and I like the idea it would probably

255

piss Mick off. I won't even tell him. It will be our little secret."

"Oh my God, you are so ridiculous." She laughed. "Okay—I'm indulging you. But this is it, all right? Then you make a concerted effort to find a beautiful girlfriend who will embarrass you with fantastic phone sex on road trips, got it?"

"Deal."

She cleared her throat and then said, in her most sultry, sexy, husky bedroom voice, "Good night, Jake. Sleep well."

"Damn." He paused. "I suddenly understand why he didn't let me talk to you last night." Another pause. "I'm so tempted to tell him."

She laughed. "You are a pain in the ass, Zee. Good night."

"Good night. And thank you."

"Any time. You know that."

Chapter Thirty-Two

She heard the key in the door and ran across the room, sliding on the tile in her socks so she careened into him sideways when he got through the door. Tom laughed with her—and at her—caught her before she fell over, and pulled her into his arms for a welcome home kiss that went from sweet to passionate in record time.

"Hi." She finally stepped back and looked up at him. "I have Chinese food. Are you hungry?"

"Hi, beautiful."

That little smile. She might die.

He pushed her hair behind her ear and just looked at her for a while. "Damn, I missed you."

"You *know* I missed you." She smiled, looking a little sheepish. "Hence the phone call."

"Ah, yes." Tom looked up toward the ceiling and then back at Liz. "The phone call." His eyes were twinkling, and that damn smile. "We definitely need to discuss that."

"We do, huh?" Liz wasn't sure where this was going, although he was clearly feeling playful.

"We do."

His eyes were getting sexier by the minute.

Bringing her hand up to his waist, he asked, "Do you like the new jeans?"

"Oh, shit, are you serious?" She started undoing buttons…two down, and she slipped her right hand around to put it down inside his jeans and grab his ass. She started breathing faster and reached up to kiss him.

He said, "You're two buttons down with your right hand on my ass." His voice was husky, and he was breathing hard. "Please do the rest."

"Do you want it just like the phone call?" She started slowly unbuttoning with her left hand while asking. "Or maybe slower, with more teasing?" She slid her left hand down inside and cupped him, leaning her head against his chest for a moment, breathing as hard as he was, and then started fondling him, rolling her fingers, and gently tugging.

"Shit, that feels amazing." He closed his eyes, humming softly in pleasure as she shifted up to grip the base of his shaft.

"So, teasing?" she asked, stroking up with her pinky, "Or straight to business?" She ran her pinky back down again. She moved her right hand over to grip him and moved her left hand back down to continue fondling.

Tom appeared to have forgotten she'd asked a question and was just standing with his eyes closed, breathing in measured breaths.

Liz smiled and said, "I guess it's dealer's choice."

She played with him, using his lubrication to make his shaft slide in her hand, spending time focusing attention around the head, until he was moaning every time she moved her hand along his length.

When she wasn't sure he would last much longer, she pulled his jeans and boxer briefs down far enough that she could run her tongue along the underside of his hard shaft and then took him into her mouth. She circled the head of his cock with her tongue as she stroked and fondled him with her hands, moaning slightly in her own pleasure, as he rested his hands on her head and began moving his hips. She used her tongue to press him against the roof of her mouth and, very suddenly, began sucking hard.

"Shit. Oh, shit. Liz, I'm gonna come," and he roared, caught almost by surprise by the suddenness and intensity of his orgasm. He slid down the cabinets to the floor, saying, "Holy shit," under his breath over and over, until his breathing came back to something that resembled normal.

"That was...I don't even know what that was." Tom looked at Liz and laughed. He had his head back against the cabinets. "Fuck, Liz. You're like every wet dream I ever had, wrapped up in a best friend." He turned his head to look at her, the corner of his mouth quirked up in that devastating smile, his eyes still hazy with pleasure. "I don't even know how to deal with you. You're not supposed to exist."

Liz stood up and grabbed the Chinese food and beer off the counter and brought it down to them.

"You already know you're my personal fantasy. You're definitely not supposed to exist." She thought for a moment. "By the way, the best friend part is included in the fantasy. My fantasies are very thorough and specific."

He chuckled and started eating.

"Eat up. You're going to need your strength. You've got a long night ahead of you."

Tom looked confused for a moment. "What are you talking about?"

Liz squinted over the bowl of Chinese food and spoke with her mouth full. "I told you I keep score. You're gonna be busy."

Tom smiled as he took a drink of beer and grumbled quietly, "A real wet dream wouldn't keep score."

Liz almost choked as she tried not to laugh. She tried to stifle the snorts. She looked over at Tom and saw his eyes were bright with suppressed laughter. She waited as he took another drink from his beer and said, very seriously, "A real fantasy wouldn't be eating bare-assed with his junk hanging out."

He lost it and spewed beer. Liz shouted in victory, and they both laughed until their sides hurt and they couldn't breathe. It started up again when they tried to stand up, because Tom stopped, grabbed the counter, and said, "Shit, my ass is asleep." They were both laughing so hard it was a minor miracle that Tom ended up wearing his jeans, and the kitchen floor ended up somewhat clean by the time they were done.

Chapter Thirty-Three

They spent Thanksgiving with Chris and Paige, as usual, and later that day, after driving back to Liz's apartment, Tom surprised her by saying, "I would love it if you would come to Minnesota with me for Christmas. My parents want to meet you."

Liz stared at him. "Really? Are you sure?"

Tom laughed at her. "Am I sure my parents want to meet you? Yes. They've only asked me about fifty times."

"No, not that. Are you sure you want me to go?" She looked worried, and Tom got concerned.

"Yes." He held her face and looked in her eyes. "Yes, Liz. I want you to come with me to Minnesota to meet my family. Please." He pulled her in for a hug.

"Okay." She looked up at him and smiled. "I'm a nervous flyer, though. I get very anxious. I'm just warning you well in advance."

"Really?"

She nodded.

"Huh. I'm surprised. You don't seem to be

261

intimidated by much of anything. I didn't realize you weren't completely fearless."

She smirked and gave him a playful slap on the arm.

"Guess I'll have to come up with some strategy to keep your mind otherwise occupied during the flight."

He stood over her, looking down, emphasizing how much taller he was, making her feel the magnitude of his presence, and she shivered. Tom brought his hand up to cup her jaw softly, gently, and stroked his thumb across her cheek. His sheer size and strength contrasted with the soft tenderness of his caresses in a way that had Liz breathing faster within heartbeats.

"I think I can come up with a few things that might take your mind off of the plane trip."

He brought his lips to hers but didn't kiss her. He brushed his parted lips against hers and then back again, slowly. They were breathing together, his lips sliding over hers, almost not touching. He captured her lower lip with his mouth in a grasp so light it melted against her as he moved to do the same to her upper lip.

Bringing his other hand up to cup her jaw on the other side, Tom slid his hand to the back of her neck, into her hair. He tilted his head slightly, and his whisper soft kiss continued to move across her lips.

Liz didn't know how long she would be able to stand it. She slid her hands under Tom's shirt, around his chest and up his back, touching him softly, letting her fingers play over his muscles as he was letting his lips play over hers, and as his fingers were brushing over her face and playing in her hair. There was already a pulsing between her thighs, and when Tom softly and ever so lightly touched her tongue with his, the resulting shock and spasm made her press her legs together, and she briefly wondered if it would be possible she would have an orgasm just from this—this unbelievable, slow, sensuous, delicate, erotic, teasing kiss.

She must have made a whimpering sound, because Tom stopped to look at her. His eyes were dark with lust, clearly as aroused as she was, but the one in control. "So I think something like that might help you on a plane ride," he whispered.

Liz looked completely confused. "What?" she whispered back.

Tom chuckled deep in his chest and pulled her into his arms firmly. "If I managed to make you forget we were even talking about plane rides with one kiss, I think I will be able to keep you occupied on our way to Minnesota."

"Was that a kiss?" She looked at him, still flushed and breathing hard, and tangled one hand in his hair. She dropped her voice back down to a whisper, "You almost made me come with that kiss, Tom."

"Really." He looked very pleased. And horny. But definitely pleased. "Then your plane trip should be lots of fun." He nuzzled her neck and said, in a voice that was now low and growly, "So you're turned on." He started undoing her jeans. "And I'm hard as a rock." He was still speaking into her neck, pulling her clothing off. "And I can't stand another

263

minute of teasing." He tangled his hand in her hair, looked up from her neck into her face. "And fuck if I don't just want to bend you over the back of your couch."

"Holy crap."

Clothing vanished, and the same man who had just been touching her so delicately now turned her around, bit the back of her neck where it met her shoulder, pushed her over the back of her couch, and entered her in one hard, deep thrust. She spread her legs wider, angling so he could reach as deeply as possible, and held on as Tom rode her, bucking back to meet his thrusts. He held her hips and pumped deeply and powerfully, stroking in and out of her with the steady rhythm of a man wanting to make this last.

"I've been wanting to do this all day. All fucking day."

Liz was gasping and starting to moan with his thrusts. Her earlier arousal meant she was close to coming already.

"God damn, Liz, you are so fucking sexy." He paused, adjusted her, leaned over, and bit her gently again as he started moving. The change in angle was good for both of them; Liz was incredibly close to an orgasm, and Tom changed his pace, thrusting faster and deeper.

"Tom." It was a groan. "Oh, Tom." A moan of pleasure.

"I want to feel you come. I want to feel it. Come on my cock, Liz."

Liz put her head down and yelled into the cushion as she climaxed around him. He continued to pump into her, holding her hips, and growled in victory as he felt her pulsing around him. Pausing one more time, breathing hard, he made one more change of angle and then began thrusting into her as fast and hard and he could, sweating, grunting with the exertion, and finally shouting out his climax in the primal roar Liz loved so well, gripping her hips so hard there was a chance of bruises, pounding into her with each surge, until he was utterly spent.

"Holy shit." Liz was still speaking into the cushions.

Tom started laughing and stroked his hands on her back. "Every wet dream I've ever had, Liz." He placed kisses down her spine and said, "God, I love you."

She turned around and smiled as he pulled her up for a real kiss. "I love you too." She looked at him under her lashes. "Every one, huh?"

His eyes got smoky again, and he growled. "Shit, I really, really love you. If I think of any others, I'll let you know."

***

"Everything is set for our trip. With one issue." Tom looked at Liz. "My mother has decreed we have to have separate bedrooms."

"Okay."

Tom looked a little irritated, so she asked, "Are you upset?"

"Yes! I'm a grown-ass man! This is so fucking irritating."

Liz smiled and said, "Well, what if Colleen was

bringing a boyfriend home?"

"What?"

"Would it be okay if she brought a boyfriend home and they shared a room?"

Tom looked shocked. "Hell, no!"

"Why not?"

"She's twenty-two! That's not the same at all."

Liz thought for a moment. "How about Erin? She's twenty-five. Would that be okay?"

Tom's eyebrows furrowed. "It's still not the same."

Liz's mouth twitched. "Because she's still too young at twenty-five? Or because she's a girl?"

"No! Maybe." He gave her a half-hearted glare. "Why aren't you just letting me rant about this?"

"Because your mom is trying to be fair *and* trying not to compromise her beliefs. I can get behind that."

Tom just stared at her. "You are so fucking confusing."

Liz laughed. "Hey, I'm just a guest. I'll follow whatever rules are laid out for me." She wrapped her arms around his waist and looked up. "Besides, we can probably find time to slip away at some point, right?" She took a breath and then squeezed him a little tighter. "Are you sure this is all going to be okay?"

Tom was surprised. "Of course. Why not?"

"I don't know. I'm finding this scary. It doesn't help that I don't like flying, but honestly, I can't remember the last time I actually cared this much whether people like me or not."

He took her face in his hands, looking in her

eyes. "Really?"

She nodded.

"Sweetheart, it will be fine. I love you." His eyes twinkled. "And I have a pretty good feeling my family is going to love you too."

***

Liz knew Tom's parents immediately when she saw them. His father was an older version of Tom, minus a few inches and the beard and with grey hair rather than light brown. His face showed age, but the lines appeared at the corners of his eyes and mouth, as if they were mostly from smiling, rather than from worries. His blue eyes sparked with a twinkle when he caught sight of his eldest son.

Tom's mother was lovely and rather petite by comparison. Where Tom Sr. stood around six-foot-one, Kathleen looked to be closer to five-foot-five, perhaps a little bit shorter, but carried herself with the bearing of a woman who knew her worth. Her hair was also greying but looked to have been blonde when she was younger, and it framed a face that was kind, with a warm smile. Rather than the dark blue of her husband and son, her eyes were a beautifully light, and surprisingly bright, shade of blue.

The greeting was warm and loving between Tom and his parents. They were clearly a very close family, and his mother and father both pulled Liz in for hugs to welcome her, insisting she call them Tom and Kathleen. When she asked about confusion between the two Toms, they laughed, and his dad said, "Oh, no, there's never a problem. That one there," he pointed at his son, "is Tommy. I'm Tom."

Her Tom smiled and shook his head, looking a little sheepish, as if he had been somehow transported back to childhood. Addressing Liz, he said, "You can never grow out of what your parents and siblings called you when you were a kid. Believe me, I've tried. I even tried to get them to call me Micky, but that never stuck, either."

Kathleen turned back around as she was walking, saying over her shoulder, "I didn't name him Micky, or Michael. I named him Thomas, and we called him Tommy."

"The only other choice I was given was the full 'Thomas Daniel McCullin,' and hearing my parents calling me that was never good news…"

Liz laughed at the image that created.

"…so I put up with Tommy." He bent down and whispered in her ear. "But not from you. I have always loved hearing you call me Tom. From the first day we met."

She looked at him under her lashes and smiled.

His parents drove them to a rental car place closer to their house—Liz and Tom could have taken care of all of that on their own near the airport, but his parents had wanted to come meet him, so they had agreed. When they arrived at the McCullin house, the rest of the siblings and spouses were already there.

Liz had "met" some of them online—she was Facebook friends with Joe's wife, Anita, for instance—but meeting everyone in person was chaotic and wonderful, and overwhelming, even for a confirmed and dedicated extrovert. If this had been a random party full of people, she may or may not ever see again there would have been no stress, but she was actively concerned that these folks might not like her.

Liz firmly believed that people who enjoy each other's company would gravitate together; people who didn't would drift apart, and that's fine. It's human nature.

But this group of people right here...she wanted them to like her. Logically, she knew there wasn't a damn thing she could do about it, except to be herself and hope for the best. And logically she also knew there was no way that Tom's family was going to be a bunch of jerks. But the emotional centers in her brain didn't always like to listen to the logic circuits, no matter how much sense they were making.

Interestingly enough, the one person who she had felt pretty confident she would connect with, Tom's youngest sister, Colleen, was very standoffish. Rather obviously so. Not quite to the point of being hostile, but enough that Tom pulled Colleen aside after a while to ask her what was going on.

"Nothing, Tommy. I don't know what you're talking about. I'm tired and have a headache. Maybe that's it."

***

Liz snuggled under the covers on the day bed in

the small guest room. It looked like Tom's mom might use it as a sewing room—the table on one wall looked like it might house a sewing machine, and there was a stack of fabric on another smaller table next to it. And Liz thought she had seen a few quilts around the house; maybe Kathleen was a quilter? She filed away the question to ask at breakfast.

The day had been long, and the anxiety over the flight, and the trip in general, had taken its toll. She yawned, stretched, and flexed her feet and legs, luxuriating in the crisp sheets, and smushed her face into the soft down pillow.

Tom's family had been lovely, of course. The logical part of her brain had known they would be, even while the emotional part had been doing a tap dance all over her nerves.

The doorway cracked open, and a familiar six-foot-four silhouette briefly blocked the light before slipping in and closing the door behind him.

"Are you awake?"

It was a quiet whisper, very low, very sexy, and Liz was suddenly very, very awake.

"Yes."

He moved quietly through the dark room, not saying anything further. She just waited and watched in the moonlight as he took the chair from in front of the sewing table and silently tipped it under the door knob. He came over to the bed, took the pillow, and put it on the floor. The floor was carpeted, and there was a soft, fluffy throw rug on top of that, as well.

Tom gently took her hand and stood her up. She

was wearing loose pj's; he eased the bottoms off, and she stepped out of them. Tom was wearing a t-shirt and flannel pajama pants, which he also stepped out of, pulling her hand to himself gently for her to feel the extent of his arousal, breathing in sharply when she wrapped her hand around his hard shaft and stroked lightly.

He sat down on the rug, lay back on the pillow, and gently pulled Liz down to straddle his abs, his erection behind her. They kissed, lips parted, tongues dancing, breathing deepening...she could feel his hard cock twitching against her back, and Tom could feel her heat and wetness against his torso.

He put his mouth next to her ear and practically breathed the words to her. "I was going crazy knowing you were two rooms away. The bed squeaks, and the floor probably does too."

They kissed again. Tom's hands wandered up Liz's sides, brushing the undersides of her breasts. He moved so his thumbs gently caressed her nipples, feeling them tighten under his touch, and she gasped.

"We have to be seriously quiet," he breathed in her ear. "Light sleepers and a wakeful baby." He kissed her again. "Can you do that?"

She kissed him and pushed her tongue deep into his mouth, moved over to nip his earlobe, and whispered, "Yes."

Liz shifted down Tom's body, putting his erection in front of her. She wrapped her hand around his shaft and stroked a few times, enjoying the feel of the soft skin covering his hard cock. She leaned her other hand on his shoulder and lifted up enough to rub the precum-covered tip of him against her clit for a few moments. Tom made a small hiss.

Liz shifted so that the head of his cock was at her entrance and pressed down. She was wet, and he was slick, but they had not been fooling around very long yet tonight, and she was still very tight. She worked him in and out slowly, a little deeper each time. Each movement was creating more lubrication; each deeper thrust slipped inside just a little more easily. On the last downward stroke, when she finally took him all the way in, she bent forward and ground her clit against Tom's public bone. She was shaking as she leaned over to kiss his chest and realized that he was sweating and had the throw rug in a death grip.

Tom opened his eyes as Liz sat up and smiled down at him. He had begun to doubt his ability to go through with this plan the moment she had grabbed hold of him. Wild thoughts had crashed through his head all at once—how bad would it really be if his parents and siblings knew he was banging his girlfriend in the next room?

Would his sister really care if the baby woke up because the bed was rhythmically thumping into the wall?

Did he even care anymore if anyone heard what he sounded like having sex?

What if he just grabbed Liz, threw her on the bed, and...

She put her hands on his chest and started to move, riding him in a slow back and forth grinding motion. Her smile was gone, replaced by slightly parted lips. Her eyebrows were knit together in a look of concentration, and her eyes were no longer focused on his face. She leaned on him, holding his shirt in her grip, and caught her bottom lip between her teeth as she continued to move, grinding against him, ever so slowly increasing speed and pressure.

Her head dropped down so her hair framed her face in the moonlight. Tom let go of the rug and grabbed her hips, breathing heavily through his nose to try to avoid groaning and growling with each breath. He was having to focus to keep from making his normal pleasure sounds; having to keep silent was taking an unexpected amount of effort. It was as if not having the vocal outlet was causing physical pressure. He gripped her hips tighter, trying to maintain control while he felt himself building toward orgasm.

Liz leaned down to her forearms and balled her hands into his shirt, pressing her forehead against his chest. She was grinding on him faster now. Leaning forward put more pressure on her clit and meant that she could feel Tom's cock sliding in and out of her further than before with each forward and backward movement. She increased the rocking motion, pulling her hips further under each time she pressed forward, and pushing them further up on every backward stroke. The friction was sending her climbing toward release, and she tried not to pant and moan.

Tom put his feet on the floor and started thrusting against her with a silent urgency, and her movements became erratic, almost frantic. He tipped his head back into the pillow, eyes squeezed shut, feeling the pressure building.

Her climax slammed into her. She felt every muscle in her body spasm at once. Thighs squeezed, core compressed as if she was doing a sit up, hands almost tore his shirt, and every internal muscle clamped around Tom. And then pulsed again. And again. And again. She took a gasping breath. And then she felt him.

Tom felt her orgasm squeeze every part of him, and it pushed him over the edge. He felt his balls tighten and gave a final thrust. He held Liz tight to his body as he ejaculated, his face screwed up in what looked almost like agony, trying not to make a sound, digging his fingers into her hips. He felt as if all of the pressure of keeping silent was forcing itself out through his cock, surging into her as he erupted.

Liz collapsed on his chest, and they lay there breathing for a few minutes trying to recover. Liz finally let Tom slip out of her and rolled partially off him. She felt boneless. She snuggled up to Tom's ear and whispered, "I don't think I can walk."

She felt him smile, and he quietly made an amused sound. In a very gallant move, he picked her up and put her back into bed, tucking her in with a kiss.

"You're amazing," he whispered in her ear.

He picked up the pillow and tucked it under her head. He put his pants back on, picking hers up and putting them under the covers with her, so she could put them on later. He then quietly moved to the door, unhooked the chair, and returned it to its place by the table. Liz watched this all through half-lidded eyes.

He opened the door a crack, and she saw his silhouette framed in the doorway for just a moment before he closed the door behind him.

He turned down the hall and almost walked directly into Joe. Joe looked at Tom, looked at the doorway, raised an eyebrow, and smiled.

"Shut up," whispered Tom.

"I didn't say a word," Joe replied in a whisper, still smiling. He let Tom get two more steps down the hall before he whispered after him, "By the way, Tommy, your pants are inside out."

Tom flipped him the bird as he disappeared into his bedroom, but he was smiling as he lay down on his bed and was asleep in moments.

Chapter Thirty-Four

Colleen was sitting at the kitchen table when Liz joined her. It had become increasingly obvious she was not happy with Liz's presence, and Liz wanted to figure out if there was anything she could do to ease the tension between them. Everyone else except Tom and his mom had gone out for various last-minute errands, so this seemed like the perfect opportunity.

"Hey. So, it feels like we've gotten off on the wrong foot, and I'm not sure why. Do you have any questions for me? I think Tom has probably shared some of my history, and I can certainly understand that being a cause for concern." She paused for a moment and chucked, "Objectively speaking, on paper, I guess I can seem sketchy as hell. If you want to ask me about anything, I would be happy to talk to you about it."

Colleen looked at her skeptically.

"If you ask something I don't want to share, I'll let you know. But I'm pretty open, and there aren't many topics that are off limits."

Colleen sat up straight and met her eye. "Are you going to hurt him?"

Liz blinked. "Yes. Certainly."

Colleen looked shocked.

"And he's going to hurt me," Liz continued. "And hopefully we will find ways to forgive each other, until the next time it happens. Because we're human, and we screw things up. Those parts suck. But the parts in between are pretty amazing."

Still meeting her eye without any hesitation, Colleen asked, "Do you love him?"

"So much that it scares me sometimes."

"Does it scare you enough to run?"

Liz sighed. "It scares me to think that he will."

Colleen's look hardened. "He won't."

Liz tried to keep any look of doubt from her face, but must have failed, because Colleen sat forward with her elbows on the table, and her voice was angry. "He will let himself fuck up his entire career. So if you're not serious about this…"

Several things happened at once. Liz reached out and put her left hand on Colleen's arm and saw movement in the hallway to her right. Tom had apparently walked up just in time to hear that last bit of conversation and was ready to walk in to stop his sister from attacking his girlfriend.

Liz caught his eye and motioned subtly for him to stay, not to interfere, that she was okay and would handle this. Colleen couldn't see him from where she was sitting.

Turning back to Colleen, she said, "I'm serious." She paused, and she and Colleen looked at each other. Liz said, "Can I ask you something?"

"Yeah."

"How old were you when Tom and Michelle started dating?" Colleen was so startled by the question she sat completely back in her chair. "You must have been young."

"I was ten. Why?"

"So you were, what, fourteen when everything fell apart?"

"Yes. Why are you asking?"

"Because this," she gestured, indicated the interaction that had been taking place between the two of them, "feels really personal, even though we just met." Liz paused for a moment, thinking, and then asked, "Was she your friend? Did you like her?" Her questions were kind, and curious, not accusatory, and Colleen answered almost without thinking about it.

"Yes. She treated me as if I were important even when they started dating, not just like I was a little kid. I was going to be in the wedding." Colleen smiled sadly. "I was helping to pick out colors and dresses."

Liz sat quietly and waited for her to continue. Out of the corner of her eye she saw that at some point Tom's mom had joined him in the hallway.

When she continued, Colleen's voice was a bit rough. "She didn't say goodbye, you know. She just disappeared. She treated him like shit and then vanished." Her eyes looked a little haunted by the memories of it.

"And you were just fourteen." Liz paused, her look gentle. "You weren't even old enough to truly understand what had happened between them. It must have been so confusing." She leaned forward. "Colleen, did you talk to anyone about this when it happened? Besides your friends?" Colleen shook her head, and Liz pressed. "Not Tom? Not your parents?"

Choking out a strangled laugh, she replied, "God, no. Everyone was worried he was going to lose his career. Or do something even worse. He was so hurt and so angry. It was awful."

"It was probably scary as hell too. I can't even imagine. But you were hurting too."

Colleen shrugged.

"They love you. *Tom* loves you like crazy. You must know that."

This time Colleen smirked. "I'm ten years younger than he is. We're not very close."

"Really? Because I've heard more about you than any of your siblings. He talks about you all the time." At the skeptical look from Colleen, Liz continued, "Brilliant, full ride to UConn, internship in New York City," ticking off the points on her fingers. "He's so proud of you." And she added with a grin, "And he and Joe were seriously considering coming up to beat the crap out of the last guy you were dating, because apparently he was really not good enough for you."

This earned a laugh from Colleen. "Okay, that last part definitely sounds like him."

"Will you talk to them?"

"My parents? Or Tommy?"

"Both."

This earned a sigh from Colleen, but she agreed.

"Promise me. I won't say anything to them, but

279

promise me that you will."

Another sigh. "I promise."

Liz sat back and smiled. "Good." She paused for a few seconds, weighing her options, and then said, "So I'm about to do something that might really piss you off. I'm going to save you some time. You've already told them."

She looked over at Tom and his mom just long enough to see that both of their faces were a mess of confused emotions. Kathleen was crying; Tom had his head back against the wall and deep furrows in his brow.

Liz made sure they were moving into the kitchen as she walked out the other way and looked back just long enough to see them both wrap Colleen up in a hug that threatened to squash her. Colleen was crying now too.

***

Tom knocked softly on the bedroom door before letting himself in. Liz was sitting on the bed, reading a book. She had retreated there, wanting to give the family time to talk and sort things out if they needed to. He sat down on the bed next to her.

"I'm sorry, Tom. It's a huge downside to my 'no regrets' policy. I accuse Paige of meddling, but I'm so much worse in so many ways."

"How did you know?"

"That I'm worse than Paige?"

"No." He shook his head, frustrated that she wasn't following his train of thought. "About Colleen. How did you know?"

"Oh. I didn't. Not really. I just knew there was something more than her just being worried about you. She was too angry at me for it to be only that." She smiled. "I hadn't been here long enough to piss her off that much yet."

Tom stared at her and shook his head.

"She's a lot like you, though."

"Really? How so?"

"She can't hide anger, either. It's written on her face, and it looks just like your anger does." She smiled at him, and he pulled her in close to him. "Are we okay, Tom? I just poked into your family in ways I really had no right to. Should I be making new plane reservations?"

He laughed. "Holy shit, Liz. No." He held her so he could look her in the eye. "No. We're good. You and I, and you and my family. I promise. Col wants to talk to you. I came up here to get you."

"You promise I'm not going to get locked out of the house? It's cold outside."

"God, you can be an idiot." He grabbed her hand and dragged her out of the room. "Come on."

He brought her back to the kitchen, where Colleen and Kathleen were sitting together at the table, talking. Colleen got up and came over and gave Liz a huge hug.

Liz said, "I'm sorry. I poke where I have no right to."

Colleen said, "Don't be an idiot. Thank you."

Liz laughed and looked at Tom, with a "see-she's-just-like-you" expression. Kathleen hugged her too, and they managed to turn the conversation to mundane things and funny stories about Tom, or

281

rather, Tommy, as a kid. Before too long the rest of the family returned, and the house was noisy and busy again.

Tom pulled Liz away to stand near the Christmas tree and looked down at her, tucking her hair behind her ear and stroking her jaw with his thumb.

"I don't understand you." He smiled. "Not even a little. But I love you a whole lot."

He kissed her then, in the soft glow of the tree lights, pulling her close to him, his arm snug around her waist, his other hand now tangled in her hair. He felt one of her hands gently stroking the back of his neck and playing with his hair as they pressed closer together. Their tongues were meeting softly, gently moving together, when a deep-voiced throat was cleared nearby.

Tom released her and looked up to find his father trying not to look directly at them.

"Your mother could use some help." He started to walk away and then added, "I was going to wait until you finished kissing her, Tommy, but I was starting to doubt I was going to live that long."

Tom chuckled, and then, to Liz's surprise he called after his father, "Anything worth doing is worth doing right." They heard big Tom's laughter in return, and Tom gave Liz a lopsided grin that made her heart flip before heading off to help his mom.

Chapter Thirty-Five

"Why the hell do you even know that?"

Tom yelled in laughing frustration as Colleen and Liz high-fived, and the group of family members playing a trivia game laughed. Liz had just won another round because she had correctly answered that a group of jellyfish was called a "smack."

"I warned you, Tom. My competitive side is small, but highly focused. And I know stuff. About things. Lots of stuff about lots of things."

"Don't mess with her at 'Words With Friends,' either," said Joe's wife, Anita. "She's currently trouncing me, and I'm usually the one beating all of you guys at that game."

"Small, but highly focused."

"I can't take this anymore. I'm out." Tom got up and grabbed his jacket to walk out on the front porch for some fresh air. Joe was outside drinking a glass of whisky and smoking a cigar. "You have another glass out here?"

"It just so happens I do." He poured a glass for

Tom and then offered him a cigar. "Did you want one of these as well, or would that be sullying your temple?" he asked with a smile, gesturing up and down at Tom.

"Shut the fuck up." Tom took the cigar, and they stood together quietly, smoking and sipping, watching their family through the front window. The girls inside were laughing and talking, the game obviously forgotten by this point. "Oh, geez, I know which story she's telling just by the body language," said Tom, watching Colleen exaggeratedly flail about and the others laugh.

Particularly Liz, who had never heard the story before. She was lying on the floor holding her stomach she was laughing so hard. It was about Tom, of course, when he was a young teenager. "Col was like two years old when that happened. She can't possibly remember it. Why does she always tell that story?"

"Because she tells it the best. I mean look at that." He gestured through the window for the finish. "It's fantastic. She captures that moment perfectly. Better than a video camera."

"Man, you are such an asshole," Tom said, grinning. "Sometimes I forget that, you know? And then I come visit, and it all comes back to me..."

The two of them stood quietly for a few more minutes, enjoying the scene. Things were quieting down, and folks were wandering off. Liz and Anita had gotten up off the floor and were sitting on the couch talking. Nothing serious, by the look of it. Anita had pulled out her phone, so she was probably showing pictures of the house they had recently purchased.

Joe finally broke the silence when the cigars were about half gone and they were on the second glass of whisky. "You going to ask Mom for Grandma Ellie's ring?" They were still watching inside the house, not looking at each other.

"I was going to originally." This comment earned him a mildly surprised look from Joe, although Tom continued to watch Liz and Anita inside the house.

"What happened?"

"Mom stopped me in the hallway and handed it to me." He turned to Joe finally and saw Joe with one eyebrow raised and a smile on his face. "She said, 'Your dad and I thought you might need this.'"

Joe stubbed out his cigar, chuckling to himself. "Shit." He tossed back the remainder of the whiskey in his glass, slapped his big brother on the back, and said, "You're doomed, Tommy. Welcome to the club."

***

The entire family attended midnight mass at the McCullins' church. Liz had brought a deep navy business suit to wear and a dark red silk blouse, plus heels. She was rewarded by Tom's surprised, and very amorous, look when she came out of her room.

"Wow."

"Just because I don't do it often doesn't mean I don't know how," she teased. "I can change a tire too. I just don't want to do that every day, either." She winked at him.

285

"You look beautiful. Truly." He kissed her and then was interrupted when his father yelled down the hall.

"Don't start, Tommy. We don't have that kind of time before we need to leave."

Tom laughed softly, took Liz's hand, and they joined the rest of the family to head to the church.

The service was beautiful, with candlelight and carols, and the warmth of family. It was almost overwhelming to Liz—Tom's family had included her, made her feel like she belonged with them, and she was standing next to the man she loved, who loved her. It felt magical, almost fragile.

This was something she had never felt before, had never experienced before. Not with her family, not with Jimmy's, not with Chris and Paige.

Tom happened to look down at her and saw the awe, bordering on fear, in her face, and touched her cheek to turn her to him. His eyes questioned hers, asking silently if she was all right. She smiled to reassure him, her eyes bright with tears, and leaned against his shoulder, feeling the strength of his presence and the warmth of his body.

They rode back to the house together with his parents, content to listen to Christmas music on the radio and hold hands in the backseat of the car. It was peaceful, and there was a quiet contentment neither one wanted to break by talking too much.

Tom and Liz sat together on the couch in the glow of the tree lights as the others got started off for bed, not quite ready to call it a night yet. She was nestled against him with his arm around her, sitting together in the way that had felt right and familiar from the very first night they had sat together on her couch.

"I want to give you your present now rather than tomorrow morning."

Liz looked up at him. "I thought we said the trip was our gift to each other? Changing the rules, sweetheart?" She was smiling, though, as if she had known it would happen.

"Yeah, well." He looked more closely at her face. "Ah, you can't fool me, Williams. You did it too."

His crooked smile twisted her heart. Every time. "Maybe. But you'll have to wait until tomorrow to find out." She blinked with feigned innocence. "You might be a very disappointed young man."

"Oh, somehow I doubt that," he said, moving toward her to kiss her. "You have yet to disappoint me." He stopped himself. "But if I start this, you won't get your present tonight, because there's no way I'm going to remember what I was trying to do."

She looked at him with her best bedroom eyes.

"Minx."

She started at his knee and began to walk her fingers up his thigh, smiling at him playfully.

He grasped her hand in his, and said, "Everyone is still awake. I can't get away with visiting you tonight. And just thinking about that is making me consider taking you out to the backseat of the rental car." He looked seriously into her eyes for a minute and then shook his head. "It's like five degrees out and that still sounds like a great idea right now, just because you're looking at me like that."

She smiled and her eyes twinkled.

"Shit, now I'm thinking about the last time we were in the backseat of *my* car." He grabbed her by the shoulders and pushed her so she was sitting next to him but not touching him. "You. Stay there." His mock severity was adorable.

"Yes, sir. Six inches of separation." Her eyes were still sparkling. "Although I seem to recall someone telling me that wouldn't be enough for some reason…" Tom just shook his head at her.

He reached into his pocket and pulled out a smallish cardboard-type jewelry box and handed it to her with a shy smile. "Merry Christmas, Liz."

"Oh my goodness! No way," she said when she opened the box. "Tom, this is beautiful! I've never seen one like this. Where did you find it?" The necklace inside was a sterling silver chain with a sterling silver pendant in the shape of the Guardians logo, which was an homage to the armed forces—a stylized eagle head profile with outspread wings. The bale of the pendant was attached at a wingtip, so the pendant hung down at an angle. It was very beautiful and quite unique. It was clearly the Guards' logo if you knew what you were looking at, but otherwise it was an interestingly shaped silver pendant. She had never seen anything like it before.

"I had it made. So you like it?"

"Are you kidding?" She looked at him, and he could see in her eyes he had hit a home run with this. "I love it. Thank you."

"Turn it over."

She did and saw "#40" etched into the center.

He leaned down and in his deep, low voice said

into her ear, "*My* number, Liz."

The result of this was immediate. Her pulse raced and blood rushed toward all important erogenous zones. She started breathing hard. And fast. And she grabbed his hand, holding onto it for dear life, so she wouldn't do what she wanted to do, which was to grab other parts of him, right there, on his parents' couch.

Tom noticed all this and asked curiously, "Liz?" He was still talking into her ear. His voice was still the sexiest voice she had ever heard, and it made every part of her insides melt. "Am I imagining this, or did you just get really turned on?"

"Not imagining." She was trying not to think about what it felt like to grab his inner thigh.

Tom moved his lips to just below her ear and brushed them there.

Liz shivered through her whole body and whispered, "Tom, you are making me crazy."

He brushed aside her hair and moved his kiss closer to the back of her neck. She let go of his hand, turned to him, and pressed a kiss to his parted lips.

They had just reached a deep tangling of tongues when they were interrupted by a deep-voiced throat clearing behind them.

"Honestly, Tommy, either you were less trouble when you were seventeen, or you were better at not getting caught."

Tom's laughter was quiet but genuine. "Or maybe I just never dated anyone this much…fun."

"You did not just blame me!"

Tom just smiled that damn little smile that

twisted her heart, and big Tom laughed.

"I'm going to bed. You two…" he pointed at them, "Tommy, I know your mom is being a little over the top about not sharing a room here, but try to keep it together for one more day, okay?" He chuckled as he walked away and added, "Besides, it will make it that much better when you get home."

Liz stared at Tom, wide-eyed, and whispered, "Did your dad just give us sex advice?" She giggled, then snorted, because the look on Tom's face was a mixture of humor and horror.

They both started laughing, using the pillows to try to be quiet, eventually calming down enough to speak again.

"I love the necklace, Tom. And now I'm going to go to bed." She leaned in to kiss him, stopped, and said, "I'd better not. Although I really want to."

Tom stood up, pulled her close, and kissed the top of her head. "Merry Christmas, Liz. I will see you in the morning."

***

Christmas morning with a big family was a completely new experience for Liz, and she enjoyed every minute, from coffee and cinnamon rolls to weird, friendly, sibling rivalries and traditions (which brother was more inept at wrapping presents, whose job it was to get stockings down from the mantle, or hand out presents, et cetera). It was fun. Just plain, silly, loving fun.

Tom was handed a smallish, flat box with his name on it. Liz said, "It's possible that's from me," with a wink and a smile. She was wearing her new necklace.

"Ah, so you did break our agreement."

"I saw it as…not so much an agreement as a suggested course of action." She raised an eyebrow. "As did you. Open it."

Tom opened the box to find an envelope. The envelope was addressed to Joe. There was nothing else in the box. "Really?" He looked at Liz. "That's mean."

"Give the envelope to the addressee."

Tom handed it to Joe, who looked confused. Anita did not, Tom noted with interest. Joe's wife had a smile and a look of happy anticipation on her face.

Joe opened the envelope and pulled out and opened a folded page. A Guardians ticket was inside. He looked at the page, looked at Liz, and said, "Are you serious?" He turned to Anita. "Did you know about this?" She nodded, smiling like crazy.

Tom said, "What? What is going on? Liz, why is Joe so happy with my Christmas present?"

Joe said, "It's a plane ticket and a game ticket to come see you play in February."

Tom felt his heart catch and a knot in his gut.

"You can stay in my apartment while you're there. I'll stay with Paige and Chris in their guest room." Liz smiled and added, "There is one catch. I have the matching game ticket. You have to sit next to me, and I yell. A lot."

Tom looked at Liz, while the rest of his family chattered about this development. All his feelings showed on his face. "For his birthday?"

She nodded. "He hasn't seen you play since that night, has he?"

Tom closed his eyes. Liz stroked her thumb across the right side of his forehead, trying to smooth out the furrow that had started, not from anger, but from anxiety. "I did give you full and fair warning that I'm a pain in the ass, Tom."

He smiled a little, opening his eyes.

She looked at him, took his face in both her hands, and said, "What can I say, sweetheart? I get jealous too."

He looked confused.

"She's living in your head, and I want her to move out."

Tom leaned over to kiss her. It lasted long enough for Joe to say, "Oh, for God's sake, Tommy."

Standing up, Tom pulled Liz into his arms and held her, bending to say, "Thank you."

The rest of the family continued with other activities, allowing them to talk for a few minutes.

"Are we okay?"

"Yeah." He took a deep breath.

"Are you okay?"

Another breath. "I think so." He paused. "I will be."

Liz looked up at him from under her lashes. "I will be at the game. If you want, I will come out with you guys after the game." She smiled and winked and said, "Hell, if you want, we can arrange ways to sneak off and fool around while we're out." More seriously, she said, "Anything to change that narrative in your head. You should be able to have your brother come see you play any time without only having bad memories attached. That's your present, Tom. Merry Christmas."

His hug was almost crushing.

Chapter Thirty-Six

Tom hadn't been in a mood this foul in quite a while. Bad game last night, bad practice today, bad traffic, and an encounter with Zee, which had just pissed him off beyond reason. Sometimes he wondered if Zee goaded him on purpose, to see how many of Tom's buttons he had to push before Tom really did take a swing at him. It hadn't happened yet.

That didn't mean it wouldn't.

He arrived at Liz's apartment, trying to shake it off, but was still feeling ill-tempered when he let himself in. Liz greeted him with a hug, and he was standing holding her when her phone rang on the kitchen counter. Tom glanced over and saw it was Zee calling.

"Motherfucker!" Tom was instantly ramped up to full-tilt angry again, and Liz looked up at him in surprise, wondering what was going on. She looked over at the phone and shut the ringer off as Tom started pacing, letting off a stream of cursing that even she found impressive.

This had all happened quickly enough that she hadn't even asked what was wrong yet.

He turned to her, jaw set, voice angry, and said, "I'm walking out of here."

She looked instantly panicked, but he continued in the same tone without allowing her to say anything.

"I'm pissed off beyond reason, and I need to walk around, or I won't be able to think straight. I will come back. I love you, and I know you love me." He turned around and walked out the door.

Liz stared at the door. She tried to process what he had just said. Leaving. Coming back. He loved her. Knew that she loved him. These were all the things he knew she would need to hear so she wouldn't feel panicked and freaked out.

But she was panicking. And freaking out. Her heart was racing, and she felt like she couldn't quite catch her breath. It took her a few minutes to realize that was because she was crying.

He was angry and he left. But he said he was coming back. And the love thing. What the hell was going on in her head? The logical part of her brain was active and telling her that her reactions were making no sense, but the rest of her brain was steadfastly ignoring that part and telling it to fuck off while she had this complete meltdown.

Tom came back about forty minutes later, looking more relaxed after walking off the majority of his bad mood in the brisk weather. He was slightly dreading the encounter waiting back at the apartment but was hoping he had said enough before he left to alleviate some of Liz's fears.

When he got back in the apartment, he found Liz sitting on the couch, brow furrowed, holding her head in her hands as if trying to ease a headache. She had obviously been crying. A lot.

Shit.

"I'm sorry, Liz. I was so angry. I just needed to walk it off."

She looked up at him, almost confused. "You came back."

He sat down on the couch with her. "I said I would." He held her hand. "I love you. I wasn't leaving you. I just needed to clear my head."

She was still looking at him, brow furrowed, and said, "No. You don't understand. You came back. Twice. You weren't even supposed to come back the first time." Tom gripped her hand tighter. She wasn't making sense.

"Liz, are you okay?"

"No." She looked at him and then gave a choked half-laugh. "I think I broke my brain."

Tom looked so alarmed that she reached out to him. "Not in that way. I don't need an ambulance." He relaxed some but still looked worried.

"You're a fantasy, Tom. *My* fantasy. This was never supposed to be real. I don't think you understand, I always expected this to end, I just didn't know when. So when you walked out the first time, I was so sad, but not surprised. No one gets to keep their fantasy."

Tom was staring at her. He had a knot in his stomach and another one in his chest.

"When Paige first figured out about us, I explained to her that when the universe gives you a chance to fool around with your fantasy for a little while, you say, *'Yes.'* No matter how nice it is, he's still going to go back to his real life, and you're going to go back to yours. So you enjoy the hell out of it while it lasts, and you don't worry that it's not going to.

"So when you left, I just hoped we would be able to stay friends, because I really had such a good time with you. And I hoped that falling in love with you hadn't screwed up that part. But I didn't regret that, either. I didn't regret any of it. I could never regret loving you."

She knew she was babbling at this point, but she wasn't sure exactly where she was going with this, or even really what she was feeling, and she was hoping that if she just let the words out, somewhere, somehow, something was going to make sense.

The knot in Tom's stomach wasn't getting any smaller.

"But then you were such a bastard, and I thought, shit, we aren't going to be friends, and I don't even know why. But, *then,"* she stared at him, "you came back. You totally weren't supposed to do that." Everything about her softened, and her eyes were bright with tears. "And I was so happy. Because I love you so damn much. But it's confusing, because you're the hockey player, and I'm just me, and you weren't supposed to want that."

"What? Liz, I don't understand." The knot in his chest wasn't getting any smaller, either.

"So, here we are, months later, and you just left again."

He was staring at her.

"And you said you would come back, and you fucking came back again." She was crying now. "And my brain snapped, because if you keep coming back, then that means that this is real. And if it's real, then I can really lose you." She started crying harder. "If I could never really have you, then I could never really lose you." She looked startled, and he did too. "Oh, shit."

She looked scared.

Tom wrapped her in his arms and held her close. "This is real, Liz. *We* are real. You might be the most real thing I've ever had in my life."

She put her arms around his neck and sobbed as if she might never stop. "I love you. Oh God, I don't want to lose you."

Tom held her while she cried, stroking her hair. The knots in his chest and stomach had evaporated. This had obviously been a long time coming. It was the first time he had seen her completely vulnerable in this way.

***

Liz was bone-weary tired when she finally stopped crying. "I feel like I've been run over by a truck."

"Emotional shit is exhausting."

Liz looked at him with surprise.

"What?" He kissed the top of her head and asked, "Did Becks ever tell you about the night after the pool party when I had acted like such an asshole to you?"

Liz sat up to look at him. "No. I never heard anything about what happened in between the party and the night on the rooftop." She thought for a moment. "Oh, except for the slap. Paige did tell me that."

"Oh, shit. Yeah, that was impressive. She's tiny but fierce." He smiled at Liz. "Becks forced me to see that I had been treating you as if you were Michelle. Actually, that I was treating you worse than I had ever treated her. The realization made me sick. Like, vomiting sick."

Liz's eyes got wide.

"And then he managed to make me realize that the reason I was doing that was because I had fallen in love with you. More puking. It was exhausting."

Liz gave a tired, half laugh. "Oh, my sweetheart. You just told me that realizing you loved me made you puke. You are so romantic. I shall treasure this moment."

Tom barked out a laugh and said, "I hadn't been in love since Michelle. Although, God, I look back and I can't even compare what I felt for her and what I have with you." He pulled her close, and she sighed.

"I hadn't been with anyone since Jimmy."

Tom caught the phrase and asked, "Wait, no one?"

"No. I mean, I went out to a few dinners, but there was nothing."

Tom turned so he could look her in the eye.

"What?"

"But…" he looked confused. "I thought…wait…was I the first?"

299

She smiled. "Since Jimmy? Yeah."

"But that's been…"

"Years. Yes."

His eyes were huge. "Holy shit." He smiled and said, "Damn, Liz. Don't take this the wrong way, but how?"

"How what?" She was genuinely confused by the question, but he was adorable in the way he was asking, like this was something he didn't believe was possible.

"How did you not…I mean…" He struggled for words, and Liz started smiling. "You're rather insatiable. Years? Really?"

She laughed out loud. "Insatiable?"

He grinned.

It was adorable, and she kissed him and then climbed to straddle his lap. "Well, McCullin, at the risk of continuing to inflate your ego," she leaned in and whispered in his ear, "I've only ever been insatiable with you." Tom closed his eyes as she put her lips against his neck and then bit down gently. "You smell so good." She sat back for a moment and said, "That first night outside the restaurant, when you bent down so I could smell you…" She closed her eyes and sighed. "I wanted to bury my face in your neck."

He made a humming sound. "Mmm. And I wanted you to. I felt your breath on my neck and had already lost track of what we were talking about."

"And then, when you kissed me, I wanted to push you up against your car."

He pulled her in close and spoke in a low, husky

voice. "I held you away from me, because I started getting hard almost immediately when I started kissing you. If you had touched me, we would have had our first time in the backseat. Or maybe standing against my car."

"It's never been like that for me with anyone else."

She had pushed further forward, so she was riding on what was developing into a lovely, hard bulge in his jeans. "I have never wanted anyone the way I want you. All the time." She pressed against him and said again, "All the time, Tom."

"Insatiable. I told you."

"Yes, sweetheart. I'm your insatiable puck bunny."

Tom laughed out loud and pulled her in to kiss her.

***

"Paige, do you have time to get together? I need to talk to you. In person." She took a breath. "There's nothing wrong, I just need to sort some things out in my head and I need a sounding board."

"Yes. Yes, of course. I'm on my way over."

"No, let's meet for coffee somewhere. I have a feeling I would think better in public, where I have to stay more logical."

Paige blinked. "Okay…you promise everything is all right?"

"I promise."

They met at the same Starbucks where they had talked after the charity formal. Liz was waiting for

Paige this time, with two cups of coffee in front of her. She told Paige about what had happened the night before, from Tom leaving in anger to her realization about still not believing the relationship would last. Paige listened quietly.

"He promised me this is real. He said I'm the most real thing he's ever had in his life." Her eyes were a little too bright, and she looked at her friend for help.

"Do you believe him?"

Liz covered her mouth, blinked a few times, put her hand down, smiled a small smile, and whispered, "Yes." A few tears leaked out that she wiped away.

Paige smiled and blinked away a few tears of her own and asked, "How does it feel?"

"It's scary. I'm scared, Paige."

Paige reached across the table and took her hand. Liz tried to control her breathing, gripping Paige's hand. Paige looked worried for a moment but then started smiling at her.

"What? Why are you smiling?"

"Just breathe, Liz. Give it a minute. You'll be okay."

Liz slowed her breathing, looking at her friend.

Paige's smile was just getting bigger.

Liz let out a tiny laugh and whispered, "Holy shit."

"Right?"

Liz put her hand back up to cover her mouth, and her eyes got wide. And then she laughed. "Holy shit, Paige." She sat back in her chair and looked at Paige. "The hottest, most amazing man I have ever imagined in my entire life is completely in love with me. Holy. Shit."

"So how does it feel now?"

"Fucking amazing."

Chapter Thirty-Seven

They had just arrived back at Liz's apartment after dinner out with Chris and Paige.

"That was so much fun," Liz said.

They had spent the entire evening talking and laughing. Chris and Tom had been in rare form, telling team stories that were actually fit for sharing, digging deep into the past from when they were much younger kids. The locker room pranks were just ridiculous.

"I haven't laughed so much with them in a long time. Very therapeutic."

Liz took off her jacket, draped herself on the couch, kicked off her shoes, and stretched out, taking up much more room than was necessary.

Tom stood looking at her quietly for a few minutes, just drinking in the sight of her. He was still wearing his jacket, his hands in the pockets. He looked at the shape of her face, the way her eyes always appeared as if she was just about to smile. He followed the contour of her neck and collarbone and looked at the spot just under her ear. That was where he breathed in her scent when he held her. Or her hair; he loved to smell her hair when he was holding her with her head tucked under his chin.

Liz said, "I promise I will make some room on the couch for you." When he said nothing, she turned her head to look at him. "Tom? Are you okay?"

He said yes, but it didn't sound quite right to her. "You haven't taken your jacket off, and you're still standing by the door."

"Oh, sorry." He took off his jacket and came over but sat rather stiffly at the other end of the couch.

Liz's nerves were on edge by this point. Something was wrong.

"Please, Tom. You're suddenly anxious as hell, and I don't know why. I'm not sure what's gone wrong in the last five minutes."

"Nothing! Shit. Nothing is wrong, Liz." Everything about him softened. "There is absolutely nothing wrong. Except possibly what I'm doing right now."

She took a breath. "Okay. But you do realize that's really confusing, right? I'll take confusing over scary, don't get me wrong," she added with a smile.

Tom leaned back against the back of the couch. He looked at Liz, and with the half smile that melted her heart every time, he opened his hand. There was a small, well-worn box in his palm. Of the jewelry variety.

"I'm not doing this very well."

"Oh." Liz stared, her heart beating in weird

patterns. She felt lightheaded. "But you're so anxious. I don't ever want there to be that much anxiety between us. About anything." She looked at him. "Will it make a difference if I tell you that, if there's a question attached to that tiny box, I am going to say yes?"

I feel like I'm having an out of body experience.

Tom smiled at her, saying, "That definitely helps." He shook his head. "Liz, this is the strangest conversation I have ever had, and that is really saying something." He took a deep breath, let it out slowly, and said, "I am afraid you won't like it."

She blinked, trying to process this information. She moved closer to him, put her hand on his face, and stroked his beard. "All of this anxiety because you are worried I won't like what's in that tiny box?"

He nodded, closing his eyes.

"Tom, I am going to say yes. But this just means we don't know each other quite well enough yet. When you *know* I will love it before I see it, *that's* when we should do this." She kissed him and then said, "Please tell me I haven't just screwed up everything."

Tom wrapped her up in his arms. "No, it's all right. We'll wait." He backed up and looked at her. "But just for the record, a guy is supposed to be anxious during this. Nerves are part of the deal. Hell, I still get nervous before games." He held her, stroked her hair, and kissed her on the top of the head. Then he pushed back again and looked at her. "Wasn't Jimmy nervous?"

The question caught her so off guard that at first

she had no idea what he was talking about. Once her brain caught up to the question, she answered rather cautiously. "Actually, he was. Terribly so."

Tom smiled and said, "Tell me."

Liz searched his face for signs of anger or jealousy.

He took her hand in his and said, "Liz, tell me. He was important to you."

She blinked back tears and said, "It was stereotypical and so sweet. He took me to dinner at a very nice restaurant in Old Town, and then we went for a walk on the waterfront. I remember the weather was beautiful that night. He did the whole down-on-one-knee bit." She laughed, reminiscing. "I was utterly shocked. I said yes, obviously. But he had been so insanely nervous and weird all day I'm pretty sure I said the phrase, 'What the fuck is wrong with you, you idiot?' at least once."

Tom laughed, saying, "So apparently you insult all men who want to marry you. Good to know." Then he said, "Tell me more. What did the ring look like?"

She smiled. "We were young and totally broke; we really couldn't even afford to be going out to dinner at a restaurant that nice. The stone was from the ring from his mom's first marriage—she had kept the diamond specifically to give to him. He had a jeweler set it into sterling silver. It was a simple setting, low, not super tall or anything. I'm not sure how to describe it. It looked like an engagement ring."

"Do you still have it?"

Liz sighed. "No, after a while I gave it back to

his mom. She said I should keep it, but I could see how much it meant to her. He was their only child."

"Did you stay in touch with his parents?"

"I tried to, for a while. We had only met a few times before he died. He was from California, I grew up around here, and we met at college here. I only knew college and adult Jimmy. They knew child Jimmy and had barely had a chance to know him as an adult. It was like we didn't even lose the same person when he died." She looked at Tom. "I was never part of their family, not really. They tried. I tried. But ultimately, we needed to grieve separately. We slowly lost touch."

Liz hugged Tom tight. "Thank you for asking about our engagement. I haven't thought about that in forever. I'm not sure you know how much that means to me." She sat back and looked at him. "I'm thinking that asking in return would not be a kindness, so I won't pry into that. But I'm happy to listen if you'd like to talk. And you're right—this is definitely one of the strangest nights of conversation I've ever had. And my bar for that is set pretty damn high."

Tom surprised Liz by saying, "I bought Michelle the biggest ring I could afford when I graduated from Minnesota and started in the AHL. I had been a fifth-round pick for Montreal. She just heard 'NHL draft pick' and figured she was going to be the wife of a pro hockey player. But I started in the minors. Minor league players don't make a whole lot of money. She seemed fine with that, at first, although it was pretty clear she was disappointed. I heard her on the phone one night with her friend saying, '…and once he gets called up to the NHL, I can get finally get a big ring.'"

Liz cringed.

"I wasn't called up during my first season. I actually didn't get a break until my third season, and I was lucky at that. But during that first season Michelle got tired of waiting and started sleeping with one of my teammates right after he got called up the first time, figuring the Lynx would bring him up permanently soon. Which they did. She got her NHL pro, her big ring, and two years later her big divorce after she found him sleeping with one of his many puck bunnies." He looked at her. "I'm not even going to pretend I wasn't viciously thrilled by that. Thank God he had already been traded to Tampa Bay by the time I was playing in Montreal. I don't know what would have happened. I'm not sure I would have had a career."

Liz sat back for a moment and stared at him and then got up and got them each a beer from the fridge. She handed one to him and took a big drink of her own.

"I feel like I just met an entire part of you I have been missing this whole time," she said with a look of wonder on her face, taking another big drink. "Seriously, Tom. Holy crap. It's like you just handed me the last piece of a jigsaw puzzle, and I hadn't even realized there was a piece missing."

She finished her beer, chuckling to herself, and Tom said, "What?"

She looked at him, put her empty beer bottle on the floor, moved to stand in front of him, and took his beer from his hand. Drinking most of his beer too, she placed it on the side table and then very carefully and gently took the tiny jewelry box, which he still held in his hand, and placed it on the table as well. Then she straddled his lap and placed her arms around his neck.

"You." She laughed. "You, Tom. My sweet, wonderful, jealous, possessive," she started kissing him in between words, "suspicious, girlfriend-hiding, gorgeous," the kisses were getting longer, "spikey with your teammates," deep kiss, "smart, funny, talented," lots of tongue, "hard-working, formal event hating," he was beginning to forget what she was talking about, "passionate man," she breathed against his mouth. She was feeling fuzzy and warm from drinking the beer so fast, and deliriously happy, almost giddy.

She leaned close to his ear. "I think I finally understand, Tom McCullin."

Tom smiled and rubbed his beard and lips against her neck. He slipped his hands under her shirt, running them up her sides, stroking the sides of her breasts gently. Moving his lips to her ear, he asked, "What is it that you finally understand, Liz Williams?"

She pulled back and looked him in the eye. "That you're mine." His hands gripped her a bit more tightly in surprise at her answer.

"What?"

"You heard me, Tom. You're mine." She pressed a hard, searing, devouring kiss into him. "I love you so much it physically hurts sometimes." She moved closer, pressing her chest against him, bringing their groins together. She felt his hardness and pushed into it, saying, "I want you so much it makes me crazy."

He was breathing faster, and his heart was pounding.

"I'm yours, Tom, in every way. You know that. You've made me yours." She bit his lower lip, "But I don't think you understand that You. Are. Mine." She laced her fingers through his hair, pressed into him, and kissed him hard, like she was trying to climb inside of him, and then sucking on his tongue, pulling it into her mouth. A consuming kiss that left him breathless.

"Someone can take from you what's yours." She held his face in her hands and looked him in his eyes. "No one can take me from you, Tom. Not because I'm yours. Because you're mine."

Tom felt something give way inside him that he didn't know was there. Liz was still holding his face, looking at him, waiting.

When that barrier came down, she saw it. She saw it happen on his face, where he showed her everything even though he tried so hard to keep it all inside.

She smiled, and his hands gripped her tightly. "It's a little scary, right?"

He didn't say anything.

"It's okay. In a few minutes this is going to feel un-fucking-believable. Because you're stuck with me, McCullin."

He started laughing. "Holy shit."

"I know, right? Starting to feel awesome?"

He stared at her with an enormous grin on his face.

"This is how I started to feel after crying my eyes out with you. When I finally believed that this…" She kissed him, slow and sweet. "…is real."

Chapter Thirty-Eight

Joe's visit was fun. He was staying for a few days, so he was able to spend time together with Tom, and the two of them spent some time together with Chris. Liz took him to see a few sights in DC, as well.

"I'm giving you a pass on the zoo this time, because it's February and the weather is gross. But next time you're in DC I will make you go." They had just entered the Udvar-Hazy Center of the National Air and Space Museum in Northern Virginia. "And bring Anita with you. She's fun."

"She definitely wants to come." Joe turned toward Liz and asked, "How did you two coordinate this, anyway?"

Liz laughed. "You can't possibly think that I would give away state secrets that easily." She took his hand and pulled him past several exhibits and toward a special hall across from the entrance. The museum was enormous—it was an old airplane hangar—and was filled, literally top to bottom, with planes and other flying craft of all shapes and sizes, including the *Enola Gay* and the *Blackbird*, which Liz was pulling Joe past without looking.

"Hey, wait—the *Blackbird*…"

"Yes, I promise we'll see that. But you have to see this first." They entered the back hall, and Joe looked up to see the Space Shuttle *Discovery*. "*Enterprise* used to be here," said Liz, "but when they retired the Space Shuttle program, *Enterprise* moved to another museum, and *Discovery* moved here. It was amazing. I have pictures from the day they flew it in on the back of a 747. They flew around DC a few times. We watched it fly over the White House twice."

They walked slowly around the big craft, taking it in. "*Enterprise* was awesome, but this one…" She sighed. "*Discovery* has been to space. And back. Thirty-nine times." She looked at Joe. "This. Right here. It's not a model. Every part of this," she gestured at the craft, "has been to space and back."

Joe looked at the shuttle with definite awe but looked at Liz with curiosity, as well.

Liz turned to see him looking at her with a questioning expression. "What?" she asked, smiling. "We can go see the *Blackbird* now. It's awesome too—broke a speed record getting here, by the way—but it hasn't been in space."

Joe chuckled, and Liz caught the hint of the family resemblance in the way he shook his head and laughed.

"Okay, I'm getting a better picture now." He gave her a big hug. "Tommy tried to explain you and museums, but it didn't translate. I had to see it in person."

They strolled around, enjoying the museum, and then headed back so they had time to get ready to go to the game that evening. Liz dropped him off at her apartment and then headed over to Paige's house to get changed. On impulse, she texted Tom—one red heart emoji. Nothing else.

In a few moments, she received a response.

Tom: I love you. See you tonight.

She laughed out loud.

Liz: Two full sentences, with punctuation. You certainly do love me.

The response she received was a string of emojis, including a heart, a kiss, and something that looked like a party horn celebration thing.

***

The game was great. Tom seemed tight in the first period, not playing as well as he usually did, but he loosened up as the game went on and got to take care of business for the team with some well-placed open-ice hits, one of which sent the Columbus Union player head over heels to the roar of the crowd at the arena. The game was a two-nothing win for the Guards.

Joe and Liz waited for Tom after the game. When Tom came out, Joe was right there, shaking his hand, hugging him, saying, "That was fucking awesome, Tommy!" Tom introduced him to his teammates as everyone was filtering out while the three of them were standing and talking.

Zee was one of the later guys out. Tom caught him by the arm and said, "Zee, man, this is my brother, Joe. Joe, this is one of Liz's best friends, Zee."

Zee managed to hide his surprise at the warm greeting and introduction, especially being identified specifically as a friend of Liz, as he shook Joe's hand and said hello. Liz stood slightly behind Joe and smiled at Zee, eyes sparkling.

She came over and gave him a huge hug, saying, "Holy crap, you had a great game!" Zee had scored one of the two goals and assisted on the other one. He laughed and picked her up, spinning her around, and then looked over at Tom...and saw Tom grinning.

Zee put Liz down, looked at her, looked at Tom, looked back at her, and said, "What the fuck have I missed here?"

Tom slapped him on the shoulder, put his arm around Liz, and said, "Not a damn thing. We're going out for drinks. Want to join us?" Joe, not sure what was going on with this interaction, simply watched to see what would happen next.

"Sure. Why the hell not? I'm having a good night. I'm going to roll the dice that you're not plotting my untimely demise."

Tom laughed out loud, causing another look of confusion from Zee to Liz, and they decided where to meet for drinks.

***

Zee arrived a few minutes after the rest of them and joined Joe on one side of a booth at the bar.

"Micky, I've gotta know. What happened at the end of the first between you and Simmons?" He turned to Joe to explain. "The last time Micky had a run in with Simmons in a game last season, he ended up with a game misconduct call. I don't know what happened then, either. But this time, something happened. Simmons looks pissed and Micky here is skating like he owns the place."

Tom grinned.

"You gotta share."

"Simmons is an asshole. And he knows guys I used to play with. He heard I was seeing someone, and in that game last season, he was chirping at me all night about how he heard I had found a puck bunny, how he was going to have to meet her, how he knew I liked to share. So when I had the flimsiest excuse in the game, I attempted to put him in the hospital."

Liz was looking at him in horror. "Oh shit, Tom! Did he know...was he a teammate...shit, I'm sorry!"

"Not your fault, and yes, he was someone who knew what happened."

Zee blessedly let this go without asking for details. Tom was talking about this without anger. He looked, from what any of them could tell, completely relaxed. No one wanted to break this spell.

"So, tonight, he starts in chirping at me again. I hear you've still got your puck bunny, are you sure you're the only one hitting that, I think I'll look her up after the game tonight and get some." He took a drink of his beer. "You know what I did? I swear to God, Liz, I didn't even think about it. I laughed and said, 'It would be funny to watch you try.' He was so surprised he missed the pass that was coming to him."

Zee laughed, looked at Tom, who was grinning like crazy, and laughed again. "Holy shit, Micky."

Liz was staring at Tom, wide-eyed with her hand over her mouth, like she couldn't believe it, and giggled.

Joe sat back and said, "It's about fucking time, Tommy."

In a playful tone, Zee asked, "This doesn't mean that you're going soft, right? Because you and I might have our differences, but when we're on the ice, I always know I can count on you to beat the shit out of someone who puts me into the boards with a dirty hit."

Tom looked a little surprised and pleased at the comment, while Joe threw his head back and laughed.

"Christ, they don't know you at all, Tommy! How is that possible?" He turned to Zee. "Tommy has been his team's self-appointed enforcer since before they were old enough to even be allowed to body check in games. God, he got himself in trouble." He was still laughing. "I used to wonder if he liked the hockey or the fighting."

Tom was grinning.

"Don't worry, Zee. He could always laugh *and* fight." He looked over at Tom. "He just forgot how to laugh for a while." He shared a brief smile with his brother.

Liz put her hand on Tom's thigh under the table and leaned against him; he wrapped his arm around her shoulder and kissed the top of her head.

Zee turned to Joe and said, "So did they tell you about the time Liz called him on a road trip?"

"Seriously, Zee?" Liz protested. "I'm right here. I can hear you."

Joe said, "Is this something I actually want to hear?"

"Yes, definitely. I'm a younger brother too, ya know. You want this kind of dirt on your older brother." Zee was in his element. The two of them got off on a brief tangent about the perils of having older brothers.

Tom was watching this exchange with a twinkle in his eye.

"What has gotten into you?" Liz asked quietly, squeezing his inner thigh gently and smiling at him.

"You." He turned his head and looked down at her. "It turns out that it's a hell of a lot of fun being yours." He bent down and kissed her, taking his time about it.

"Jesus, you two!"

Zee laughed at Joe's protest.

"Okay, I'm out." Liz gave Tom one more firm kiss and said, "You guys have fun. Joe, please remember that Zee exaggerates and that I can neither confirm nor deny any knowledge of whatever he tells you." She looked briefly at Tom and added, "And based on this one's mood tonight, I'm going to add that I can neither confirm nor deny anything he tells you, either."

Tom just grinned at her.

Joe and Zee stood up for goodbye hugs, and then she leaned back into the booth for one last kiss from Tom.

As she walked away, she heard Zee say, "So we end up sharing a room on this road trip…"

***

Liz woke up to hear her phone vibrating on the nightstand. Bleary, she answered when she saw that it was Zee calling. "Everything okay? What's going on?" She looked at the clock and saw that it was two a.m.

"Holy shit, Liz. He's funny!"

Zee was definitely drunk. Liz could hear Joe and Tom laughing in the background and heard Tom asking to talk to her.

"Oh my God, Zee, are you guys still out? You sound plastered. Please tell me you're getting cabs home."

"Yeah, of course, we're waiting for an Uber or something right now. I'm not sure. Some ride. Somewhere." He giggled. In a very exaggerated whisper, he said, "Micky sang karaoke. It was awful."

Liz started laughing, not sure whether to believe this drunken banter or not, until she heard Tom say, "Give me the phone," and then directly to her, "It was awesome. You have never heard me sing. It was glorious."

"What did you sing, sweetheart?" She was laughing, secretly hoping someone had taken a video of this.

There was a pause, and then she heard him ask the other two guys, "What did I sing? I don't remember." Pause. "No one remembers. Doesn't matter. It was awesome."

"Is Joe conscious?"

"Hang on." Then muffled, "My brother, she wants to talk to you."

"Hey, Liz."

"You sound almost coherent. Where are you guys going?"

"Oh, I'm drunk, just not like these two. We're all going back to your apartment."

In the background she heard Zee call out, "Slumber party! Liz, come join us!" followed by Tom laughing and explaining to him there was no fucking way that was happening.

"Aspirin, Tylenol, and Advil are in the medicine cabinet in the bathroom. Drink water. I'll talk to you tomorrow, Joe."

"Hey…wait…Tommy wants to talk to you again."

Tom got on the phone again. "I love you. You know that, right?" He suddenly sounded concerned, in the way of the very drunk.

"Yes, sweetheart. And I love you. Keep having fun."

"Oh, and Zee's okay. You were right. He's only mostly an asshole." He started laughing as Zee started complaining and took the phone back from Tom again.

"I was going to say something nice about Micky, but now I'm not."

"Good night, Zee."

"Wait! Wait! I want a sexy voice good night!" She heard Tom saying, "Fuck no!" in the background.

"Sorry, sweetie, that was a one-time deal. Love you, have a good night."

She disconnected the phone, trying to remember how long it had been since she had gotten a drunk phone call from friends out partying. It had been a really long time.

***

She was already at work the next morning by the time she heard from Tom. She answered the phone with, "Hey, handsome. How's that headache feeling?"

He grumbled, "Fuck. Please sound less chipper."

She laughed.

"Zee and I just left your apartment. Joe is flying out later tonight. Can we get together for dinner before he goes?"

"Of course. Just let me know where and when."

"Sorry about the late night call. I know you had to get up early for work today."

"Totally worth it. I'm really hoping that one of the other guys took a video of you singing karaoke."

There was a long pause. "Fuck." Another pause. "Are you sure that happened?"

"All three of you seemed to agree last night. You said that you were, and I quote, 'glorious.'"

Tom barked out a laugh and then groaned from his headache. "Shit, that was a hell of a night. The only thing missing was Becks."

"Yeah, but that wasn't for lack of trying."

Another pause. "What do you mean?"

Liz laughed. "Really? You drunk dialed him last night too. He already called me this morning to tell me about it. Apparently you tried to get him to come meet you guys at the karaoke place. Something along the lines of, 'Come sing with me, my brothah!'" She gave an imitation of the crooning voice Chris had used, which made him laugh again.

"Shit, stop making me laugh. God, I haven't been this hungover in a long time." He chuckled. "Thank you. That was awesome."

"I'm so happy, Tom. I've got to run. Drink a lot of water, all right? I would like you to be feeling good tonight, when I'm back in my bed in my apartment."

"Got it. Water. And a nap before practice. Love you, sweetheart."

"Love you too."

***

They had a lovely dinner. Joe convinced Tom that he did, in fact, sing karaoke, although there was no video, much to Liz's disappointment. Apparently, he sang "Cherry Pie" by Warrant.

"I would have paid good money to see that," Liz lamented.

"It was…special." Joe smirked. "But holy shit, it was great to see you really having fun again, Tommy." He chuckled. "Wait until I tell Col about your new singing career…" He started a horrible imitation.

"Don't you dare! Bastard!" Tom was laughing. "Shit, the stories she already tells are bad enough." He got a sudden horrified look on his face, as if he just thought of something. "You wouldn't." Joe was grinning. "Fuck, no. Joe, you wouldn't."

Liz had no idea what was going on.

"Let's just call that collateral, then, shall we?"

Tom closed his eyes. "What do you want?"

"Game tickets. Of course." Tom laughed. "And whatever else I think of as time goes on."

"Fuck." He shook his head.

Liz finally said, "Do I want to know what this is about?"

Tom glanced at her, looking a little uncomfortable. "I don't need my sister hearing some of the things that Zee shared last night."

Liz laughed out loud, and Tom added under his breath, "Jesus, what would she do with *that* story?"

Tom and Liz walked Joe to his rental car to say goodbye. Joe hugged Liz tightly. "Thank you." He looked at her. "I feel like you gave me my brother back."

She smiled back at him, just a little teary. "Safe travels. Remember, next time bring Anita."

Tom and Joe shook, hugged, Tom put Joe in a headlock and rubbed his knuckles in his younger brother's hair, and they finally said goodbye.

As Joe drove off, Tom pulled Liz close to his side, breathed in her hair, and kissed the top of her head. "That was amazing. Thank you."

Chapter Thirty-Nine

Chris and Tom thoroughly enjoyed watching the women come down the stairs dressed for the formal. Even knowing from last year how transformed she could be, Tom was still struck speechless when he saw Liz. This year's gown was a sea-foam green, at least that was what Paige had called the color, and it was a one-shoulder design that made Tom think of something a Greek goddess would wear.

"It is very satisfying to see my fantasy man speechless," she teased.

"You are so beautiful." He said it so sincerely she blushed, which made Paige laugh.

"Wow, Micky, you've still got it. You're still the only person I've ever seen who can make her blush."

As they were heading toward the front of the house to get coats and wraps to get ready to leave, Tom put his arm around Liz and said, "We could skip this whole thing, and I could just take you home and make you blush more."

Liz smiled up at him but noticed that, as much as

he was trying to be playful, there was already an underlying strain in his face. She turned to look at him. "Do you have something for me? I'm thinking it would be a little bigger than a business card? Perhaps magnetic?"

He smiled, fished in his pocket, and handed her a card key. "I got 403 again. Good memories."

"Definitely." She smiled and slipped it into her purse.

He clenched his jaw for a moment and said, "I don't know why this is so fucking hard for me. We're not even there yet, and I can already feel myself getting pissed off."

Liz tilted her head and looked at him. "Well, according to both you and Chris, you never liked this kind of thing, even when you were kids, like awards ceremonies and such, right?"

"Right. But I never wanted to randomly kill people at them, either." He was still making an attempt at joking.

She gently took hold of the lapels of his tux coat, looked him in his eyes, and said, "This was the part that Michelle wanted."

Tom grabbed her by the wrists suddenly and almost violently, holding her hands still. "What?" he asked, his voice and face a mix of confused emotion, anger, and hurt chief among them.

Chris and Paige had walked back to see what was keeping them and heard and saw the exchange. Liz heard Chris say under his breath, "Jesus, Liz," and he started toward his friend, but this time Paige was the one who put her hand on his arm. She looked at Chris and whispered, "Wait."

"This. The formal events. The charity balls. The press attention. Meeting important people. All the trappings of being with a famous pro-athlete. That was the part that she wanted."

He slowly released her wrists, staring at her.

Liz took a chance, hoping she wasn't going to push this too far. "And she wanted it so badly she didn't want to wait for it to be with you."

Tom spun around, looking for the nearest chair. He was feeling dizzy and slightly sick. They were near the kitchen, so he sat at the table.

Liz followed him and sat down next to him. Tom had his elbows on his knees, looking at the floor, breathing hard. Chris and Paige moved to the doorway; after a few seconds, Paige got a glass of ice water and put it on the table next to Tom before retreating back to the doorway with Chris. Chris's face was strained, still looking like he wanted to rescue his friend.

After a few moments, Liz reached over to stroke her hand through Tom's hair, tucking it behind his ear, touching the way it curled slightly at the back of his neck at his collar. She wanted to speak, to tell him he was worth so much more than this, how wrong Michelle had been, to reassure him how much she loved him. But she had the sense that Tom just needed to work through this in his head, so she stayed quiet despite the pressure in her chest and simply continued to stroke his hair.

After a minute or two, he sat up, drank the ice water, and looked at her. "Would you care?" he asked, his voice raspy, his face rather pale.

"About what?"

"If we never went to another formal event. If you never met the owner of a pro sports team. If there were never any press pictures."

She put her hand up and stroked his beard. "Of course not. Tom, I'm only going to this thing tonight because you're going. If you weren't there, I'd rather be wherever you are."

He took and gripped her hand and said, "And if I retired from hockey tomorrow?"

She searched his eyes, surprised by the question, and said, "Then I would get to see you a whole lot more. And we could watch games together."

"And I would no longer be your fantasy hockey player."

She felt everything in her chest twist at his words. "Oh God, Tom, is that what you think?" She smiled and felt tears gathering and knew she wasn't going to be able to stop them. "Sweetheart, quite a while ago my fantasy stopped being a six-foot-four hockey player and started being Tom McCullin." She sniffled. "You idiot."

He smiled that half smile and said gruffly, "You're supposed to call me a bastard first."

She punched him in the shoulder. "Paige, I am in desperate need of tissues. Please. Because this guy is a bastard."

He smiled. "Yes, and an idiot."

"Yes." Paige brought her a box of tissues.

"And I love you, Liz."

"I love you too. Are we okay?"

Tom stood up, stretched, and took her in his arms. "We are okay. Thank you."

As they walked toward the cars, Chris pulled Liz

back for a moment. "How did you know?"

"Which part? That it was Michelle who was making him insane about these things, or that he wasn't going to put his fist through your wall when I said something?" She gave him a wry smile.

"Both."

"The first was an educated guess. The second—I had no idea. I just hoped."

Chris smiled at her and gave her a kiss on the forehead. "Magical fucking superpowers, Liz."

***

On the drive there, Tom glanced over and said, "I'm concerned about something, and I want to clarify."

"Anything, sweetheart. What's wrong?"

"I just want to make sure that, in case our talk this evening has helped me and I am not feeling as angry during the event tonight…well, I want to make sure that doesn't mean I'm getting laid less. Because I'm not sure that's a really good trade." His crooked smile was adorable.

Liz was so relieved she laughed out loud. And then ran her hand up the inside of his thigh. "Oh, no. I'm good with that." She ran her hand higher. "Shit, I love that you wear silk boxers under these."

Tom floored the accelerator as her hand started tracing patterns around the silk and everything underneath it. She was enjoying the changing shapes underneath his fly altogether too much, and he was suddenly very interested in arriving as quickly as possible.

"You're making me crazy."

"You're the one who asked if you were still getting laid. I'm just making sure you understand. Completely." She squeezed gently and then started making slow complete strokes through his pants.

"Jesus, Liz." He was starting to sweat. "I do want to make it to the hotel."

"Oh, I'm pretty sure I could make this last a long, long time." She slowed down and lightened her strokes, so he was being teased by her fingers and the silky fabric. And then she reached lower between his legs and cupped him, rolling and squeezing very gently. He was fighting to keep paying attention to the road. They weren't very far from the hotel, but he was having trouble remembering the directions for some reason.

She dragged her nails across him from the bottom of his balls all the way up to his tip. If he hadn't been wearing clothing, it would have been agony, but through the two layers of fabric, one of them being silk, it was making him throb.

She let him go as they pulled up to the valet and smiled at him wickedly, and they made a very fast trip to the room before even heading to the event.

***

Tom was indeed much more relaxed all evening and would have been even without their regular trips to visit Room 403. But true to her promise, Liz did not skimp on her distractions. By the time they sat down to dinner, there had already been the pre-event encounter plus one more, so Tom was feeling very mellow already.

He pulled Liz's chair close to his and tucked her under his right arm as soon as the speeches started, and she enjoyed his closeness, feeling warm and fuzzy and still slightly sex-drunk herself. She had her left hand on his thigh under the tablecloth, gently caressing him just because she could, not even really in a flirty way. Just because he was here next to her, and she could touch him.

Tom shifted slightly in his seat, turned his head, and looked down at her. This beautiful, surprising, confusing woman had turned his entire world upside down. She had done it again tonight—their earlier conversation had shocked the hell out of him. He felt his chest contract thinking about how much he loved her, how much his life was different, better, because they had found each other.

Liz felt Tom shift his arm off her shoulder and back next to her, in between them, to hold her hand on his thigh under the tablecloth. She shifted her absent-minded caress to his fingers and palm, loving the way her hands felt small in his very large ones. Then came a sensation she couldn't identify at first—he was holding her hand still, but his other hand was moving. She had just figured out what the feeling was and was starting to turn to look at him when he leaned into her and whispered, "Will you marry me?"

She had never felt her heart beating so hard, and it sounded so very loud in her ears. Surely everyone in the room could hear it and knew what was going on.

He bent down to hear her whisper back, "Yes.

331

And it's perfect. I love it."

He smiled and whispered, "I knew you would." He moved his arm back around her and tucked her back into his side. She put her hand back on his thigh, caressing him, feeling the change of the weight of the ring on her third finger, and feeling her heart racing.

He wasn't nervous or anxious. Or angry or irritable, for that matter. He had been planning on giving her the ring later that night, after the event was over. In private, maybe in their hotel room, maybe at her apartment. But then, this just felt...right. He hadn't overthought it, he had just done it, knowing she would love everything—the ring, how he asked—everything. Not because she had some preconceived notion of how she thought it should be done, but because *he* had done it.

As the speeches ended and the music started up again, he covered her hand with his and said, "I want to look at you when you see it. Come dance with me."

She laughed as he pulled her away to the dance floor.

Paige looked at Chris questioningly. "Do you know what's going on?" Chris shook his head. "Something happened after dinner," she said. "During the speeches. I looked over and something was different."

"I have no idea, but *he* just pulled *her* to the dance floor. To *dance.* I feel like I'm in some sort of bizarro world."

Tom draped Liz's left hand around his shoulder and began swaying with her. "It belonged to my

Grandma Ellie. She was amazing and tough and funny, and I loved her very much. When I was little, she promised me I could have her ring for my wife if I wanted. You are just the kind of woman she would have loved."

"You realize I already feel entirely like I'm watching myself from somewhere slightly up and to the left of me, don't you?" Liz had tears in her eyes. "And now you're going to make me cry on top of this? I feel like my heart can't even fit inside me anymore."

"Please look now."

Liz was shaking a bit as she brought her left hand down to rest on Tom's chest as they danced. He was watching her face. Her eyes grew wide, and then her brows knit together a bit and her head tilted down and to the side as she looked, trying not to cry. She looked back up at him, and he thought he could die a happy man from what he saw in her eyes.

"Oh God, Tom. It's perfect, and I love it. Truly." She blinked back the tears and laughed.

"I really knew you would. You have no idea how much fun that made this." He smiled down at her and then wrapped his arms around her waist and picked her up off her feet as she wrapped her arms around his neck. They stood there like that for a good ten seconds before he put her back down again.

***

Tom led Liz back over to the high tables, getting

her a drink along the way. "You look like you could use this," he said, chuckling. "I've gotta say it's a very different experience looking to take care of you at one of these events." He kissed her on the top of her head and added, "I want to kiss you very badly, but I know I won't want to stop once I start—and I have to go take pictures right now." His voice was getting low and his eyes were getting smoky.

It was making Liz's heart start to race.

She rubbed her hand on his beard and said, "I still don't feel I'm properly connected to the floor. I'm going to sit right here and wait for you, if that's okay."

He laughed out loud, a joyful sound, and turned just as Chris was walking up to the table with Paige. Chris said, "I was just coming to get you for pictures. Everything is okay, I take it…?"

Tom laughed again and clapped Chris on the shoulder. "Fantastic, my brother. Let's go take pictures."

"Christ, if I didn't know you better, I would swear you're high." They walked off.

Paige sat down across from Liz. Liz turned and stared at her.

Paige looked very concerned. "Liz, what's wrong?"

"Nothing. There is absolutely nothing wrong. Unless I was accidentally dosed with LSD. Then I'm on an acid trip, which would explain some things. But it's a good trip, so I don't want to come down."

It was Paige's turn to stare. "What in the living

fuck are you talking about?"

Liz put her hand on the table between them. Paige stared at her hand and then back up at Liz. *"When?"*

"During the speeches."

"During the speeches. *During* the fucking *speeches?"* She looked off into the distance. "Sweet Jesus, can't you guys do anything normally?" She looked back at Liz and then broke into a huge grin. "Oh, Liz!" She jumped off her chair and came around to hug her best friend.

Liz started laughing, then crying, and then laughing again.

Paige got her a few cocktail napkins to use as tissues and helped her clean up her makeup. Liz still wasn't sure about her legs working, so she stayed at the table and finished her drink. The guys came back a little while later, Tom still grinning and Chris still looking confused.

"Micky, seriously, you didn't tell him? What the fuck is wrong with you?" Paige started swatting Tom with her purse. Tom was laughing and trying to fend her off, and then he just grabbed her and pulled her in for a huge hug.

"What the hell am I missing?" Chris was starting to get irritated. "God damn it, I'm getting sick of being the last person to know shit around here."

Tom wrapped his arm around his oldest friend and said, "Becks, you know I would tell you, but I'm about to kiss my fiancée, and this is gonna take a while."

He walked over and pulled Liz to her feet as Chris tried to process what he'd just said.

Tom put one hand on Liz's waist, gently cupped her face with the other, and began to kiss her. Slowly. Like their first kiss. He pressed his lips against hers and then pulled back slightly and then brushed against them again. The third kiss he parted his lips, breathed against her, finding her lips parted to meet his. He tilted his head slightly and slid his hand up into her hair. They brushed their parted lips against each other again, he pressed in closer...and time stopped.

He was careful to keep one hand on her waist and the other hand in her hair—he didn't want to lose himself completely while standing in a crowded ballroom and do anything utterly inappropriate or vulgar; he was even careful about tongues getting too involved, and that was difficult to resist—but he was going to kiss her until he was done kissing her, and that was going to take a bit of time to do properly.

When he finally stopped, he heard Chris say with a laugh, "Are you quite through, Micky?"

"For now." He turned around and was startled to see quite a few more of his teammates, including Zee, standing around behind Chris, who had gathered there during his little show. Some had noticed the kiss, but Chris and Paige had grabbed the closest guys and told them and had spread the word that way. So when Tom turned around, he got cheers and whistles. And he laughed.

Paige looked at Liz and mouthed, "He's laughing! Holy shit!"

One of the guys had told one of the organizers of the event, and there was an announcement, and suddenly they were getting congratulations from everywhere.

"We are going to have very little luck sneaking out at this point, I'm afraid." Liz twined her fingers into Tom's. "That's what you get when you turn yourself into a big hero." She winked at him.

"No rest for the fantasy man, I'm afraid."

She had never seen him in such a good mood. He was relaxed and confident, and nothing seemed to be able to bother him. It was astounding. And wonderful.

She grabbed the front of his jacket with both hands and brought him down to her so she could say, "You'd better fucking believe you're getting no rest later, fantasy man. When can we leave?"

He stepped behind her and put his arms around her. He pulled her close and pressed against her, sliding the hardness of his arousal against her rear and hip. Bending so that his deep voice was directed into her ear, he asked, "Do you feel that?"

She gasped and nodded, not trusting her voice.

"That," he said, pressing again for emphasis, "has been that way since I kissed you. So the second we can leave, I'm going to have you naked in our room."

She was breathing hard.

"I don't want you wearing anything except that ring." He slid his hand over her stomach and gently bit her neck, then calmly took her hand in his and walked to find one of the event organizers.

"I just wanted to apologize—I actually tried to be very quiet about this and didn't intend for it to become a distraction from your event. I didn't count

337

on the reaction of my teammates."

The organizer smiled and shook his hand, saying, "Not at all. This kind of thing tends to be very good for fundraising, so I should be thanking you. Something about happy people feeling good makes for open wallets. It would be very helpful if we could use this—along with pictures—as part of a press release. Would that be okay with you two? We would certainly get more social media attention, and it would probably help us raise even more for the charity."

Tom looked at Liz for her approval.

She said, "This is all you, sweetheart. I'm just along for the ride."

He told the organizer, "Sure, whatever you'd like. I don't know that there are any pictures, though."

The woman laughed out loud. "I think you have no idea how long you two were kissing. There are a *lot* of pictures. Probably some video too."

Chapter Forty

Liz had arrived at the pool party early to help Paige out with some final preparations. Apparently one of the people she had hired had become sick at the last minute, so reinforcements were needed, and Liz was happy to assist. There wasn't really that much to do, anyway; Paige and Chris had hosted this enough times that they had everything down to a science at this point.

It wasn't too long before Tom arrived and asked if he could steal Liz away for a few minutes.

"Really, Micky?" Paige rolled her eyes at him, and he somehow managed to grin and look sheepish at the same time. "Oh, for heaven's sake. Go. You two are ridiculous."

Tom grabbed Liz's hand and pulled her away, sneaking them off into a back bedroom, shutting the door behind them, and then locking it.

"What has gotten into you?" Liz teased as Tom started kissing her neck and nibbling her earlobe, pressing her up against the door.

"I always feel this way when I'm with you." He

stopped and looked at her, his eyes still playful, but with more heat than before. "I thought you would have noticed that by now." His hands were beginning to roam around her midsection, teasing her stomach and back under her shirt.

"Mmmm, that's true," she replied, "and I always feel this way with you." She captured his mouth for a kiss, which lasted somewhat longer than she had originally intended. "But you don't, usually, randomly drag me off in the middle of a party."

"Oh, really?" He shifted to her other ear, paying attention to that earlobe and running his tongue along the sensitive skin underneath her ear and down her neck. "It seems to me that you were the one that started all this, with hotel rooms…" He kissed her. "…and amazing blowjobs." He kissed her longer and with a lot of tongue. "And insanely hot sex up against the back of a door." His hands had reached her breasts, and he teased her nipples through the fabric of her bra.

"Oh," she breathed, head back against the door. He took the opportunity to place kisses along her throat, biting her neck gently. "That was me, wasn't it?"

"Yes." He removed her shirt and bra and bent to take her nipple in his mouth, running his tongue around her peak as he sucked gently, while she gasped and moaned. "That was definitely you." He moved to her other breast and repeated his attentions, while she ran her fingers through his hair.

"So," he said, now dipping his fingers into her waistband and opening the button of her shorts, "I really want to take you right here up against this door." He pushed off her shorts and underwear. "Unless you have another preference?" He took a step back for a moment and looked at her face to see if she had anything else in mind as he stripped off his clothing. "No?"

She was speechless watching his chiseled body.

"Okay, then." He pushed her up against the door and kissed her, deep and hard, bent his knees to angle himself properly, and entered her, pulling one leg up over his hip, and then stood up, pulling her other leg up, supporting her ass with his hands.

She wrapped her arms and legs around him and whispered, "Oh, crap."

Tom laughed in his deep voice, and she blushed.

"I love making you blush." He started moving, pressing her against the door, sliding in and out of her in a steady pace that was making her lose herself. She put her head back against the door, and Tom gently kissed her neck as he continued to stroke himself into her. "I've been wanting to take you this way for a long time."

Liz made a small short humming sound, her breathing picking up speed.

Tom continued talking to her, knowing it would make her crazy. "You're beautiful and sexy, and I have wanted you wrapped around my body."

She gasped, and he sped up just a little, shifting his hips.

"I can't wait until Monday." He breathed into her ear and heard her moan, felt her grip him with increasing desperation, grinding against him. Tom sped up, stroking into her quickly and deeply. He could tell she was close. He started losing his rhythm, and knowing he was close, too, he growled into her ear, "I can't wait to fuck you as my wife."

She spasmed, clutching her arms and legs around him, vocalizing against his neck, trying to be quiet, feeling her internal muscles grasping around him over and over, as he used his knees to push her harder into the door, thrusting as deeply as possible, emptying himself into her, gripping her hard, not breathing through the pulses to keep from yelling.

They were both panting and gasping, muscles shaking, trying to come down from the high. Liz put her feet back down on the floor and giggled as she found she really couldn't stand very well. Tom leaned against the door and pulled her into him, chuckling with her.

"That was amazing," she said as she kissed him. "Excellent idea. I love you, Tom." He grinned at her, looking sated and pleased. "I suspect we need to get back out to the party, though…" She began the process of gathering her clothing.

"Oh, if we must." He came up behind her and put his arms around her waist and said, "But I do love making you blush." He turned her around. "I'm glad we're not waiting."

"Me too."

They had decided on a civil ceremony at the courthouse, so they had gotten their marriage license on Friday and were going to say vows on Monday with Paige and Chris as witnesses. They would have a big reception in Minnesota with Tom's family, but neither one wanted the formality of a wedding. Liz had insisted on getting the wedding rings—they were simple bands, but inside each was engraved, *"I'm yours ~ You're mine ~ I'm yours ~ You're mine"* around the entire band. Tom had loved it.

She had known he would.

***

When they came out of the house through the sliding glass doors, Liz saw there was a good crowd already.

Paige saw her and came over. "Jesus, Micky. 'A few minutes?' I don't even want to know what the hell just went on."

Tom just grinned.

Zee spotted Liz before she spotted him, and she ended up on his shoulders with a surprised shriek as he carried her to the diving board. She laughed, wondering if she was going to end up in the pool this time or not.

He stepped onto the board and then put her down, allowing her to step down. "You're losing your touch, Zee. You didn't even make people vote."

Zee grinned and then stood up, puffed himself, and said in a grandiose fashion, "Dearly Beloved, we are gathered here today…" and Liz burst out laughing.

Tom was standing next to her and put his arm around her waist. She looked up at him, and he gestured up to Zee, who had resumed in a normal voice, "I have been authorized by the Commonwealth of Virginia to perform the marriage ceremony of Thomas McCullin and Elizabeth Williams."

Liz said, "No." She looked at Tom. "No, you're kidding."

Zee said, "Geez, Micky, you said she was willing to marry you." The people in attendance, who were now clustered around the diving board, were laughing. "I can't be party to some kind of forced marriage."

Liz was looking closely at Tom.

"I told you I couldn't wait until Monday." He smiled at her with that cooked grin.

"Really?" She shook her head. "No. You would not have an actual wedding without your parents. You just wouldn't." Chris and Paige had moved to stand next to them.

Tom turned her around by her shoulders, so she was face to face with Kathleen and big Tom, who hugged her. Liz started shaking and laughing and looked around at the other guests, realizing suddenly they weren't all players and their families. Just in her brief glance around, she saw Jason and Paul and several other of her close friends. She looked at Chris and Paige, standing with them as she had been expecting them to do Monday morning. Paige was smiling and looking a little teary, and Chris looked so happy.

She turned back to Tom, who had the biggest smile she had ever seen. And then she looked at Zee.

His eyes were twinkling as he asked, "Are you quite ready? Can we please get back to this? It's my big moment here, Liz."

She laughed, gestured to him, "Please, continue," and snuggled under Tom's arm, accepting that this surreal experience was actually happening.

Tom breathed in her hair and kissed the top of her head. They said their vows and exchanged rings.

Zee boldly said, "You may now kiss the bride!" and everyone cheered.

Tom turned to address the guests. "Please feel free to go, eat, drink, enjoy yourselves." He looked down at Liz. "Because I'm about to kiss my wife, and this is gonna take a while."

Liz heard big Tom start laughing and then was lost in kissing Micky.

About the Author

Law firm office cog by day.
Writer of steamy romance by night.
Hockey fan all the time.

Ellen lives in the Northern Virginia area with her husband and two sons, along with various furry and scaly creatures.
Life is good.

Facebook:
https://www.facebook.com/ellen.devlin.5494

Twitter:
https://twitter.com/ellendev_author

Website:
http://www.ellendevlin.com/

Join our Reader Group on Facebook and don't miss out on meeting our authors and entering epic giveaways!

Limitless Reading

Where reading a book
is your first step to becoming
limitless...

LIMITLESS PUBLISHING *Reader Group*

Join today! *"Where reading a book is your first step to becoming limitless..."*

https://www.facebook.com/groups/Limitless Reading/

www.ingramcontent.com/pod-product-compliance
Lightning Source LLC
Chambersburg PA
CBHW020355260626
47156CB00007B/2119